Capturing the Last Welsh Witch
by
J.M. Davies

Copyright © December 2015 by J.M.Davies
Visit J.M.Davies official web-site
http://www.jenniferowendavies.com/ for the latest news, book details, and other information.

Printed in the United States of America
First Printing, December 2015
ISBN-13: 978-1519576590
ISBN-10: 1519576595
Author J.M.Davies
Cover Art provided by G.S.Prendergast.
Copyediting provided by Faith Williams from the Atwater Group.

Acknowledgments

I would like to thank Faith Williams my editor, and my cover artist Gabrielle Prendergast.

I want to mention my cohorts from my writers group the Writers Connection and in particular, Rachel Knox Alesse and Jennifer Smith, very talented writers who share my passion, and provide invaluable feedback, and proofing before I pushed the button for publication.

I want to thank all my friends and family who always encourage me to keep going and keep writing. Finally, I have to say writing wouldn't be possible without my brilliant husband Paul Davies, who believes in me and refuses to let me give up. Writing a book is a process that involves a team of people committed to its success, and I am grateful for each one. Thank you!

CHAPTER ONE

Ella handed the taxi driver the folded bills, replaced her wallet back inside her elegant ivory and diamanté studded purse, and snapped it closed. She clutched it tightly in her sweaty hand as she stepped onto the empty sidewalk and shivered not only from the brisk coolness of the wintry night that greeted her but from an ever-present need to watch the ghostly shadows. As a five-hundred-year-old soul-shifter, being alert ensured her survival. She had learned a long time ago—after discovering she was the last of her kind from the clan of Ariana, Moon Goddess—to be prepared for anything.

With a deep breath, she stepped forward. Being a soul-shifter with magic filling her veins, there were perks for sure, but this was her fifth life, and if legend proved true, the end was in sight. She sensed it. With each life, new queens, kings, and presidents ruled, and she remembered them all. Each moment of death or torture was tattooed on her brain. Memories she'd sooner forget of how each lover or husband betrayed her were clearly imprinted on her heart.

It was therefore ironic to Ella that her continued existence depended upon finding her Mr. Perfect soul mate. Without him, the next time her life ended, she wouldn't experience that moment of clarity as all her lives merged into absolute silence in her body, and then, as if taking a deep pause, she breathed once more, reborn and like a butterfly, the transformation startling!

No, this time it would be eternal darkness unless she found true love. But as every man in her life to date was in some way responsible for her previous deaths, rushing to find him hadn't been a priority.

As she pulled her long, black velvet coat tighter to protect her scantily clad body from the cool night air, she glanced right and left and inhaled the air. Aidan, her sort-of boyfriend, had arranged an impromptu dinner date, which was not like him at all. Usually, he was too busy with work as a professor of archeology at the Andover museum, with his head buried in some ancient textbook or scroll for anything remotely romantic, which was fine because they didn't have a typical relationship, to say the least. Ella pushed down the sleek silver handle on the tall glass door and walked straight up to the mahogany front desk. A pretty brunette greeted her with a warm smile and direct eye contact.

Ella tried to relax, offered a smile back and gave her name as the woman perused the guest list and nodded. As her gaze lifted away, Ella's eyes wandered around the overflowing and busy restaurant. The heat and array of conversations swirled around and stifled her for a second but a waving of frantic hands drew attention to the center of the room.

Aidan's frowning and bespectacled face studied her from his table directly in the middle of the popular Italian bistro as the smell of garlic and tomatoes surrounded her. For a moment, their eyes met. His steel-gray eyes narrowed, and before she took a step, he pushed his chair back, leapt up and strode toward her impatiently. His gaze, directed only on her, was stern and unemotional. Ella wished she had stayed home, instantly sensing tonight wasn't going to end well. Aidan, tall and with a slim build, towered over her as he gave a brief brotherly hug and dropped a perfunctory kiss to each cheek before he placed his hand in the small of her back to lead her to their table.

"You're late, so I've already ordered to save time."

Ella sighed and peered at him in an attempt to gauge his mood. They rarely dined out alone; not knowing the reason for the sudden night out, she had taken extra care in choosing her outfit—a rather sexy, revealing dress. The short black lacy dress fitted her curves and now as the heat climbed into her cheeks, she wondered why on earth she had bothered. Her usually swept-up and tied-back into a severe chignon hair was left loose and tousled, but Aidan's pale, gaunt face bespoke an impatience to get the meal over with. She frowned, wondering why he had even suggested a restaurant or for that matter, why she had agreed; they didn't have that type of relationship. She opened her mouth to say she was leaving, but stopped, staring at the dark, handsome man with a strong square jaw in the far corner. A twinkle of recognition made her stare longer than normal, but the man in question was in shadow and her vision of him was not clear. He didn't move in her direction, oblivious of her perusal, intent on the menu and in full conversation with someone on his cell. Shaking her head and dismissing him, she looked away.

"Ella, you're not listening to me. I've ordered some antipasti and Cacciucco."

She swallowed. The thought of fish stew left her wiping her hand over her mouth and she forced a wave of nausea down. Something was definitely off, and she prayed it was only the fish.

Aidan loosened his collar and pulled his tie down, as if uncomfortable. His conversation rambled and his voice sped up like a runaway train. Ella noticed his temple beaded with a dewy sheen. He was nervous. He was never nervous.

A need to escape rose over her so quickly that she pushed away from the table, scraping her chair on the floor, and stood up but froze as the diners around her stared at her. Aidan leaned forward and clamped his hand down on hers, bringing her attention back to him.

"Ella. Forgive me. I'm sorry…I confess, I'm a little nervous. May I say how lovely you look tonight? I don't think I've seen you in a dress before. Please forgive my impatience. I brought you here because I have something I *must* talk to you about. But forgive me—where are my manners? Please, have a glass of wine. It will help us both relax." He sat back, released her hand and removed his glasses to wipe them with his microfiber cloth.

Ella looked at his face, which softened as their eyes met. She sat back down, not wanting to make a scene and wondering what he wanted to discuss with her that could make him so on edge. A glass of wine might settle whatever jitters he had and she nodded before she glanced back over her shoulder at the man she had stared at earlier but who now was absent.

"Are you all right, Ella?"

Ella turned back to face him and sighed. "A glass of wine would be lovely, and then you can tell me what's going on."

****

Hours later, Ella blinked as rays of golden sunlight streamed down upon her face and warmed her cheeks. Birds chirped merrily around her. *What on earth?* The last thought in her mind was that Aidan was being impatient in the restaurant but beyond that, there was nothing. Normally when Ella woke it was in a soft bed, with the aroma of coffee wafting up from the kitchen and Aidan was there, but she shivered as the cold blast of air hit her shoulders.

Ella peered at a blurry view of a distorted world and what looked like skyscrapers were tall, leafy trees. Lying on her side on the cold and damp earth with grass stuck to her lips wasn't helping her feel any better. She lifted her head, and shook it to clear her mind and vision. Pushing her hand into the moist, spongy earth to force her body up, needing to move, but a wave of bile rose up and the dizziness stopped her. In the distance, water gurgled, and instantly she knew she needed its healing energy to clear her confusion.

Allowing the dizziness to settle and the nausea to pass, she tried to recall last night but without result. Usually, those last moments of her life remained etched in her brain, but as she pressed her fingers to her temple, there was nothing. Right now, the black scraps of materials that had once been her dress wasn't covering her well and she was in the middle of a forest, with no recollection as to how she ended up there. Frosty kisses from the early-morning breeze touched her bare shoulders as she clamped her arms around her shaking body, and pain coursed through her.

When she removed her hands from her waist, she stared at them trembling and turned them back and forth. Dried blood covered them. Biting her lip, she let her gaze roam over the rest of her body to study the trail of dark bruises and screaming red welts that littered her pale skin. A hazy image of a furious Aidan flashed through her mind and screams surrounded her.

"What did you do, Aidan?" she whispered to the wind, as if it would answer.

Needing to move, Ella pushed herself off the grass quickly, but her legs wobbled and threatened to give out. Grabbing the nearest tree next to her to lean on, she retched and emptied the contents of her stomach. Ella clawed the bark of the tree with her fingernails for support, and a wave of energy sizzled through her veins like caffeine. Her vision cleared and she had enough strength to stand. After she wiped her mouth with the back of her hand, Ella moved toward the stream, which was mere feet away. Clean, invigorating water was exactly what she needed to revive her, and to know whether she had changed.

On weak and wobbly legs, she staggered toward the water. None of this made sense. Ella was usually prepared, but last night was a complete blank. Each step increased the pain throughout her body; even breathing hurt. It was as if she had fought in a great battle and lost. White dots danced merrily before her eyes.

Just get to the water and drink.

Ella pushed forward to the edge of the stream, but her legs finally gave way, and she dropped to her knees. Leaning over, she stared at the ripples of water and her reflection.

"Ow." She moved her jaw and lifted her hand to examine her face.

She traced an outline of a large, black bruise on her cheek with her fingers and winced. Dried blood congealed by her nose, and her mousey hair was a wild mass. One eye was swollen and as she peered downward; a collection of dark polka dots decorated her neck. She lifted her gaze and sighed as she stared into familiar dark eyes. She was still Ella Masters.

Despite looking battered, and as though she'd been raised by wolves, she was alive—at least for now. Sitting back on her haunches, she glanced down, and followed a succession of bruises on her arm that resembled fingerprints. Ella ran her hand over them as an ugly memory roared to life.

An angry face loomed into view. Turbulent gray irises, like a stormy ocean, gazed at her. There was no warmth in his expression; he pulled his mouth into a narrow line and gripped her wrists so tightly they hurt. Ella twisted and pulled at them, but he wasn't letting her go. A cry escaped her lips. "Aidan."

The memory vanished, and Ella shook her head. They had been fighting. That alone was not unusual, but why was she terrified? Her glance roamed all over her body for clues. Her lungs stung as she breathed, and a large purple bruise on her torso confirmed the reason. Maybe a broken rib; she couldn't be sure. What was certain was that these weren't just sparring injuries. Had Aidan tried to kill her?

She closed her eyes, inhaled a deep breath, and began to visualize each injury. Ella could see several cracked ribs, a small open wound at the back of her head, and bruises on her back, legs, and arms. As she observed the injuries, her warm blood soared toward them. Her hands moved impatiently around her body to apply pressure. As her fingers connected with the broken bone or wound, an immense internal energy flowed toward it. Her body glowed as her healing spirit worked on her injuries. Ella's breathing increased and became more rapid, until at last her body sagged.

Most of the pain eased, and her wounds started to heal. Some injuries would take longer than others, but at least she could move. Her body trembled with the exertion, but she closed her eyes, and willed herself to remember last night. *Pain.* All she could sense was pain. She wondered why she couldn't recall the night clearly.

As a soul-shifter with nearly five hundred years' worth of memories—memories she'd sooner forget of how each lover or husband betrayed her—she remembered their smiles, their gentle words of love. However, last night was lost to her.

There was nothing.

A tear rolled down her cheek, and she wiped it away. The pain eased and in its place, a blazing anger rose. Someone betrayed her. The wind swept the leaves off the ground and they rose high into the air to dance around her. She clutched her bare right wrist, and rubbed the skin where the amulet had once been. The skin was whiter than the rest, as she always wore it. The innocuous-looking amulet was her only link to her people and her means of escape. Now it was gone, and she was alone. The gauzy wisp of material that had been her dress was ripped to shreds and covered in dirt. Her fingers touched the torn edges of the material and she stared into the distance, blinking as an old memory shook her.

"Come here, before I come and get you." Aidan's voice was deep and hoarse. His piercing eyes glared into hers, and she looked back as she contemplated her options. She glanced toward the door; if she moved, he would grab her. She could try to seduce him. However, that would be hopeless with Aidan. No, the only way was to trick him.

Aidan inched closer. So close, she could smell his musky aftershave. Ella let him get closer still. Let him think he had won. Her heart pounded violently against her ribs, but still she waited, barely breathing. Aidan inched closer, his eyes never leaving her face.

"Are you ready to admit defeat?" He raised one eyebrow, and his mouth spread into a lazy smile.

"Never, Professor." She flicked her leg outward and kicked as hard as possible, just like he had taught her.

"What the..." He fell to the ground, doubled over and clutched his stomach.

Sucking on her lower lip, she hesitated before she turned away. That split second of doubt was her undoing. Arms came from nowhere and grabbed her legs. Whoosh. The view of the room shifted, and the floor went from under her feet. She ended up flat on her back, with Aidan's body impaling her to the floor.

"Never trust the enemy," he said.

She spluttered and coughed as the memory swirled away. Professor Aidan O'Connor was an enigma: a historian, friend, pretend-lover, and expert at martial arts. He'd taught her how to use her body as a weapon.

"But last night wasn't practice, was it? Aidan, what have you done?"

Staring at the crystal-clear water, she dipped her head to submerge it and the shocking coolness washed over her. Moments later, she jerked her head back, raising it out of the water, and shook it to let her long, wet tresses cascade down her back. Ella jumped up and was pleased the world didn't swirl around.

I have to find the amulet. Which means I have to go back.

The wind moaned through the trees, and the breeze pushed her onward. One foot lifted in front of the other, and before she knew it, she sprinted effortlessly through the forest. Oblivious of the stray branches and bushes that whipped against her skin, she continued to push through. Even the screeching birds were ignored. She simply kept running. Running was freedom, a lesson she had learned many times. The wind was hers to beckon, and it helped her by clearing the way and cushioning her weight as it carried her forward. Until a small log cabin came into view.

****

"Christ, what the fucking hell is going on down there?" Jackson shouted.

Marcus sighed. The shit had hit the proverbial fan in the last twelve hours, and now his boss, Philip Jackson, was breathing fire at him down the phone, blaming him for this mess. The man sounded permanently angry, but today he'd hit an all-time high. From his first meeting with his boss Jackson, nicknamed the Controller, Marcus knew he was trouble. He reeked of intolerance. His gray eyes and face looked like the ash from the tip of his cigarette that was permanently wedged in his mouth. He looked much older than his fifty-seven years, and rot had settled in. At least that was what he sensed. Marcus had heard the rumors about the burnt-out senior who'd simply gone crazy after his wife's death and had felt some sympathy toward the man, but now he suspected he was reaching for the bottle far too often, and was a ticking time bomb.

Marcus knew when he was moved into Jackson's team that his career was going nowhere fast. And who could blame the powers at the bureau? He was labeled a risk taker, not a team player. He suspected he was onboard a sinking bloody ship. Well, he would be damned if he was going to go down. Jackson promised that if he brought in Ella Masters, then he would get the team leader position, with his own crew in New York. He'd worked hard, and had put up with a truckload of tedious assignments and all because he wanted this promotion. It was all he wanted.

Shit, and now it had exploded in his face.

Marcus took a deep breath to stay calm. "I'm sorry, sir."

He ran his hand through his unruly mop of thick, dark hair, and rubbed his chin where stubble formed a nice five o'clock shadow. In truth—and he couldn't admit this to his boss—he didn't know what the hell had happened. He'd been working this latest assignment for around four months working undercover as Nate Williams, the new manager at the Ultimate Perk, a local coffee shop. It was a track, observe, and when requested, extract the target. Simple. At least it should have been. Ella Masters, alias the Witch, was on the surface a young preschool teacher, with no exemplary achievements. Nothing smacked out of the ordinary. Except that she was on the FBI's Most Wanted list. She had no priors, zip. For four months, he'd been babysitting, and all of a sudden it went berserk. He'd scoffed when he'd first been given the assignment and the overwhelming non-information in her file. When he'd questioned the insignificant details, requesting more on her background and priors—of which there was none—Jackson told him in no uncertain terms to, "Stop looking for problems and do the job you're paid to do. Don't balls this up."

Marcus rubbed his temple; his job was to investigate the truth, no matter where that might lead. His boss had serious problems, and he didn't trust him one bit, but Marcus didn't want to dig too deep. He just wanted to get the job done, so he could go to New York and catch real criminals. Marcus stared at the bare cream walls of his apartment and relayed the events of the night again.

"I was watching them eat in the New Seasons restaurant. They ate and left. The professor looked uneasy and all the while Ella was distracted, fussing with her hair and not really looking at him. At one point, their voices rose and it sounded like they were arguing but they still left in a taxi together. I followed them back to Ella's house. At first it was quiet, but it wasn't long before it turned nasty. I did my usual perimeter check, and it was quiet. I circled round the back, but by the time I reached the front of the house, she was yelling at him. I listened, but their voices were muffled. There was interference on my listening device and the sound kept breaking up. I only managed to catch snatches of the conversation. As I watched them, the atmosphere tensed and he started shaking her. She was struggling and there was silence. The professor gripped her shoulder, and smacked her across the face. I was about to intervene, but some son-of-a-bitch knocked me out cold."

Jackson started to reel off a long list of complaints, and Marcus shook his head. From the moment he'd arrived back at Ella's house, his gut told him something wasn't right. He should have simply marched in there and taken her, there and then. Instead, Marcus took his eyes off the target and ran another sweep of the perimeter. He'd messed up big-time. Marcus's intuition was telling him that he was being played, even though he had no proof—just his sixth sense, and he didn't like what it was telling him one bit.

If there was another agent there, then why wasn't he told? If it wasn't an agent, then who and why didn't they help Ella?

Marcus scratched his head.

"Are you listening, Drayton? I've had enough of your *incompetence...*"

Marcus stared out his long window. "Yes, sir, I understand." He walked over to the large wooden dresser, opened a drawer and picked up a picture of Ella, staring hard at it.

Where are you?

His fingers traced her heart-shaped face. Her face was scrubbed free of makeup, making her look young and innocent. After being knocked unconscious, Marcus had woken to discover the professor battered to death. There was blood spatter all over. During his time as a Navy SEAL, he had seen plenty of harrowing scenes, but the thought that this petite and seemingly defenseless woman could bludgeon to death a man until he was unrecognizable was the reason he had emptied the contents of his stomach. He simply could not believe that she was responsible. The last image Marcus saw was of Ella crashing to the ground, after that bastard's hand walloped her. There was also the fact that there were several unaccounted-for hours. The only possible explanation was that he'd been drugged. As he rubbed the whiskers on his jaw, he stared at Ella's picture. Someone had gone to a lot of trouble to keep those hours free from interruption and he intended to get to the bottom of it.

Jackson's voice bellowed through the phone.

"Well, you'd better fucking sort this out and quick. Headquarters is looking for your blood. You were told to bring her in *last week*. I gave you the extra time, and the crazy bitch kills her lover. Jesus, I'm not going down for this. Do you hear me?" There was silence.

Marcus knew without a doubt, had always known when push came to shove, he was on his own.

"Yes, sir, loud and clear." He pressed End on his cell. "Jerk."

Marcus had a clear picture of Ella Masters in his head. She definitely was not his type. He preferred blondes, for a start. Her mousey hair was forgettable, like all her features. He mostly thought her plain and ordinary. Her eyes were a muddy brown or hazel—it was hard to know for sure behind the thick glasses she wore. But her smile: something about her smile made you stare. It had taken weeks of small talk, and careful planning to ensure that only Marcus served her, before he glimpsed it. Her face lit up like the sun, and her cheeks flushed with a pink glow, as if she felt guilty for smiling. He was so wrapped up in her smile that he'd spilled her skinny vanilla latte all over the counter, but was rewarded by her carefree laughter. Something he suspected Ella rarely did and he wondered why.

When he introduced himself as the new manager of the coffee shop, his cover for this assignment, Marcus remembered how the corners of her mouth lifted tentatively as he shook her hand. She was hiding something, that much was obvious—but what? In that instant, a sliver of protectiveness rose inside him. He wanted to know more about Ella, and why she was a national security threat. That smile was the reason for the delay in his bringing her in. Once, his mother told him he was gifted with knowing people. He cursed and checked his side arm before he strode for the door.

"Damn it, Ella. What have you gotten yourself involved in?"

What was he saying? Why should he care? This job was the last step in his plan for promotion, and he was not going to let some con artist stand in his way. He grabbed his coat and keys and headed for the only place he could think of, the Ultimate Perk, hoping against all odds, she would turn up.

CHAPTER TWO

The discovery of the deserted cabin was too convenient. Ella hesitated but the chance of a shower, even a cold one, was too good to pass. Before she walked inside, she channeled her energy to search the vicinity for any human presence. Using her enhanced senses this way was easy. Her nose lifted to inhale the slight breeze that floated around; she could gauge whether a human was near. Their sickly-sweet odor was distinct. Detecting other life-forms was getting harder as there were more than she ever realized. Vampires were easy. They smelled like you would expect, metallic like blood, whereas werewolves smelled damp and woodsy. Her own kind, she believed smelled of the fall, but again it could change according to their moods.

After convincing herself there was no immediate threat, Ella touched the handle with her palm, and the door clicked open. A shower, change of clothes, and food if there was anything edible: that was the plan. She fully intended to pay the owners back and would leave a note to say so. After she charged upstairs, she quickly found the compact bathroom and searched for supplies to help restore her appearance. She opened the drawers in the large vanity, ignoring the two boxes of hair color and array of accessories. Ella grabbed two small travel-sized bottles instead and shoved the drawer closed.

After she stripped off her little more than rags for clothes, Ella stepped into the shower. The streaming water was freezing. Normally, she would raise the temperature simply by running her hands through the spray, heating the flowing liquid, but her reserves were low after repairing her injuries. However, at least, she had the bottle of shampoo and conditioner that would tame her matted hair. The smell of coconut soothed her senses as she massaged her scalp with her fingertips and softly explored a lump at the back of her head.

A picture of Aidan zoomed into her mind, and she winced at the memory. She was shouting, and he was trying in vain to calm her down. Suddenly, his patience evaporated, and his hand whipped across her face. Blinking, her tears intermingled with the water from the shower. Aidan's slap was forceful enough to knock her out and send her crashing to the ground.

It wasn't a friendly spar.

She let the icy-cold water cascade over her face and numb her. She stretched her thin arms out to lean against the tiled wall of the shower. The water flowed over her supple body, deadening every nerve ending, until the pain—both physical and emotional—disappeared. In its place, a blinding fury filled her, and she went into survival mode. Ella stepped out of the shower, determined, and she twisted her hair to expel all the water before she wrapped it in the small white towel from the hand rail. Standing in front of the large rectangular mirror, she touched the still vivid bruise on her cheek; her fingers gently soothed the skin. With a sucked in breath, she visualized the bruise fading and shrinking. Within seconds, the bruise did just that; in an hour, it would be completely healed. Her face would cause too many questions, questions she could ill afford.

Padding barefoot into the pale green and minimally decorated bedroom, she opened the heavy closet doors and checked through the few items of clothing left hanging, discarding each one until she pulled out a pair of skinny black velour pants and a matching jacket. With a grimace, she wiggled her long, lean legs into the pants. When she looked in the full-length mirror, she observed how they clung to her curves around her slender hips and bottom. Finding shoes that would fit was a problem. Eventually, she settled for a pair of plain black flip-flops that would just have to do. After she closed the doors to the closet, she swiveled around and left the room.

Ella raced down the stairs as her stomach growled for attention. She needed food. Spying the large white fridge, she walked and opened the door but apart from some condiments, it was empty. Disappointed, she turned to search the cupboards. As each door opened, she stared at the meager choice: either a can of tomatoes or creamy chicken soup. Ella grabbed the soup and pulled all the drawers open until she found what she was looking for, and lifted up a can opener. Pouring the liquid into a cup to drink, she inserted her finger, twirled it around in the contents until she was happy with the temperature; she removed her finger and licked the dripping broth. Making the soup a warm temperature was about as much as she could muster at the moment. As she checked around the room, Ella homed in on the radio and automatically reached over to switch it on to gain some sense of the day and maybe her location. The ticking clock on the wall read ten thirty, but she couldn't be sure of the day. With the cup held between her hands, she listened as the music changed for a news report. She sipped the warm liquid and relished its comforting taste.

The newscaster was reporting live at the scene of a vicious crime, a murder in Andover, the town where she lived. She froze, unable to take another sip, listening instead to the report. Her heart raced and missed beats as details of the savage attack was relayed over the radio. The victim's name was mentioned. The cup of soup slipped through Ella's hands and smashed on the tiled ground. The radio continued and all she could do was listen. It couldn't be.

"Professor Aidan O'Connor was well-known for his work in retrieving ancient artifacts and worked at the Museum of Archeology in Andover. He also taught at Boston College. His body was discovered in the early hours of Saturday morning in what can only be described as a frenzied and gruesome attack. His girlfriend, Ella Masters, is currently a person of interest. Any information about her whereabouts or indeed, anything to do with this case..."

The soup she had just enjoyed rose back in her mouth as her stomach heaved, and before she was sick where she stood, she dashed toward the sink to vomit in the bowl. Her head reeled as the news sank in and tears sprung from her eyes.

Aidan was dead! Remember, damn you! Remember.

She slid to the ground, her head cradled in her hands, and sat there for some time as she listened to the rest of the report. Ella learned that it was, in fact, now Saturday afternoon, almost twenty-four hours after that fateful evening. Learning that, panic set in, and she jumped up, needing to move and fast, because if history repeated itself, like usual, then the Elusti would be coming for her. The Elusti were an old religious sect comprised of influential humans that throughout history had hunted her kind, *soul-shifters,* down. Over the centuries, they had done exactly that, leaving her in the belief she was the last of her kind—except for her soul mate. Instinctively, if he was dead, she would know but she couldn't be sure. Anyway, Aidan's death couldn't be an accident and that meant they were involved and would be hot on her trail, if they weren't already.

Ella knew the drill—stay alive and disappear—but first she needed to figure out where she was. Her gaze flickered over the kitchen countertops, searching for mail, newspapers, anything that would give her location. Nothing. She raced to the front door, remembering she'd stepped on some magazines on the floor as she walked in. There on the carpet lay several pieces of junk mail and a Lands' End catalog. Ella flipped it over and there in typed letters was a name and address. She was in Lincoln, New Hampshire. About two hours away from her home. For some insane reason, she and Aidan had been fighting, and now he was dead and she was in New Hampshire.

Was it possible that she had killed him?

Ella let the magazine drop to the ground. Aidan was a good seventy pounds heavier than her and athletically strong. They had sparred many times, and he never gave an inch because she was a woman. There was no way she could have overpowered him, but what if she was given no choice? Rubbing her temples didn't make the events any clearer. The last memory she had was of Aidan hitting her and blacking out. There was a void where her memory should be. Whatever had happened, Aidan didn't deserve to die, and she was as certain as she could be at this point that she wasn't to blame.

"Aidan, what did you do?"

Spinning around, she fled back up the stairs and took them two at a time. She needed to transform her looks in some way if she headed back to the scene of the crime. Fiddling with her colored contacts as she tried to remove them, a sudden burst of laughter made fresh tears appear.

"I love you, Ella. I've tried hard not to, believe me, but I can't help it. I love you. I need to tell you something, but not here." *His eyes were pleading, and he looked nervous. Aidan was never nervous. From the first moment they'd met, he'd literally swept her off her feet, refusing to give up no matter the countless times that she told him to leave her alone. He pursued her ruthlessly.*

"I have a secret I need to tell you, but it could kill us both. Will you just listen to me, before you launch in, and please try to understand?"

As painful memories rained down in her mind, she frantically pulled open the drawer in the bathroom, to find exactly what she wanted and lifted up the pair of scissors. She stared at her reflection as she hacked her long tresses short, as quickly as possible. Clumps of hair fell into the sink as she chopped crudely over her shoulders and when she was satisfied, she grabbed the box of hair color she'd seen earlier and lifted out the plastic gloves.

Tears fell as she saw them shouting at each other back at her house. He grabbed her arm and was trying to explain something, but she wouldn't listen. That's when his hand struck. Her hand wiped the tears away from her cheek. The next picture chilled her blood to ice. Memories flooded her mind, horrible snatches of last night.

She sat strapped in a wooden chair. Aidan was there. He paced back and forth across her room, his hands behind his back as if he was giving a lecture. His face was composed and waiting. When his eyes met hers, he moved swiftly to her side. However, he didn't release her.

" I didn't want to have to do this, but you've given me no choice. They told me if I took a sample of your blood, they would leave us in peace, so I agreed. We can move away, go anywhere, and they'll leave us alone. Damn it, Ella. Keep still.

I don't want to hurt you anymore." Aidan pulled out a sterile packet, ripped it open, and then held up what looked like a butterfly with a silver needle at the end. Ella ignored his words and tugged against the arms of the chair. She tried to kick out, but duct tape secured her limbs.

"How could you!" She spat the words out. Her heart galloped like a wild stallion and she wriggled to loosen her ties. He inched closer with the needle, and she screamed as loud as she could, only to feel the sting once again from his hand.

"Ella, please, you're making me do this. I don't want to hurt you or your lovely body, but if you don't comply, they will kill us both. When things settle, you will understand. You see, I know who you are, Ella Masters. You're a soul-shifter, born into the clan of Ariana. Most people would think you're a freak but not me. I think you're fascinating."

His eyes bulged like a toad, and she blinked to rid herself of the repulsive image. Aidan seized that moment to stab the needle into her vein. Stunned by the shocking turn of events, she sat there, unable to react. This slimy man had earlier been declaring his love. Revulsion rose inside her, and she wanted to kill him but her body went limp. She couldn't fight anymore. He wiped where the needle punctured the skin, covered it with a Band-Aid and dropped her arm.

Aidan shook the glass vial that contained her blood, and then placed it into a small black case. A holler from the other room sounded out, and he turned and stared at the doorway. A bulldozer of a man filled the doorway. His face was covered in acne, and his surly brown eyes stared lasciviously at Ella as he wiped his mouth with the back of his hand. She started to turn her head away, but caught sight of a large triangular tattoo with an eye in the center on the man's wrist. Her gaze traveled once more upward to study his face. She'd never set eyes on him before, but remembering every detail would be important, later. Once more, she tried in vain to move, pushing her body forward, which made the chair pivot and scrape against the wooden floor, but it was no use. Instead, she concentrated on imagining flames consuming the *building. The flicker of orange sparks danced to life. She shut her eyes to close off the world, and called to the forces of nature. She called out to her fire elements but it was too late. Her eyes flew open as panic swamped her veins. Her time ran out.*

"It's no use, Ella, love. Relax. It will be alright. You'll see. Now, I just want you to sleep. Grab her legs. I don't want to miss her vein." The two of them approached her, and Aidan loomed across her with a full syringe. He flicked the top, and the tattoo man gripped her legs to reinforce their hold. A sharp sting dug into her arm, and all sensation left her.

"Ella, it's pointless trying to fight me. You'll only make it worse."

His words were hazy and her body sinking fast. The tiny ounce of energy dissolved into a mushy puddle. The world started to spin and collide, until there was nothing but dark space. No stars, just darkness.

The memory faded, but the terror and hurt stung as fresh as when the needle penetrated her flesh. She clutched her arm where the needle was thrust several hours ago, and there was a dark ugly bruise the size of her fist.

She gasped, "Son of a bitch."

Why did this keep happening? Why did all the men in her life turn against her? Or die? Would she never learn?

Staring at herself in the mirror, she realized she didn't know Aidan at all. Her eyes were now bright blue without the contacts and she stared at the label on the hair dye. "Inky Black, hm."

****

The Ultimate Perk's crowd was in its last wave of customers desperate for caffeine before closing. It was almost eight o'clock and Marcus pulled awkwardly at his collar. His gaze fixed on each customer as they entered. He wasn't sure coming here was a good idea, but he just knew that Ella was a creature of habit, and he hoped by some miracle, she was still in the vicinity. God, he'd hated this assignment from day one. Hell, if she was a cold-blooded murderer, she would be long gone. As he pictured the slim and introverted woman, he couldn't imagine her killing any living thing. But if by some stroke of luck she did turn up, he had no choice. She was his. But then what? Hand her over to his prick of a boss or help her? His hand smoothed the lines on his forehead. What was wrong with him? Marcus shook his head. Absolutely take her in. She was a suspect in a murder and a national security threat, for God's sake. Although, the vagueness of why she was on the FBI's Most Wanted list prickled his senses. He strode over to the counter and wiped the top down with a cloth until it shone. He couldn't wait to be out of New England, with its quaint charm, and get to the bustling city of New York, where it was easy to stay lost.

A soft feminine voice prickled Marcus's ears, and his back stiffened like granite. Even though she came in most days, no one at the coffee shop except him knew her name. It struck him as odd from the first time he set eyes on her, how she tried to blend in. Her voice was low and she never gave any pleasantries. When she visited the coffee house, her order was the same. And it was always to go. From the beginning, she had been his assignment and that required him to develop a quick rapport. Normally, he wouldn't have glanced at someone as meek and quiet as Ella twice. However, being his target, each detail about her was engraved on his mind; as he heard her voice now, the hairs along his neck stood up to attention. Marcus turned slowly. This was it: his last chance to redeem himself, and he'd better not mess it up.

When he swiveled around, at first the face that appeared before him made him continue to sift through the last remaining customers for the woman he knew but his gaze snapped back to the figure at the counter, and his hands clenched into balls at his sides. Ella's normally swept back, long brown hair was cropped bluntly at the shoulders, and now it was a striking ebony. His gaze slowly swept over her from head to toe. It was definitely her voice, but…when she spoke again, his glance wandered to her thick rose-bud lips and up squarely at her heart-shaped face. He gasped and held back a laugh as his heart roared inside his chest, beating furiously with anger at his foolishness. Sweeping his gaze up to her eyes, he blinked. Hers were a startling blue, like sapphires.

A black velour tracksuit clung to the soft curves of her body, and for a moment, he was dumbstruck. A memory of a dream resurfaced and seized him. Since he was a child, dreams plagued him, but he always dismissed them. However, today he was wide awake, and he couldn't ignore it. A picture of a woman with soft, flowing locks swamped his mind. Her smile stopped his heart, but it was her twinkling blue eyes that were filled with desire that held his breath in his throat. A soft hand caressed his cheek, and an unusual feeling tugged in his chest. Marcus stammered, and exhaled as if winded.

"Ella Masters?" Her name escaped from his lips like a whisper.

She turned a fraction, but kept her gaze low. Marcus knew it was Ella. Her voice sang to him like a siren and she moved in a swaying motion, gently moving her hips. He knew as his eyes drank in the contours of her trim body and long legs it was her. He'd never paid much attention to her shape, because it was always hidden beneath loose-fitted and baggy clothes. He opened his mouth, but nothing came out. Unable to stop staring, he simply tracked her movement like a hunter.

Ella continued to avoid eye contact, leaving her order on the counter and slowly moved away, but Marcus kept his gaze pinned on her. He needed to make his move and soon, before she bolted out the door.

"Ella."

His voice rose against the din of the coffee machine, and Ella lifted her head to stare directly at him. She tugged at her lower lip with her teeth, a nervous reaction he knew by heart; he watched as she darted for the door. He slammed the mug of cappuccino down on the counter, grabbed his jacket, and moved the customers out of the way to get close to the front just as she reached the exit.

As her hand touched the silver handle, he stood at her back and breathed fast against her neck. Ella didn't turn around, and instead of pulling her away from the door,

Marcus caught hold of her elbow and whispered, "Keep going, Ella, and don't make a scene. I know who you are."

There was no response; she simply pulled the door open and he moved along with her outside. Neither spoke until they were farther down the street. His hand tightened around her arm roughly, and he dragged her into a side alley. Marcus towered a good head and shoulders taller than Ella, and he guessed she wasn't more than a hundred pounds or so in weight. Assessing her features closely, he eased his grip. The alley was a dead end, and there was nowhere for her to run, but he wanted to set up some ground rules before they proceeded. He lifted a finger in front of his mouth as she opened hers to speak, motioning for her silence.

"Ella, you're not going to say a word. I don't have time for any games. You have the right to remain silent, but anything you say or do may be used against you in a court of law. You have the right to consult an attorney before any interview and to have an attorney present during questioning now or in the future. If you cannot afford an attorney, one will be appointed for you before any questioning, if you wish. If you decide to answer any questions now, without an attorney present, you will still have the right to stop answering at any time until you talk to an attorney. Do you understand what I have said to you, Ella Masters? Are you willing to answer my questions without an attorney present? Do you hear me?"

Her mouth snapped closed, and she frowned at him.

"If you understand, just nod."

Ella tried to pull her hand free and struggled fiercely against him. He pulled her five-foot-five frame against his solid chest. Marcus couldn't risk losing her now. Her blue eyes sparkled like precious gems, and her cheeks flushed a bright crimson.

"Keep still, damn you. Just nod, Ella, or so help me."

His temper was on a short leash, and God help him, she was yanking it. Ella stopped moving and nodded silently. Marcus sighed and eased his hold again.

"Good. You will not fight me, or I'll have to use other means to restrain you, and you won't like it. I work for the FBI, and I'm bringing you in for questioning."

She moved her head to the side, stunned as she stared at him. Her look penetrated his gaze and he softened his stance as she shook her head, bowing it low as if in defeat. In an odd way, he felt as if he'd let her down and he shifted position to step back slightly.

"I don't have time to listen to a connived explanation of what happened to the professor. My orders are simply to bring you in."

His gut told him that wasn't entirely true, but he needed to stick to the mission; it was easier to push any conscience he had away. In the Navy SEALs, he never questioned an order even when frustrated; he'd been completely loyal to his country, his team, and mission. Only now there was no team. He was alone and this mission didn't make a damn bit of sense. Underneath his shirt, he wore his tattoo of a frog skeleton with a fierce pride but his last tour as a SEAL in Zabul, Afghanistan was brutal and ended badly. He'd lost good men and with them, his sanity—although he wouldn't admit that to anyone. It was also the biggest reason for zero attachments. The ghosts of his past haunted him at night: his friends and enemies both kept him awake.

Ella stumbled against him, and Marcus grabbed her narrow waist to steady her. Swallowing the rising disquiet toward her, he acknowledged how tiny she really was. It would have been virtually impossible for her to have overpowered the professor and killed him. He stared into her almost violet-blues that were framed with long brown lashes, and the picture of the girl from his dreams flashed again. She didn't look like Ella, apart from the eyes. Marcus shook his head to dislodge the image but inched instinctively closer. So close that as he breathed, the smell of coconut from her hair teased his nostrils. His gaze wandered downward, entranced and captivated, as her tongue flicked out across her rose-bud lips.

Before reasoning took hold, he stared at her luscious full lips as a need to claim them rose so fierce he couldn't think for a moment. But she was his target, his acquisition. A murderer! For a moment, he simply studied her innocent wide blue eyes, which were misty pools that drew him in. As if bewitched and even knowing it was wrong, he invaded her space, gripped her hard against his chest and lowered his head to stare into her eyes.

Their gaze locked into each other as the world around them suspended.

The moment Ella watched Nate's expression change from intolerance and anger to a heated need that flared from watching her lips, she knew her moment had arrived. Ella knew this was her moment of freedom. A kiss was so not happening but as his head lowered, their lips brushed against each other's and a delicious friction rippled through her. That was unexpected, to say the least. As soon as Nate's lips touched hers, a trail of fiery sparks erupted from the pit of her tummy right to her toes. Her body trembled in his arms. In all her lives, she had never responded to any man like that. If the mere touch of his lips had this effect on her, what would it be like to have him touch her all over? It was clear this man was a menace in more ways than most—plus, he was far too good-looking for his own good. She never fell for pretty boys. And he had arrested her!

This was utter madness. He was the enemy.

Swiftly refocusing her thoughts onto the task at hand, she lifted her right knee a fraction, and concentrated hard before she rammed it exactly where it would have the greatest effect, impacting sharply in his groin. Nate jerked his head upward, shock written across his face as it twisted in pain. Instantly, Ella threw her right hand upward, pushed his chin and then thrust her left fist into his ribs. Finally, her left leg kicked into his side to knock him sideways. Stunned, Nate didn't respond but went down to the ground like a felled tree. Ella didn't look back. She was running for her life.

CHAPTER THREE

Ella ran until her legs threatened to buckle from under her. In the past, Ella knew that making friends or taking lovers was a risk as much for them as her. It was her undoing, countless times, and it was why she avoided relationships like the plague. Men, in particular, couldn't be trusted. They always let her down. Even though magic enabled her certain skills, like healing a broken bone or fading a bruise, it didn't seem to stop her making the same mistake over and over in each of her lives. She had allowed Nate into her life and she had fallen for his good looks and schoolboy charm. At six foot plus, with chiseled good looks and rock-hard muscles that made him look more like a male model than a barista, she had considered Nate a friend.

He'd never really flirted but he'd shown her genuine concern and interest; at least, she'd thought so until now. She choked and coughed. The last time they had talked, he'd scolded her for the bruises on her arm, telling her that no woman deserved to be hit. Dumbstruck at his obvious discomfort when she'd mentioned Aidan's name, a deep-seated anger bubbled and she struggled to explain that the bruises were from self-defense classes with him, nothing more. His eyebrows arched as he shook his head and cursed as he walked away. She should have trusted her instincts that told her he was out of place in that tiny coffee shop.

He was an FBI agent. How could she have been so blind and stupid?

Ella sighed. She always thought his Latin looks would have been more comfortable spread across a glossy magazine than serving chai. But his rich, whiskey voice and easy manner had seduced her into believing him. When his gaze penetrated hers, there was a connection that she knew would be dangerous to explore and therefore she had tried to keep her distance. Shaking her head, she wanted to scream to the gods above for her stupidity. When Nate had held her in his arms, a spark of yearning flickered. Even now, running away for her life, the unsettling tingles still prickled inside. However, she'd been nothing more than a mark to him. She was his assignment. Ella paused in the deserted street, her hands on her hips as she breathed fast but forced her rhythm to slow down.

It seemed laughable to Ella that her effort to remain inconspicuous failed miserably. Everyone knew exactly who she was. Nate had known from the beginning. As he held her, and casually read her her rights, his voice was cold and devoid of any hint of emotion. He was detached. His demands rolled off his tongue without hesitation. The harsh words made her flinch: "I don't have time to listen to any connived explanation of what happened to the professor."

His acid tone and words left her in no doubt that he clearly believed she was guilty of murder. Chest heaving and heart banging against her ribs, Ella regained her composure. Running aimlessly would do nothing except get her killed. She bent over, resting her hands on her knees, and lifted her head to study her surroundings. Instantly she recognized where she was. Yards of bright yellow crime-scene tape decorated her front door and house.

What if the police were still around?

She listened carefully, glancing around the area to watch for the slightest clue that someone lay in wait for her. The neighborhood for a Saturday evening was quiet, and to Ella, it appeared more so than normal. Even the noisy dogs next door and the kids' laughter from down the street were missing. It was eerily quiet. She sucked on her lower lip. If there was another way, she wouldn't be here. She had no choice; Ella needed her amulet. Watching for any signs of life, she cautiously slid into the neatly trimmed backyard and deftly lifted the plant pot. After she snatched up the spare house key, she walked toward the back door.

Once inside, Ella forced herself to ignore the fact that the house she had lovingly made home, and had felt safe in, was obliterated. As she walked through the war-torn kitchen into the living room, glass crunched under her feet. Ella had painted the whole house white to maximize the feeling of space. Color was added in the accessories that now lay vandalized and in tatters on the floor. Pictures were slashed and ripped apart. The side tables were overturned, and the stuffing from the armchair lay strewn across the floor. Ella gazed around her unrecognizable living room, and she refused to let any tears fall, even when she saw the taped outline of a person marked out on the floor. She should hate Aidan, despise him, but in his own sick way, he'd loved her, even if it was only as a curiosity. Now, he'd paid the ultimate price with his life. This was her fault; she'd let people get close to her and this is what happened when they did. Fragments of last night continued to splinter into her mind. She saw Aidan standing in the living room, holding her at arm's length to keep her still.

"They've told me, they only need a small amount of blood, and then they'll leave us alone. Ella, you have to listen. If you don't agree, they'll kill you...I've told them I'll get the sample and bring it to them. Then we'll be free."

Ella digested what he said. Was Aidan part of the Elusti or were they coercing him? He looked sincere, which if it was real, then he had no idea who he was dealing with and what they were capable of. They were an ancient, merciless sect that stretched over continents. They believed anything outside of their order was fair game: either you converted to accept their beliefs or you died. Their corrupted thirst for power and greed involved murder of the innocent and destruction of anything in their path. For centuries, they hunted not only her kind but other innocents, slaughtering them in the name of their faith. A wave of nausea swept over her. She wanted to scream. Did he realize what he'd done?

In a reflex action, Ella turned and kicked out, but he was ready. Aidan grabbed her foot and twisted it hard. Flashes of the fight morphed to life and last night burst into her mind with a clear snap of clarity. They had fought each other until bones were broken, mostly hers. He didn't hold back and neither did she. And now he was gone.

Ella inhaled a deep breath. Aidan had taken her blood, and then drugged her, but what was his plan? Why was she still alive? It didn't make sense. The Elusti had for centuries hunted her people like savages. This fanatical group dated back to the sixteenth century, and was involved in the witch trials in the United Kingdom, Europe, and later the United States, burning and hanging innocents across the world. Over time, their faces changed but the determination of the cult never altered course. It grew and gained more support, remaining hidden behind their wealthy benefactors and seemingly protected behind one government organization or another. They had decimated the clan of Ariana to the point of extinction as far as she knew.

Shaking her head free of the hazy memory of last night, she blinked. Knowing that Aidan had betrayed her and was somehow involved with this group froze her blood to ice. She needed to find the amulet and disappear, fast. Ella remembered knocking it free when she was fighting. As she scanned the room, she wondered whether the amulet had been stolen. To ordinary eyes, it was a striking and unique gold bracelet. In reality, it was her talisman, forged with magic. The bracelet had followed her into the next life gifted to Ella by her mother. In fact, Aidan had once commented on it, saying its jeweled design was similar to one from the nineteenth century. She'd simply smiled and said it was a good replica, keeping the fact it was indeed an original from the Victorian era a secret. It was a gift from a friend who had it fashioned so that the center cabochon opened like a locket. At one time, it was used to hide messages and then later a key. The key was her link to freedom. It opened a safety deposit box that gave her numerous identities and money. Time had taught her to be prepared.

Crawling on her hands and knees over the floor, she checked under the coffee table, the rug, and the fallen magazine rack. As she neared the stone fireplace, slowly a picture formed in her mind of the bracelet: its intricate and delicate crisscross design across the slim band, to the pretty flower shape on top that was inlaid with one large circular diamond and several teardrop diamonds surrounding it. Ella called to it, reaching out to find its location. She narrowed her eyes and then closed them, moving on instinct. The bracelet had been crafted for her by Barnaby who had known who Ella was and what she was, before even she did. Now, it was part of her.

A soft steady beat thrummed in her ears and her fingers tingled. She stretched her slim digits forward over the rough and dusty surface of the fire grate, gazing back at the door to the kitchen and her exit before she turned around to continue her hunt. A sharp sting of electricity charged through her, letting her know she was close. Her hand sifted through the soot and rubble; she finally touched a solid object. Ella inched her fingers forward and tightened them over her discovery.

"Gotcha."

The smug masculine voice boomed close to her ear and her breath caught in her throat. A clicking noise and a distinctive snap brought her out of her frozen stance. *How on earth had he caught up with her?* She jerked her body forward and curved her fingers around her prize, only to be tugged back. Cold metal jammed hard against her left bony wrist and pulled her away. Snapping her head around sharply, she met Nate's determined glare.

"I told you if you didn't behave, I'd use other means."

Ella watched the boiling inferno of absolute maleness that was Nate spew. Yanking her up off the ground, he quickly applied the remaining handcuff to his solid wrist. Stashing her find in her back pocket quickly, she tried to shove him away but he caught her free wrist to hold her; try as she might, they were shackled together.

She was his prisoner.

His dark gaze studied her face; his hand intently grabbed her chin firmly and he peered at her eyes closely. "Contact lens?" He ground the words out and the harshness startled her as they were so unexpected and for a moment she didn't understand why he was asking such a question. Frowning, he repeated the question.

"What?" She stood next to him, completely baffled by his question at this point in time.

"Your eyes, Ella. They were mud brown and now they're as blue as azure. Did you use contact lens?"

She opened and then snapped her mouth closed. She stared him down, straight into his dark, soulful eyes, unwilling to be intimidated by his size and her predicament but dropped her shoulders as if in surrender. "Yes! It's an easy way to change one's appearance. Sometimes, it's necessary."

One corner of his mouth twitched. "It must be tough being a preschool teacher these days."

If he only knew the half of it. Her childhood had been full of love. She was from an ordinary middle-class family, her mother a preschool teacher just like her and her father an up-and-coming author. She went to a good school and had a great circle of friends until a freak car accident claimed the lives of her parents, which left her an orphan at eighteen. Everything changed from then on. As soon as she was ensconced in the community college in Wells, she knew her powers were rising and she had difficulty controlling them, which drew unwanted attention to her. One terrifying night in particular led to fleeing the coastal town of York, Maine where she lived. She left to start a new life in Massachusetts with a new identity and the moderate inheritance she had been left but it had never been a choice—more necessity. She was about to scream at him as to who the hell did he think he was to judge her, but his callused hand clamped over her mouth as a succession of muffled popping noises exploded across the room and splintered holes in the walls.

Nate pulled away from the fireplace to hide in the alcove; he yanked on the handcuffs, which made her slam against his steel-like chest. She was practically kissing his chest hairs, which she could see peeking through the top of his fitted charcoal-gray shirt. Her wrist stung from the sudden force but she pushed it aside as the gunfire continued. Stepping away slightly from Nate, she glanced in the direction of the bullets but he shoved her back behind him. If it was the Elusti, pretty boy didn't have a chance.

"We have to get out of here. Someone's firing at us."

"No kidding, Sherlock."

His face loomed in close, scowling. "Be quiet." More bullet holes peppered the white walls. His hand twisted around his back to search for something she couldn't see as it disappeared under his black trench coat. Ella hoped to hell it was equal in firepower to what they were being shot at with. Whoever was firing at them was using a silencer, and they weren't shooting for fun. If they didn't move, they were dead, and the handcuffs were a hindrance. As if he read her mind, he lifted Ella's wrist, pulled out a key from his pocket and opened the lock.

"Keep quiet, and stay behind me. I'm taking these off, but I warn you, if you move from my side, you're dead. Either I'll shoot you or they will. Understand?"

She rubbed her wrist, but didn't move. Judging from the direction of the bullets, and the quantity, Ella surmised there were at least three gunmen inside the house, but she wasn't sure about outside. Nate's forehead creased with multiple lines as he briefly narrowed his gaze at her, as if trying to work out some kind of puzzle; she wondered what he was thinking. Standing straighter, she sighed as she realized her appearance was the cause of his disquiet. Did he really believe she was capable of murder, even if she was barely recognizable as the timid schoolteacher? His gaze moved away from her. For the longest time, Ella had believed being hidden in this leafy, quintessentially New England town, she had found a safe haven, but once again she was surrounded by danger. *Would it ever be any different?*

After a moment, Nate turned to look over his shoulder at her and his chiseled features appeared softer than before. He lifted his finger to his mouth, silencing her once more. He lifted his other hand with the palm facing her to signal for her to stay put. She pulled at his shirt. "I'm not staying here. I'm coming with you."

He tilted her chin upward and rubbed his thumb on her jaw. "Ella, if that's even your real name, this is what I'm trained to do. Stay put—stay alive. There are too many of them. I need to even the odds. We're sitting targets like this."

Before she could question why, she pressed her lips against his, as if to remind her of the recent electrifying effect. Instantly, a deep tingling shot through her body, firing and sparking her energy. She was about to push him away, but he did and she stood breathless and alone.

In a flash, Marcus disappeared around the corner and headed for the kitchen. He crept with the stealth of a leopard in the darkness and silence. A crunch sounded toward his left; he swiveled around as a large black mass loomed and pounced. He fired two shots from his Sig Sauer P226 and the figure dropped to the ground. He had thirteen rounds left and another magazine in his belt. Running forward, he crouched and searched the dead man's pockets. Nothing. He turned his body over and as the man's hand fell forward, it displayed a prominent black tattoo that Marcus recognized. Swearing under his breath, he stood up to search the silvery shadows, but large plumes of white smoke billowed into the kitchen from the stairs, making visibility difficult. *What the hell was going on?*

A loud explosion erupted from the same direction, knocking him back but he recovered, quickly straightening from his position to dart back into the living room. Whatever was going on, they needed to leave—now. Marcus found Ella still sequestered away in the alcove, staring vacantly as if in a trance. Maybe shock was setting in. With no time for niceties, he grabbed her arm and pulled her out. Another explosion rocked behind them and the entire house crackled with the energy of the fast-spreading fire that licked the walls a sparkling orange and gold.

Another round of shots fired, and Marcus swiveled around, raised his gun into the muted light and shot at the fast-moving shadows. The pungent smell of burning wood and plastic attacked his nostrils and stung his lungs. Covering his mouth with his arm, he moved quickly as the flames crawled across the floor to consume the sofas, rugs, and anything flammable. He gripped Ella's hand tightly to pull her through the house, keeping her positioned close behind him as he faced the enemy—both fire and man—with his weapon positioned in front, loaded and ready.

As they reached the back door, Ella screamed. At this point, they had become disconnected. Marcus swung around to face a beast of a man, several inches taller than him and wider, who dragged a struggling Ella back into the flames. Her eyes twinkled in the darkness like a beacon of hope. Slowly, he steadied his breathing and felt in his pocket, pulling out his night vision scope, which he attached to his hand piece. With complete control and precision, he raised his arm, took aim and even though his target held Ella close like a shield, shot the man dead.

"Ella." Before he could stop the words, they tumbled out as he raced into the dancing shadows and grabbed her quivering form. Killing someone was always a last resort. The act of taking a life gave him no thrill or pleasure. It was simply a necessity, a kill-or-be-killed situation. His job was always to protect those who couldn't protect themselves. Now he knew who was after her: the Elusti. That raised yet more questions that his boss definitely wouldn't like, but it changed his perspective on this mission and on what to do with Ella Masters.

Only once had he tangled with the fanatical group and that was enough to leave a permanent scar on him and his men. The incident that to this day sent shivers down his titanium backbone happened while on tour in Afghanistan. His cast-iron belly over the years faced a multitude of bad situations. He was as used to devastation, turmoil, and chaos as anyone could be, facing it in large and regular quantities. Marcus was trained to trust no one outside of his team and to suspect everyone. However, this group—at the time, an unknown band of mercenaries—hadn't just massacred an entire village. This army, he spat to the ground, had held thirty defenseless women and children hostage in this tiny hilltop community in unsanitary and unholy conditions. They had tortured, gang-raped and drawn out the deaths of their victims, as if gaining pleasure from the act. In war, death and loss of life was inevitable and soldiers knew that; few he'd met over the years enjoyed killing. It was a necessity—at least that's what they told themselves, dealing with the mistakes and consequences later when they weren't on the battlefield or pushing them away and pretending they didn't exist.

But walking into the camp on that bitterly cold Sunday morning, there was nothing holy about what they discovered that day. It was a death camp. For the first time, he wondered how the human civilization still existed. How could people wreak such violence upon each other? This army had no respect when it came to human life. He was told his mission was to help the hostages escape to freedom. However, after arriving in the early hours of the morning with his team, they executed their plan, stealthily making their way to the compound. But even using the thermal night vision goggles, they didn't realize until they were deep inside the brick buildings that they were too late.

Way too late!

The tortured bodies of women and children were stacked in heaps, some smoldering, some left rotting for the flies to feast upon—the smell of death pungent and overwhelming. Many experienced warriors emptied their stomachs as they stared at the bloody sight. Bile reached the back of his throat just recalling the putrid odor. Marcus swallowed down his memory and cast a quick glance in Ella's direction. Quickly, his orders had changed from recovery to burying the bodies, along with any evidence that was found. Fighting in a hot zone where you never knew at times who the enemy was, be it a child with an innocent-looking toy only to have it explode or a female suicide bomber, few things in life truly shocked him but the grisly scenes of children and women haunted him.

They still did.

It was the reason he had left the only stable family he'd ever known—the SEALs. When he returned stateside after that last mission, he'd made a vow to the last victim who died in his arms. When he asked her who was responsible for the massacre, her final word was Sampa, which in Pashto means Devil. Since that day, it had become his personal mission to discover who these devils were. And he had. The tattoo on the dead man confirmed their continued and very active existence.

CHAPTER FOUR

Nate dragged Ella away from the house just as the bright orange flames engulfed the building and swallowed it. The windows smashed as smoke and flames spilled out around them, blanketing the view.

Ella coughed but quickly covered her mouth with her hand and tried to keep up with Nate, not wanting to look back at the inferno. Her body weighed heavily and she knew her strength was failing. Starting the fire reduced her energy. To keep it burning, after healing her injuries earlier, left her running on empty. If Nate's arm wasn't wrapped around her waist right now, she would be on the ground. It was too much. Aidan was dead. She was wanted by the FBI for his murder, and hunted by the Elusti. Now, her home was burning to the ground and would soon be no more than a pile of ash.

"Nate, I can't keep going," she rushed out between gasps. Clinging to his arm, tingles dropped from her head to her toes and her body slumped as the world around her disappeared.

Adam Levine blasted out around her, along with the strong aroma of coffee, and she jolted awake. Shifting her position so she sat up, she yanked her arm and wrenched the socket painfully. Looking sideways at her wrist, which was secured at the side and bashed against cold, hard metal, she practically exploded. She stopped herself from stomping her feet and spun her head to glare at his sideways profile. *Damn him.* Ella made a show of tugging her arm again, but it was useless. Her hand was locked in the handcuff, and it was secured to the seat belt hook. She swiveled back to peer across at Nate, who focused on the traffic ahead. His mouth tightly closed, he appeared oblivious of her frustration. Blinking away her sleep, she decided to try reasoning with him.

"Is this really necessary? Did you think I would jump out of a moving truck?" She bashed the metal cuff against the seat belt ring, and sighed with a shrug.

"Is that a trick question, Ella? The last time I served you coffee, you were a preschool teacher. Today, you're wanted for murder, and you've turned into some kind of sexy Mata Hari. I'm not taking any chances. If you behave yourself, when we stop, I'll unlock the handcuffs but for now they stay."

"That's rich coming from you, Mr. FBI. You damn well kissed me after you arrested me. Is that standard procedure these days? As for your *name* is that another of the lies you've spun?"

A muscle in Nate's cheek twitched and he shot a sharp stare at her before he repositioned his hands on the wheel, which he gripped until his knuckles blanched white. Despite his coolly delivered speech, she affected him and she smiled at this awareness as she stared out the dusty window. A lot had changed in twenty-four hours—that was true—but what was the same was the fact she was his prisoner, even though he had called her *sexy*. That needed to change and fast, but where on earth were they headed? As she puzzled over her next move, his deep voice interrupted her thoughts.

"That kiss was a mistake it won't be repeated, but I'm glad you're awake. You had me worried for a while. I wasn't sure if I was going to have to take you to the emergency room when you fainted. I thought you had been shot." He briefly turned his intense gaze toward her before he turned back to the traffic.

Hearing his words and the implication, Ella bolted upright and adjusted her coat. She shivered with the cold and noticed that her jacket was unzipped, revealing her lacy camisole and her heaving bosoms beneath. Her cheeks flared with heat. Suspicious of his words, she flicked a furious glare at him.

"And how did you know that I wasn't?"

"Before I became an FBI agent, I was a Navy SEAL. I'm used to checking bodies for injuries. Ella, trust me, I have seen a *woman's* anatomy before."

Her cheeks scorched with the knowledge that his large and capable hands had roamed across her flesh while she lay unconscious.

"Not *this* woman. Well, I hope you enjoyed your grope, because it's the last one you're going to get." She pulled the thin velour jacket closer, as if to save her modesty, even though she knew that it was too late.

He smirked and turned the heater on full blast. "Ella, I've never needed to resort to seducing an unconscious woman. Ever. Women like what they see and as I happen to like women, a lot, I'm never without a supply of *willing* partners."

God, he was unbearable. So arrogant. "Women like what they see." Ha. Ella opened her mouth, ready to protest, but as she tried to be shocked, she wasn't. Soaking in his features, she had to admit, he was a gorgeous hunk of controlled strength and masculinity with his square jaw, straight nose, and dark, intelligent eyes. She stared as his suntanned hand, which combed back his closely cropped but thick hair, and noticed the light stubble scattered across his chin and above his lips. It made him even more handsome and dangerous-looking. She believed him when he said women liked what they saw. She did. Ella also imagined that he knew exactly how to please them in every possible way, which made her mouth water. Swallowing away her growing desire, she reminded herself that she needed to figure out a way to get rid of him, and to escape.

Life was never fair.

In all her lives, only once had she came close to real love. It was her second life and the year was 1676. She had survived the squalor of a childhood in the plagued-infested city of London and the Great Fire of 1666 that destroyed thousands of houses and churches but mercifully took few lives. The upside of the fire, which started in King Charles II baker's house in Pudding Lane, was it vanquished and eradicated most of the disease-ridden rats, which diminished the plague, although it left large numbers of people displaced and homeless. However, her father, a vicar, after losing his wife the previous year, had already made the decision to move back to his family's residence in Oxworth. They lived on a modest but respectably sized estate with a housekeeper and a few servants. Life was better, the air clean and sweeter.

And Isabella grew up happy and carefree with little care for society or her place in it, but eventually she turned sixteen and her child-like features developed into that of a young woman, and it drew many stares and glances from the gentry and locals. However, when it became common knowledge that she had little in the way of a dowry, her suitors fled. Despite being told she was a beauty with a bonny personality, it seemed money carried more weight. Only one pursued her endlessly. One young ardent suitor refused to back down and overwhelmed with his persistence and the fact he was strikingly handsome. She fell head over heels in love with Sir Robert Jackson. Robbie, her nickname for him, was a nobleman by birth, but that didn't stop the love affair that blossomed.

Of course, he convinced her the romance must remain a secret for both their sakes, as both families were against any involvement. Naively, she agreed and when he suggested a clandestine marriage, it should have alerted her but she believed he loved her. Without banns or a wedding license, she agreed. After the hasty nuptials were conducted in a tavern several towns away from her home by a man dressed in ill-fitted clothes who said he was an ordained clergyman, she was blissfully happy for a few short days but the Elusti arrived and put an end to that and her life.

The Elusti spun a compelling story of how they believed Isabella was a vixen who dabbled in witchcraft and had spellbound him. Because of the lingering history of the Pendle witch trials, and hangings, he believed them. Robbie had achieved what he truly wanted, and fearing it more trouble than his worth to argue, didn't need much persuading of Isabella's guilt. He didn't need much convincing and when his parents arrived, it was clear they were instrumental in the Elusti's involvement. They threatened him with exposure. If he surrendered Ella for inquisition, they would keep the fact she was a witch a secret, sparing his reputation and honor. Deep down, Robbie couldn't survive without his fortune, which his parents threatened to retain unless he married a lady of worth; fearing such scandal, he agreed.

It wasn't until the noose was placed around her neck for the second time in as many lives that she knew she had died this way before. As the rope squeezed around her throat and the air left her lungs, a flash of her past execution rose up to greet her before everything faded away.

No, love never lasted for Ella, no matter who she was or what year she lived. Love was fleeting. It left her alone, afraid, and usually at the hands of those who wished her harm. If now her time was at an end, so be it; at least there would be no more heartache. Maybe her destiny was to be alone. Her heart squeezed and she forbade the welling tear to fall. Love came and went. She rubbed her neck with her free hand, feeling the tightening of the noose, and blinked the bitter memories away, hardening her heart against sharing it with anyone.

"So where are we headed? I thought I'd be in a prison cell by now. Not some battered, foul-smelling truck. What's the plan, Nate?" She wriggled, feeling uncomfortable, and her arm ached, but she wasn't going to say anything. She needed to find out what he intended to do.

"Hey, don't knock old Maisie. She's a classic." He turned the music down, and lifted his thermos to sip at his coffee.

"And she belongs in a museum or the dump. Doesn't the FBI pay you enough for a decent car?"

He flicked his eyes over at her,

"Look, Ella, I left my SUV with my neighbor and borrowed his truck. I did this to buy us some time. Don't make me regret it. There are a few questions I need to find the answers to and I'm not getting much help from the agency. Therefore, I'm taking a little detour, which may or may not get us killed. But either way, I will not simply hand you over right now." All the earlier easy banter faded. His voice was a dry monotone and deadly serious.

Sitting up straighter, Ella wondered why he was taking such an interest.

"What sort of questions?" She raised her eyebrows and edged closer. What was going on inside his head? Would he help her or was this another ploy to land her in more trouble? He said the word *us*—what did he mean?

When he pulled the truck over into the service station, he parked and turned his body sideways to stare intently at Ella. His arm rested along the back of the seat and he nodded casually in the direction of a small diner.

"You hungry? I know you must be. Maybe it will stop the shaking. I don't need to be your enemy, Ella. If you stop fighting me, I may even be able to help you. I feel somewhere along the way we have our wires crossed and I need to find out why. I want to know what's your involvement with the Elusti. And why are they after you?"

Ella shook and she couldn't stop when her blood sugar was low, which happened when she depleted her energy after using magic to start the fire. She needed rest and food. At the moment, Ella was cruising on adrenaline and her survival instincts, but it would not last long.

Nate dug in his jean pocket and pulled out a small set of silver keys. As he leaned over, her chest stole her breath and tickled her nose. She could smell his subtle cologne, a fresh mix of musk and him, all male. Her heart catapulted at his closeness and for a second, she thought he would kiss her. Instead, she heard the click of the handcuffs unlocking. Freedom. She could bolt right now. She might even make it; she was a fast runner. But he had taken a risk by not taking her in and he wasn't the Elusti. His coffee bean eyes flashed at her with an alertness that told her to wait, and she nodded.

"You're right. I need to eat and then we can talk."

They settled in the corner table of the mostly empty diner and a pleasant middle-aged woman with short bobbed hair took their order.

"Look, we don't have much time. My name isn't Nate Williams, it's Marcus Drayton, that was my undercover name. I want you to trust me, Ella. We're going to my friend's place in New York. He's a Navy SEAL too—well, he was. I think he will be able to help." He discreetly peered around the dated diner with the jukebox playing softly in the background. A young waitress wiped down the laminate counter, but her gaze never left them.

"Marcus Drayton, it suits you but as for trusting you, how on earth do you expect me to do that? Anyway, how can your friend help?" She grabbed his hand to gain his attention. When he looked across at her, she drew in a deep breath. Just touching his warm skin sent a zing of electricity that rippled through her hand, shocking her. Being this close to him was a hazard and should come with a warning. She removed her hand and picked up her glass; the cold, refreshing liquid steered her back on track. Ella liked his real name, why he had chosen to come clean about it now she wasn't sure, but it was simply another detail he had lied about.

"He's a genius. He's called the Gateway. He can hack into any computer system and I need information. You and the professor—was it love at first sight?" He raised his eyebrows and narrowed his gaze as he waited for her response.

Why did he want to know?

"Excuse me..." Ella choked on the water and squirmed in her seat, uncomfortable about the directness of his question about Aidan. She stared at her hands instead. Their relationship was not like any other that she had with men. She thought this time, because there were no emotions involved, no feelings of romance or love, that she would be safe. How wrong she had been. With her hands clasped together, she sighed and sat back.

"It's just you don't seem that upset at his death. That is, of course, assuming that you didn't kill him."

Her gaze darted back at him. His eyebrows furrowed together, and he leaned forward with his chin resting on the bridge of his hands as he waited. His dark eyes scanned her features as if he were trying to read her thoughts. Ella ran her tongue over her lips as she contemplated her answer and leaned on the table to face him.

"I didn't kill Aidan. I would never do that but I think the Elusti did. My life's complicated…" She shrugged.

"Try me, Ella. Complicated is my middle name and I'm sure I'll be able to keep up."

At that moment, the blonde waitress who'd been watching them intently decided to turn up with their two plates of food—steak, rare for him and a chicken salad for her—which broke the cozy spell. She put the plates down, and smiled broadly at Marcus. Her long eyelashes fluttered with a brazen look that made Ella want to scratch her eyes out. Instead, she fixed her gaze on her food and willed her irrational emotions to calm down. She stabbed her tomato with her fork.

"Can I get any sauces for you? Anything at all—just let me know." She flashed a brilliant smile, showing her perfect row of white teeth.

"Nope, we're all set." He gave a brief smile and dismissed her, snapping his attention back to Ella.

The waitress drilled holes in her with her glare and she smiled back at her sweetly as she moved away. *Jeez Louise, he was telling the truth.* The young woman could not take her eyes off him. Ella lifted her gaze once more as the waitress whispered to her friend and pointed over in their direction.

How dare she behave this way in front of her, as if she were invisible. For all she knew, she could be his wife or lover.

Ella stabbed her fork into the chicken, shoved it into her mouth and chewed to stop herself from saying anything. Swallowing the rubber-tasting piece of meat, she sucked on her lower lip as she contemplated her options. Should she tell him the truth about Aidan? No matter what he said or did, she couldn't trust him. He was playing some kind of game and this was simply delaying the inevitable. But she could play along for a bit and figure out what his role was in all of this. She continued to pick at her food.

Marcus cut up his steak and piled his fork full, swallowing his food with relish. He devoured the entire meal and cleaned his plate until he'd scraped up even the gravy.

"Aidan wasn't my boyfriend, at least not in the way you or anyone imagines. It was all for show. He wanted companionship more than intimacy. He was a historian, a writer. For all his social graces, he was rather shy and introverted. I don't think he liked people much, to be honest. Last summer, I was a student in one of his courses and I bumped into him at the museum. He's quite a bit older than me—sorry, he was. God, it's all so much to take in... Anyway, he gave me A's in my class and told me I was a bright student and should consider taking a full-time course. One thing led to another. He was persuasive when he wanted something. He was also a martial arts expert; he'd trained in Thailand. He insisted I be able to protect myself, and strangely enough, we connected. That move I made on you was called the Buffalo Punch. He taught me that—he liked to practice. The relationship was uncomplicated." Ella pressed her eyes shut, remembering scenes from the last night that now haunted her. She'd been so careless. So stupid.

"There's more but..."

Feeling his stare burn her cheeks, she opened her eyes. His face remained stiff, contemplative, and devoid of emotion. Marcus rubbed his thumb back and forth over his full lips as he patiently waited. Ella's heart slammed into her ribs, as heat infused her cheeks. How could she begin to tell him the rest? What would he think? And why should she care? Maybe he already knew? Time ticked as she weighed whether to release anything more about herself.

"I cannot help you if you don't tell me everything, Ella."

Marcus stared at her but he moved his hand to reach out and grab hers. The thumb that once had been stroking his lips now rubbed the skin on her hand and a heart-stopping pounding began in her chest. Her body responded to his touch by melting and liquid heat spread through her veins, sparking a fire in her belly. Ella's open mouth formed an *O*; she had not been caressed by a man in such a long time and she gasped at the escalating need. Right from the start, Aidan had made his intentions perfectly clear. His interest was not sexual. At first, she was shocked, and suspected that perhaps he was gay, but soon learned that wasn't the case. A couple of weeks into their relationship, when she thought he would try to kiss her, Aidan announced that wasn't what he wanted from her, and that he was not into forming emotional attachments.

He went onto explain that he had seen the effects of such relationships, and did not want to be held slave to them anymore. At the time, Ella didn't believe him, but having Aidan as a pretend boyfriend provided her with a cover that was too tempting to resist, enabling her to hide behind the facade. There were nights that they shared a bed, usually after a heavy session of fighting. But they never kissed or touched each other intimately. They became friends. Only, he had deceived her from the beginning. She was nothing more than an artifact or specimen he hoped one day to possess and keep in a glass container, like the many displays at his beloved museum.

"I *can't*, Nate. You wouldn't understand." She shook her head, feeling a fool again. Part of her longed to explain, but she could not trust him or put him in danger. She pulled her hand away from his.

He wiped his mouth with the napkin and signaled for the check. "It's Marcus, and I'm all you've got. Didn't it occur to you for one minute as to why the professor would choose you? Sure, you're beautiful, but beautiful women are a dime a dozen. You were played. He wanted *you* for a reason. You're telling me jack shit, and I know there's a whole lot more to this."

The chair scraped across the linoleum as he pushed it back. He pulled out a couple of crumpled twenty dollar bills and slapped them down on the table. Ella stood up and walked away from the table. He let her pass in front of him and once outside, grabbed her arm and turned her around to face him.

"The Elusti *kill* people, Ella, and call it a necessity. They've been protected by the government before for God knows what reason. I won't work for any organization that helps, aids, or justifies the killing of innocent people. Hell, even murderers get trials. The people the Elusti slaughtered didn't. If you're one of them, Ella, so help me, I'll kill you myself..." he whispered softly against her neck as his face nestled in her hair.

Small, warm breezes like kisses caressed her skin intimately. Shivers skittered down her spine. Her breathing stopped as her heart catapulted into the star-filled sky. In her five lives, no man ever had such a magnetizing effect on her. She blinked and her heart thudded.

"I'm not...but I do know them. They've hunted my people for centuries, and they won't stop until they have me." She stared into the inky depths of his eyes, hypnotized and unsure why she was revealing anything to him.

"Why?"

As she stared at his soft, moist mouth inches from hers, a pulsing ache for him to touch her grew. "Because I'm the last of my kind. They've killed all the rest."

Marcus pushed back and shook his head. His dark eyes, like burning wood in a smoldering fire, left her motionless and a captive. He roughly pulled her chin up. "What do you mean, your kind?"

How many times in her lives had she been asked that question? More than once and yet the irony was that in most of her previous lives, the only explanation that people accepted who'd hunted her was that she was a witch. Twice, she had been convicted and hung as one. Blinking up at him, she oddly found herself wondering how old he was as lines formed around his eyes, and one eyebrow lifted as he spoke. Sighing and unable to look at him directly, she gave him the only answer she was willing to give.

"I'm a witch."

****

Marcus gripped the stirring wheel, and twisted his hands as if he were strangling the life out of someone, namely Ella Masters. *A witch.* For one goddamn minute, he thought she was really going to be honest and transparent. He should have known. Did she take him for a fool? If her answer was meant to be amusing, it had the opposite effect. Not for the first time, he wondered whether he should take her straight in and hand her over to the FBI to sort it out. God, his head ached. He didn't believe in anything that couldn't be explained scientifically; at least, that's what he told himself, but for some unknown reason, the idea of handing her case over to anyone else was unsettling to say the least. A long held obligation to a young woman no older than Ella gripped his reasoning.

He'd given up all that mumbo jumbo, psychic crap a long time ago. Ghosts, witches, other life-forms: he'd heard it all before. Each one, he discounted and dismissed. Magic was a bedtime story, a fantasy, and he was too old and jaded for those. He knew firsthand that harboring such illusions was extremely dangerous. He'd barely lived through his mother's spaced-out journeys, or second sight as she called them. The doctors called it paranoid delusions, which meant she spent most of his childhood locked away in a psychiatric hospital, heavily medicated. Her confession of being a witch hit the mark and pierced him like nothing else could. Did she know of his past? That was impossible.

He slammed the steering wheel with his hand and let his gaze wander toward Ella, who slept like a baby and made little snorting noises. She was curled into the fetal position, but every now and then she moved, and he caught a glance of her makeup-free face, which in sleep appeared softer, more relaxed. He let out a deep breath. It was funny how in watching her, his anger slowed in tune with her breathing, and he admitted to himself how utterly captivating and beautiful she was.

A huge commercial truck honked its horn in the adjoining lane and he swiftly maneuvered his vehicle away. She literally would be the death of him. Since that kiss in the alleyway—a kiss that never should have happened— something tugged at him and twisted in his belly. Hell, even in the diner, the way her eyes focused solely on him, drinking him in, practically begging him to kiss her again and her frosty glare at the waitress should have annoyed him. Yet it had the opposite effect. Ella was hot; how had he ever believed she was plain or ordinary? Damn it, he was not used to feeling played or out of control. He did not date; he had lovers and that was the way he liked it. Anything else was trouble and took his focus off the mission.

Ella was a complication he couldn't afford. However, his body was claiming otherwise. When she came near, his body responded in seconds, leaving him as frustrated as hell. His instincts told him to protect her from harm. She clearly was a magnet for trouble. Yet, this was the opposite of common sense. But when had he ever demonstrated that? In the hot zones, he'd acted on his gut, and more times than not, his gut was right. His grip tightened around the wheel at the thought of what he should do about Ella. All that was clear in his mind despite the lies she dished out was he would kill anyone who tried to hurt her and that worried him. Maybe she wasn't entirely lying because she had definitely cast a spell over him. A low laugh escaped his lips. For now, she was exactly where he could keep a close eye on her. He would get to the bottom of the puzzle that was Ella Masters.

As he stared ahead at the virtually empty highway, Marcus wondered whether he had made the wrong decision earlier when he had phoned his boss. The whole conversation stunk and made him uneasy. However, he reasoned that it would give him more time to figure out what the hell the Elusti's role in all of this was. He told Jackson that he had acquired the target, and explained the run-in with the Elusti. He made out that he was worried about Ella's safety, and that taking a slower route on the back roads would be better as they seemed to know her every move. At the mention of the Elusti, his boss clamped down his conversation. Marcus explained what had happened at Ella's house.

"I guess this is another mess that I have to clear up, Drayton. Just make sure you don't leave a trail of dead bodies across the state. You have twelve hours to bring her in, understand?"

Marcus had expected more resistance from Jackson, and certainly more questions about what had happened, which confirmed that something unusual was going on. Was he being set up? He pulled off the highway, and prodded Ella.

"We're almost there."

She did not stir. The last twenty-four hours had been a minefield to navigate and it was not going to get any better. She must be exhausted. *A witch*, he whispered as he scratched his head. Her file referred to her as *the witch* because of two college dumb ass kids reciting that she had spelled them to do crazy stunts one Halloween night. Her story was somewhat different and involved the frat boys behaving in a lewd and borderline terrorizing way that should have ended with their arrests but their parents had deep pockets and Ella wouldn't press charges. The complaint was several years old and the only slip of information he had managed to dig up from her past. But all the boys had called her a witch and it had stuck.

He didn't know what to make of her confession. Of all the likely scenarios that he had imagined—such as she was a Russian spy, a member of the Secret Service or a wife of some big crime boss—he had never imagined *that*. Inside, his gut instinct told him whatever she was, it was not a murderer, and he would be damned if he would turn her over without more information. The sign he passed read East Brunswick. His old buddy Jake, who he had not seen in over a year, was expecting him. He hoped he would be able to help.

Jake's ranch house was at the end of the dimly lit street. It was silent apart from the rustles of the trees as the wind brushed against them. He parked in the driveway and turned the engine off. His eyes studied the house as it lay shrouded in darkness and observed the absence of any movement inside. Across the street, identical houses lay spread out in a horseshoe curve and all were equally quiet. He looked for any messages on his phone from Jake, who he'd contacted earlier, giving as few details as possible for his early-morning arrival.

Certain that it was safe, he pushed the door of the truck open and stepped out. Ella started to stir and sat up, bringing the blanket that was thrown over her up around her shoulders. Marcus walked around to the passenger side and opened the door. He offered her his hand to help her down, but she shook her head and jumped to the ground. Immediately her body swayed, but two muscle-clad arms instantly swooped under her, grabbing hold and saving her.

"I can manage. Put me down." She wriggled and pushed her hands against his chest.

"I rather doubt that. You hardly touched your food in the diner and after what you've been through in the last twenty-four hours, you're beat. Unless, hang on—was that little performance what happens just before you lift off and fly? I mean, witches fly, don't they?" He laughed and carried on despite her reluctance. Carrying her was not difficult; as a Navy SEAL, he was used to carrying his body weight plus that of his gear. She was a light weight by comparison.

As he neared the back door, it opened with a creak. A well-built man with deep set eyes and closely shaved dark blond hair appeared with a broad smile etched on his face. He remained in the house and beckoned for Marcus to enter, only speaking once they were in the house and he closed the door. "Well, well, bro, unexpected, but great to see you."

Marcus put Ella down and clutched the other man in a quick bear hug. They pulled apart, and the man punched Marcus in the upper arm but fixed his eyes on Ella. Marcus rested his hand on Jake's shoulder, as if to keep him apart from Ella when he noticed his glance didn't lift from her.

"Ella, this is Jake. Jake, this is my *fiancée*, Ella." The word was out before he could retract it, but it showed his friend that she was hands-off.

Jake instantly lifted his gaze away and glared over at him silently for a second before he shoved off Marcus's hand and lifted Ella up, easily swinging her around.

"Well, I'll be damned. Ella, it's a mighty pleasure to meet you." Jake smiled with delight, and peered across at Marcus as he kissed Ella firmly on the cheek. He placed her back on the ground, but instead of letting her go, clamped his arms around her waist and squeezed her against his solid chest.

"You even smell good." He sniffed her hair.

"Jake." Marcus growled and pulled him off her. His face leered right up close to Jake's.

"It's okay." She tugged at his sleeve.

Her touch and voice had a strange effect on him. The pulse in his neck that throbbed since Jake pawed Ella settled and he unclenched his teeth. He dropped his shoulders, and without any good reason, he marched next to Ella.

"Well, well, this is interesting. I never thought I'd see the day, you acting all possessive. I've never seen that. Engaged? Brother, you swore that there were too many beauties out there to pick just one and you sure bedded a few." His gaze flicked over Ella. "Although, you sure are a rare beauty. Sorry, I don't mean to offend you…"

Ella swung her gaze from Marcus to Jake, confused as to why he'd introduced her as his fiancée. Now, what the hell was she to do, go along and play act? She gazed at Jake, unsure of what to say.

"Jake, you don't have to explain to me. I'm not—" Before she could finish, Marcus slid his arm around her waist and reeled her in close against his heat and she closed her mouth.

"No, you don't have to explain to Ella. She's been around me long enough and knows about my past. And that's exactly what it is—the past." Pulling her chin toward him, he ran his finger along Ella's bottom lip as he stared over at Jake.

"Okay, 007…oops, didn't mean to let that slip out, sorry." His boyish grin revealed a dimple and gleaming white teeth.

Marcus sighed. Ella, still entranced with the conversation between the two powerful men, laughed, staring at Jake and then Marcus, taking in his sigh as he removed his hand from her chin.

"Is that your nickname? Seven. Well, I thought it might be a number referring to your many conquests, but it doesn't seem high enough from what I've heard." She smirked up at Marcus deliberately ignoring the double o and slapped her hand across his chest hard.

He didn't bat an eye but lowered his head and stared into her bright blue eyes as he wondered exactly how many conquests she had made. A frown crossed his face, not liking where his mind was taking him, but he kissed the tip of her nose and squeezed her tighter and refused to release her.

"Ha, she does know you. Well, he's had a bunch of names: Casanova, heartbreaker, sex god, but none he would answer to until he was caught drinking a medium dry martini. The guys ripped into him about that and from then on, it was 007 or Bond, *James Bond*. He looks like one of those suave dudes who play the spy, and I think he's slept with as many as the character does, if not more." Jake shrugged and watched Ella's face.

This time, she wasn't sure whether he was trying to goad her or get some type of reaction and she tapped her lip with her finger.

"Cut it out, Jake." Marcus frowned at him. Ella said nothing.

"You said she knew all about your past, bro." Jake pretended to punch Marcus's arm again. The boys eyeballed each other until Ella broke the trance.

"I didn't know his nickname until now, so thanks, Jake. He doesn't reveal much about himself, but we all have a past, don't we? It's what makes him who he is and I love him regardless." Ella reached up and kissed Marcus gently on the lips and hugged him.

Marcus lowered his hand down her back and squeezed her ass.

She wanted to slap him but remained stoic, staring at Jake, who she couldn't make out at all.

"Look, we need your help. Sorry to bring it to your doorstep, but I had no choice. Ella needs to sleep. Is there somewhere she can put her head down for a while?"

She struggled against his hold, not wanting to be sent to bed like a little child. Ella wanted to stay and listen to whatever Marcus wanted to say to Jake in private, but he tilted her chin to face him.

"Yesterday was exhausting and today is going to be just the same. You need to rest and besides, I need to catch up with Jake...Ella." He stared down into her eyes, willing her to play along before he released her chin and his hold around her waist as he waited for her response.

It was almost as if he expected her to fight him and because of that, she thought it would be best to give in and comply. Maybe it was better to play his game for a while.

Absentmindedly, he tucked a stray strand of her hair behind her ear. "Please..." he whispered.

With that, she gave a quick smile, pecked him on the cheek and yawned.

"I am actually really tired. A bed or a sofa would be great." Her face was still pointed at Marcus but she knew Jake watched the scene with more than idle curiosity.

"Sure, follow me. I have a spare room. It's nothing special, but it's clean." He walked down the short carpeted hallway. Ella stepped away from Marcus and was about to follow Jake, who disappeared from view, but Marcus grabbed her hand and tugged her back.

"I need to talk to him and you're beat...Ella...can I trust you not to run?" Staring at her, his face tensed and a puzzled expression broke out, as if he were trying to figure out what she was thinking.

She ran her hand through her tousled shoulder-length hair and yawned.

"You wouldn't get far. I'm trusting you... I don't want to have to handcuff you to the bed, but I will."

Red angry blotches bloomed across her cheeks; she turned sharply away and pulled her hand away, storming off. *Damn him.* She'd give him "handcuffed to the bed." Her plan took shape.

CHAPTER FIVE

The room that Jake led her to was tucked away at the back of the house. As Ella walked into the moderately sized room and stared around, she noted that it was neat and painted in a neutral magnolia with few personal possessions adorning the place, but in the middle was a humongous king-sized mahogany and wrought-iron bed. Jake pointed at the door in the corner.

"There's a shower in through that door if you'd like one. Forgive my comments earlier about Marcus but he was always with a different girl and we've been through so much shit together it's second nature to joke around."

Ella stared at the huge bed, and then glanced toward the shower. Seconds ticked by and suddenly she realized that Jake was still there, expecting some sort of reply. A hot shower would be bliss. "Jake, you don't need to explain anything to me. What's your nickname?" She turned her glance directly on him, raising her eyebrows as she sat down and bounced up and down on the comfy mattress. All the while, she watched the SEAL's expression as he stood still and watched her with his arms folded. He quickly moved to stand right in front of her, and he crouched low. His face was shut off to any emotion and his eyes were unblinking as they pinned on her.

"They call me the Gateway, and I guess it's why you're both here. Just so you know, Ella, Marcus is one of the few people I call a friend. I trust him with my life. Being in the SEALs does that to you. There's a code and it goes way beyond the missions. Seeing as you *know him so well*, I'm sure I don't have to tell you that he's the type of guy who'll defend his team and put their needs before his own. There's little I wouldn't do for the guy. So be sure you know which side you're on, little lady. He's not someone you want as an enemy, because he'll hunt you down and he never gives up." His face was inches from hers, and his baby features were masked in a razor-sharp expression of suspicion.

The door creaked and in strode Marcus.

"Jake…give it a rest. We need to talk, and it's late. Leave Ella to sleep." Marcus grabbed his arm and pulled him out of the room.

Ella released the breath she was holding. Wow, he was intense. She stared at their retreating figures and sighed. Jake wasn't fooled one bit by Marcus's show in the other room. Jake was worried about his friend and he knew that she was the reason Marcus wanted his help. She sighed. Just being with Marcus made him a target, as well as her. The last thing she wanted was anyone else getting killed. Back at the house before it had burnt down, she had managed to retrieve her amulet. She lifted the gold bracelet out of her pocket; the stones glinted in the light a rainbow of colors. Her neatly trimmed fingers lifted the clasp. Inside lay the precious key. She closed the locket and snapped the cuff on her wrist. A quick shower and she would leave. Damn Marcus. Who the hell did he think he was? She was not his fiancée or his possession. She was his prisoner. They were not a team, but enemies, and she needed to remember that because at the end of the day, he was going to hand her over to the authorities. She did not know who scared her more: him or the Elusti. They were both deadly.

"Argh." Peeling off her borrowed clothes, she let them drop to the floor and headed for the shower. Any hesitation about carrying out her quickly-thought-out plan disappeared after hearing Jake's words. Her plan would work; all she needed to do was stay focused.

The steaming water pummeled against her supple skin, easing the residual aches, and now she lay in the bed, covered with a crisp white sheet and wearing only her skimpy underwear and a white lacy bra. The plan was simple. She was going to seduce him. Ella tried to resist the hypnotic lure of sleep, but after the warmth of the hot shower, and lying now on the comfortable mattress, her well-used muscles softened and relaxed. Her eyelids grew heavy and fluttered as she struggled to stay awake. Just then the door clicked open; a small light filtered in and disappeared as the door closed. Marcus crept into the room and slipped into the en suite.

Ella was suddenly wide awake. Her heart skipped beats as she waited for him to finish. She licked her lips as the minutes ticked by. She had never actually seduced anyone before, but reasoned it should be easy enough to do with a man like Marcus. When his body had been pressed up against hers, she had felt his growing desire for her. Her touch affected him much in the same way as his did her. Smiling, her heart stalled as the tap from the shower squeaked off. The door fanned open, and steam billowed out. She blinked and stared as his smoldering gaze landed on her. He stood in the doorway like a Greek god surrounded in the clouds, and wrapped in a virgin white towel. Ella stared, unable to swallow or breathe or do anything except stare. His wet blue-black hair was slicked back, and his face was damp and newly shaved, showing his flawless olive skin. His body glistened from the steam, and she gazed at his muscled and toned abdomen that was covered in a dark smattering of hair that tapered down toward narrow hips. Together with his taut biceps, he created a powerful male picture of perfection.

"Sorry, I didn't mean to wake you." His voice was low and smooth as his hand rubbed his wet hair.

Ella swallowed an imaginary lump in her throat and watched in total fascination. Solid muscles rippled across his chest and abdomen; there wasn't an inch of fat on his body anywhere. As he dried himself with a smaller towel, Ella's gaze roamed over his physique, and fell to his waist where the towel was loosely secured. Butterflies danced around in her tummy. Her insides melted like liquid gold and she could not stop drooling over him. She clenched her legs together to stop the throb that was building between her legs.

Marcus moved closer to the edge of the bed.

"I couldn't sleep," she said huskily.

Marcus stopped what he was doing and stared at her, frowning. His eyes narrowed as they examined her face. Ella sat up, letting the sheet fall to her hips and he gasped.

"Ella…" He turned his back to her as he sat down on the edge of the creaking bed. She crawled forward, resting on her knees, and placed her small hands on his shoulders, kneading the knotted muscles.

"Ella, what are you doing?" He stiffened and glanced at her sideways. His voice quivered with barely held control.

"Easing the tension, and I was always told my hands delivered just the right amount of pressure." She squeezed and massaged his shoulders until he groaned. Kneeling, she pressed her chest into his back, and skin touched skin. Heat met heat and it set fire to her skin and blood. She breathed warm air out and stroked his shoulders with her hands and blended her body with his, trying to stay focused as she talked.

"What's the tattoo for?" Her words were barely a whisper in his ear as her fingers smoothed over the black skeleton of a frog on his arm. He moved forward but she grabbed him back and continued to manipulate his muscles. She knew he didn't want to answer her question, so she let it go. She tried to get him to relax instead.

"That's so good." He moaned as his shoulders dropped against Ella.

She continued to soothe and work on his shoulders, and then his back, releasing the knots that she could feel, while listening to his shallow breathing. Her own breathing increased to keep pace with her heart rate that beat like a drum. Ella's lacy bra skimmed across his back, and she laid a tender but brief kiss on his shoulder as her body shuddered.

In one swift motion, Marcus swiveled around and pushed her backward, pinning her to the mattress as he lay inches above her. His chest heaved in and out as the heat between their bodies steamed.

"You're playing with fire, Ella." He leaned closer and held her wrists above her head.

She lay there mesmerized. A flame of desire licked through her body, and instinctively, she arched her back upward. As their bodies touched, it ignited a fire. Ella lay a teasing kiss on his closed lips and fell back against the mattress, gazing at him with longing. Marcus watched her, at first unresponsive to her kiss, but his gaze zeroed in on her soft lips. She flicked her tongue out to wet her lower lip.

As if he couldn't resist any longer, his head descended. He devoured her mouth, kissing her hard and fast, pushing his tongue into her mouth to demand entry. The full weight of his body pushed her deep into the mattress, and his knees pinned her legs between his. All too soon, though, his body stilled and he lifted his lips away from Ella.

"Ella, this isn't going—"

She caressed the back of his neck with her hand and weaved her fingers into his hair to pull him back to her waiting mouth. Marcus succumbed and claimed her mouth, dueling once more with her playful tongue.

Passion consumed Ella like a wildfire as she clung to him, needing to be as close as possible. She moaned as his rough thumb and finger squeezed and stroked her nipple through the lace of her bra. Needing more, she pushed his chest forcefully so he tumbled back against the mattress and she rolled to straddle him, taking control. He laughed and relaxed back into the bed. She laid her upper body across his, kissing his lips, and then slowly lowered herself down his body, licking and kissing a hot trail down his neck, chest, and abdomen. She continued her downward path until she hovered above the towel.

"Ella, if you don't stop, I'm…" His voice was strained and hoarse.

She knew she was close; her hand quickly maneuvered to grab the handcuffs from under the mattress all the while her other hand stretched and massaged his skin in soft strokes around his ribs and lower. She kissed his belly button and her finger edged the corners of the towel. Marcus breathed heavily as her fingers stole under the towel, and he moaned. She lifted her body and stretched his right arm high above his head, kissing his fingers and running her hands along his flesh. *Click.* She snapped the cuff around his wrist and shackled him to the bedpost. It took seconds for him to realize what was happening. Then his body spun into action and he growled like a wild hog.

She sprang off the bed.

"Ella, this is a big mistake," he growled, as the handcuff scraped up and down on the bedpost. Marcus yanked hard and twisted his body sideways to try to break free.

Ella grabbed her clothes off the floor and jumped into her velour pants and jacket.

"Sh, baby, you don't want to wake the whole house. What will Jake think? Marcus, I'm going to leave the key where you'll find it, if you behave. I'm going, Marcus, and you need to let me go. It's safer this way." She moved away, not taking her eyes off him. She left the key to the handcuff on the table by the door and moved to open the door.

"Ella...I will find you, but for your sake, you better hope I don't."

With that, she swiveled around and grabbed a sock from the dresser. She darted over and shoved it into his mouth before he could resist. She nimbly moved out of the way like a gymnast to avoid his leg flicking out to kick her and raced out the door. Ella had already pocketed Marcus's keys, and was soon out the back door and driving away in the battered red truck. She couldn't believe how easy her departure was, but didn't stop to question why. Her mind focused instead on where to hide until the bank opened. As she stared out the windshield, she smiled at how well she had executed her plan to seduce Marcus.

Twice, she had played him and each time he surrendered to her charms. A tiny shiver of awareness blazed along her spine, and her insides warmed at the look of fury and his words: "Ella, I will find you, but for your sake, you'd better hope I don't." The images of him lying sprawled across the bed made her almost want to turn around and continue what she had started. Almost! Touching and kissing him unleashed a wild desire inside that made her long to take things further. However, she couldn't do that. He didn't even believe her when she said she was a witch. Imagine what he would say if she told him the truth: that her people were an ancient race from the stars, descendants of the moon goddess Ariana, who after hearing her name called by her soul mate, roamed the earth for five long centuries to search for him. It was a full moon and it glowed down on Ella, who rubbed her wrist and sighed. There her birthmark, the crescent moon, itched.

****

Marcus knew that Ella was planning to escape. While in the shower, he'd wondered what her tactics would be. Ella was, he was learning, an enigma and she sparked his interest big-time. When he dragged Jake away from the bedroom last night, when he'd interrupted his interrogation, the two men had exchanged their opinions and talked openly about Ella the witch.

"Damn it, Marcus, why here? Why did you bring her here? Are you insane? Her face is all over the media. Did you really think I wouldn't know who she is? Don't answer that. I'll tell you who she is—a goddamn fucking improvised explosive device, an IED. In case you've forgotten."

Marcus hadn't forgotten. Jake had every right to be angry for bringing his mess to his doorstep. Perhaps he was insane. He raked his hand through his hair and massaged the stubble on his chin as Jake continued to ramble on.

"Look, I know you have a hard time with lost causes but man, she's murdered someone. What the hell possessed you to shackle yourself to her?"

Jake was like his younger brother, only now he was trying to usurp his authority, as if he were the older sibling. Marcus smirked at his concern. "I'm not shackled to her. And when did you grow up and become all serious?" He knocked his shoulder in a friendly, lighthearted way.

"Knock it off. I am serious. She's trouble, and she has you wrapped around her little finger. She's beautiful, but she's more trouble than it's worth. Hell, she'd been here no more than five minutes before she was shooting out orders at me to collect something from the truck for her. I told her to go and get it herself. I told her that I was not her slave. She pouted her sweet mouth, but sure enough, she went and got what she wanted."

Hearing that, Marcus's face froze and he swiveled around. Ella didn't have any possessions to retrieve from the truck. What the hell? Was she looking for the keys? He felt in his back pocket and sighed. She was up to something for sure and he wouldn't have expected anything less.

"Damn it. You're right—that little witch is trouble. But, the Elusti is involved, man, and she's caught up with them somehow. She's no match for them, even if she's spirited and trouble. So as much as I hate to admit that you're right, Ella is mine and she isn't going to know what hits her when I've finished with her. But first we need to talk…" He sat down on the leather couch and stared at the empty hallway that led to the bedroom, trying to focus on the task at hand and not Ella. There were no windows in that room, so he figured that she wouldn't make her move yet. Not if she didn't want to get caught. For the next hour, Marcus discussed Ella, the Elusti, the FBI, and what he planned to do.

Something was desperately keeping Ella focused. A sudden picture of her crouching by the fire grate back at her house made him realize that she had been looking for something. That was why she had risked going back there. What it was, he had no clue, but it must be extremely important for her to keep risking her life and freedom for. She wasn't about to voluntarily confide in him and in a way he admired that. No matter what Ella was, she was a survivor, used to relying on herself. Nope, the only way to discover what the hell was going on was to let her go. Then, he would tail her and find out.

Meanwhile, Jake had agreed to break into the FBI computer system and trace any involvement with the Elusti. If there was any trail to find, he would find it. However, that would take time and a different location. Pinching his nose with his fingers, he at last felt he had the upper hand, but then a distorted vision had his heart about to stop. The air was literally sucked out of him. The image in his head had him running for the bedroom. As he walked in, all was quiet; he could hear Ella's shallow breathing, but he knew she wasn't asleep. The vision he'd seen of Ella was of her lying on the ground; a crimson stain pooled out around her like oil. As she lay on her side, her bright blue eyes stared at him, lifeless.

After a steaming shower, he had let Ella play her game, knowing she would have something planned for him. As she sat up in bed and let the sheet fall back to reveal her slim, toned body and ample breasts encased in a delicate white lacy bra, he'd almost jumped out of his skin. This he hadn't expected at all. Holding back was not his strong point, but with Ella, it was different on so many levels. He smiled as he ran slowly over the events that led up to her escape. She was right. She was good with her hands, and before long, he would get his own back. The thought of how he would extract his revenge aroused him more than he liked to admit.

Only this time he knew what was coming. This time, he had placed the keys for her to steal and planted a surveillance bug on the truck, so that no matter where she went, he would be able to track her. Jake had been ready to unlock the handcuffs, which he did but not before taking a picture and grinning from ear to ear. Then he moved like lightning; he didn't want to lose sight of her because the only image that kept replaying in his head was of her cold and stiff as a corpse. He lifted and placed the black motorcycle helmet on his head.

Jake grabbed him and bellowed, "I always knew one day you'd fall hard for some woman. Serves you right. I just hope she's worth it, man. I'll be in touch."

Marcus nodded. "Thanks for the bike." He revved the engine and left in hot pursuit, cursing loudly under his breath. *This time she'll pay.*

Marcus drove constantly as the sun rose and dawn broke. It took him less than an hour to track her on his GPS to I-95 and he stayed well back so that she wouldn't suspect she was being followed. His journey took him back up 93, headed to Boston. This crazy woman was driving right back to where they had started. What on earth was she playing at? Ella turned off and entered a parking garage right on Boylston Street in Boston. And there she remained. He parked several rows back; he'd gotten off the bike but had kept himself tucked away and hidden. His sole focus was on any movement from the truck. An hour passed before there was any change. The truck door slammed shut, and he watched undetected as Ella stepped out and scanned the vicinity before she moved away.

He ducked and weaved behind cars, following her as she exited the parking garage, but stayed back at a safe distance so that he would not be observed. She walked down Boylston Street at a steady pace, passing shops and restaurants until she was outside Bank of America. At this point, Marcus stopped and waited. What the hell was she up to? Slowly, he followed her in and watched as a young man stood far too close to Ella for his comfort. The man smiled a greedy smile like a wolf as he hovered over Ella in his blue pin-striped suit. With his hand on her back, he marched her away to a private elevator. After the doors clanked shut, Marcus pivoted around and eyed the young blonde woman at the nearby table.

The attractive woman was already smiling at him broadly. Marcus walked over and leaned his hands on top of the granite counter, giving his best appreciative smile at the slim lady, who continued to hold his gaze with her slim lips spreading wide.

"I wonder if you can you help me? My *soon-to-be ex-wife* just entered *that* elevator. Where does it go?" His voice was laced with just the right amount of bite and sexiness that he knew the woman would respond to his request; they always did. She followed the direction of his outstretched hand to the elevator in the corner.

"I'm not supposed to say, but I don't see what harm it can do. You cannot access it unless you have a key. The elevator leads to the vault and the safety deposit boxes." She shrugged and smiled.

"I see. Thank you, you've been most helpful." He lifted her hand and kissed it quickly, his stare not leaving her face, which was openly admiring him.

"Anytime. And take this, for when your divorce is final or before, if you want." She sucked the tip of her pen.

He let go of her hand and took the business card that she had handed him. "Thanks again." He flashed his even white teeth, waving the card at her, and left. Pushing through the revolving doors, he dropped the card in the nearby garbage can and paced back and forth. Another thirty minutes passed. As he studied the doors, he spotted Ella shaking hands with the man she had just been with and was now walking in his direction. It took her less than a minute to reach the doors.

Ella exited the bank, a black bag thrown over her shoulder, and her face set in a tight grimace as she searched around before she placed her dark glasses on. To Marcus, she looked as if she carried the weight of the world on her tiny shoulders and he wished he knew her secrets. Marcus stood just out of sight, but he kept a clear view of her. As she strode away, he could almost taste her fear and his need to capture her increased by the second. She had only taken a few steps when he pounced, clasping his hand around her wrist and yanking her around to face him.

"Marcus, how did you—"

He snapped the handcuff onto her wrist once again. Fearing that the couple nearby would be alerted to trouble if they saw what was happening, he wrapped his arms around Ella, holding her fast, and kissed her, putting a swift end to her chatter. Kissing her made her whole body soften against him; he felt her will to fight him recede and this made him smile. Lifting his head, he let the corner of his mouth lift. "I've missed you too, baby. Now, my little vixen, we're in a public place and you're wanted for murder. Need I remind you of the rules? I am trying to help you but the time for hide-and-seek is over. You need to come with me. There's someone I want you to meet and then you're going to talk until I have a clear picture of what is going on or so help me, I will drop you in the FBI's lap. Now, what's in the bag?"

"I'm not coming with you. You don't understand who or what I am and you cannot help me," she scoffed and struggled against him. The harsh wind increased and whistled at them. An empty soda can swept up from the ground and hit Marcus across the cheek.

"Damn it." He winced but didn't release her.

"Marcus, let me go. I'm not worth getting killed over and *they* will kill you," she whispered against him, trying to wrench her arm free. Ominous gray clouds appeared in a deep, thick formation, threatening a storm. Marcus raised his head skyward, feeling the increase in the strength of the now billowing wind, and stared back at the street as people ran for cover. Looking back at the clouds, he looked across at Ella. Her eyes seemed to match the grayness of the sky. Her shoulder-length hair danced and leapt wildly around her shoulders as she closed her eyes. The raindrops increased until they fell like a waterfall. Hailstones the size of acorns pummeled down from the sky. Still, he clasped a firm hold on her.

"Whatever you are, I'm not letting you go, not if you bring the whole damn sky down upon us." They stood drenched by the monsoon downpour that darkened the light around them. People dashed into stores at the unexpected shower but they continued to stand alone on the now deserted sidewalk. He let go of her wrist and gripped her shoulders to shake her. "You have to trust me. I'm on your side, Ella. Whatever is going on, I will do my best to help you."

Ella tilted her head to watch his stubborn and fixed expression, taking in the rain that poured down his face and drenched his clothes. She blinked as the water flowed down her lashes and cheeks, invading her thin velour outfit and chilling her to the bone. "Each person I trusted either died or let me down. How are you any different?"

Marcus stared at her, standing in the spontaneous torrential rain, amazed at her strength and resilience despite her size. A wave of admiration shook him. She was like a wild animal, hell-bent on survival and willing to do anything, but he didn't believe she was a murderer. His heart squeezed. She looked vulnerable, innocent, and alone. Not caring one bit about the weather, he stood his ground and battled on.

"I'm not like other men. I want to show you something." In all the years that he had been an agent and Navy SEAL, nothing had felt as right as the decision he was making—God only knew why. He raked a hand through his sopping hair as her face softened; as she smiled, the rain ceased and dwindled to a light drizzle and then stopped altogether, as did the wind. A churning sensation reached up into his stomach. Did she just stop the rain?

The one remaining cuff dangled from Ella's wrist and he unlocked it. "Run if you must but you won't get far. The FBI expects you in by noon and I'm guessing the Elusti are still on the prowl, waiting for you. It's your decision. You either trust me and accept my help or see how far you get. You may even make it, but eventually they'll catch you."

She examined his face and sighed. If he was being honest—and she suspected he was—she should run and keep running, but she couldn't. "Okay. I'll come with you but no more handcuffs. Why do you want to help me anyway?"

His arm swept across her shoulders and he guided her away.

"I couldn't help the last victim of the Elusti but I can help you. Now, let's move. I'm taking you to meet my mom."

CHAPTER SIX

They had been driving up the highway for about forty-five minutes with no conversation. As she sat across from Marcus in his truck, Ella tried to imagine what he was ruminating about inside his head. She'd expected anger, maybe even violence when he'd caught up with her. Of course, she knew from his parting words he would, but she hadn't expected him to be so quick. He must have known at some point she would make a run for it and had laid his own plan, letting her believe she had escaped. She stifled a chuckle as she realized that Jake must have been in on it from the start. All that brotherhood stuff and special code was not simply for show. Looking across at this now gentle giant who had moments before stood in the rain, fighting for her to trust him, the last thing she expected was a trip to visit his *mother*. Was it code for the enemy?

"Ella, I can tell by the inch-long line between your eyebrows that you're puzzled as to what's going on. Stop fretting. We need to get off the grid, and I need to speak with Jake, who will be pleased to get his bike back. We'll be safe where we're going for a while."

Safe. That word sent an alarm fizzing through her. Ella had felt safe until the other night and it was her downfall. Feeling safe had made her soft and now she was relying on a virtual stranger whose job it was to bring her in for questioning and yet, staring at him, somehow she desperately wanted to believe he would help her, which was crazy.

Marcus glanced over at her briefly and then stared back out at the road ahead.

"So am I forgiven for leaving you all high and dry?" she teased, unable to stop herself as heat coiled around her insides and sparks tingled. She squeezed her thighs tight together to stop the mounting excitement. She remembered sitting astride him on the bed, and how much she enjoyed being in control. The friction as their bodies touched. The heat. Ripples of delicious waves roared loudly. God, just the reminder of earlier turned her on and she wanted to scream out loud. What was wrong with her? She usually had more control.

"I'm a man, Ella, but don't take me for an idiot. If you go down that particular path again, I will not hold back and you'll be the one left breathless and wanting more. I know you like feeling in control, Ella, but in the bedroom, I'm in charge and I've never had any complaints." He flashed his gaze directly onto her, underlining his point, and her mouth went dry. Turning away, his hand turned the radio up.

Ella couldn't breathe as images of them tangled together with her lying flat on her back as he licked his way down assaulted her and she squirmed in her seat.

"No advances in the case of murdered college Professor Aidan O'Connor. His girlfriend Ella Masters is still a person of interest…"

As the news blared from the radio, Ella shot forward as if doused with a bucket of ice water, bringing her dreamy reverie to an end. Staring out the window at the now baby-blue sky, she whispered, "Money and a passport."

Marcus shot a glance in her direction and watched as she sucked on her lower lip, a habit that she couldn't break. "What…" The car slowed; he maneuvered it, turning right, and continued down a hidden and bumpy dead end lane. She'd been watching the signs and knew they headed north and toward Rockport, along the North Shore. He drove to the end of the dirt track and parked the truck.

She stared at her hands, which she twisted in her lap.

"That's what's in the bag—enough money to start over and a new identity. All I have to do is get a plane ticket and I'm going home to Wales. It's where I'm from. It's where my people originated from, so the legend goes, and I need to find out if there is anyone else besides me left." Her wavy hair brushed across her shoulders as she turned. Tears bubbled in her huge eyes but she refused to let them fall. She blinked and wiped them away. "I need to go home…"

Marcus undid his seat belt and shifted. He tilted her face toward him, her chin cupped in his hand as his callused thumb smoothed across her trembling lip and stroked back and forth in a gentle rhythm. They eyeballed each other and Ella's heart thudded.

"I know you didn't kill the professor, even though I wouldn't have blamed you if you had. I've never liked how the man treated you, you know that. He may have been training you but there were far too many unnecessary bruises." He continued his lazy stroking on Ella's sensitive skin and she lifted her chin, wanting him to touch her elsewhere. "That night, I saw him hit you. In my books, that's a death sentence right there. Ella, I know you're not capable of killing someone. Even though you've thrashed me, it's not with the intention to hurt or kill, merely to escape, to be free. You've been surviving for too long on your own. Look, let's go inside. You're soaking. And I need to contact my boss." With that, he turned and opened the door, ending the magical moment. His tenderness shocked her more than his cold indifference and it left Ella wishing they were in a different time or place altogether.

Inside, her body shuddered, muscles relaxed, and nerve endings lit up, crying for him to continue his caressing, to soothe her. Lifting her hand, she traced her lips with her fingers where his had just been. Her heart pounded in her chest; he was dulling her resistance and drawing her in until she was putty in his hands. He seemed to know exactly what to do to get what he wanted, which terrified Ella. She had never felt so exposed and raw. While he oozed confidence in all things, taking control, he would swallow her whole, which should make her run and hide but made her desire for him soar. Ella blew out a hot breath of air. Getting involved with him in any sexual way would be a huge mistake, one she couldn't afford even if it did relieve some of the undeniable tension. Hearing the door slam jolted her back to reality and she shivered, feeling the drop in temperature at the coast. Suddenly, his parting words vibrated inside her head.

"I need to contact my boss."

What? One minute he was reeling her in with his tantalizing caresses and reassuring words, making her believe she could trust him and the next, the noose around her neck tightened. The door of the truck on her side squeaked open sharply and Marcus stood there in his fitted faded jeans and black Henley shirt that stretched across his chiseled and firm chest. His dark sunglasses hung casually from the front buttons of his shirt. "Come on, you need a change of clothes. You're freezing. Can you walk or do I need to carry you?"

Ella wanted to refuse, to argue, feeling trapped and uneasy once again, but what would she gain? She simply needed to stay alert and look for another opportunity to leave because no matter what he said, Marcus was a man who dominated and controlled each situation. He was used to getting exactly what he wanted and she couldn't afford any more mishaps.

"I'm fine. I can manage, but thank you." She pushed herself out of the truck and studied her surroundings as she breathed in the fresh, salty air. The narrow lane was nothing more than a gravel dirt track and a dead end. The truck was parked in front of a row of neatly cut eight-foot-high green hedges, giving no view of what lay beyond. Isolated and secluded. No one would realize this place even existed from the main road. It stood alone, with no neighbors, cloistered away and completely private. Seagulls squawked overhead, and the roar of the ocean announced its closeness. Ella loved the sea; being close to it automatically calmed her body and soul. A feeling of freedom washed over her, as if just being close to the water would save her.

Marcus clasped her hand in his larger one and pulled her toward a small black iron gate and the green-hedged archway, giving the only view of the stone cottage beyond adorned with wisteria. Marcus hesitated before he pushed the gate to gain entry.

"I warn you, my mother is not what you might expect, but please be polite. She's different and you of all people should respect that." He pushed the squeaky gate wide so they could walk down the natural stone pathway that led to the quaint two-story cottage. As they walked through the black metal gate, Ella thought she was walking into an enchanted woodland as she was accosted with an array of blooming flowers of all different heights planted alongside the path on either side, which split on both sides and followed around to the back of the property. The entire dwelling was surrounded in a riot of colors and scents even though it was end-October. There were lilies, orchids, crocuses, and mums aside from the beautiful wisteria that covered the house, leaving an exotic fragrance in the air. Over to the left was an acre of well-manicured lawn that overlooked the clear view of the endless Atlantic Ocean and the blue sky.

"Wow, it's beautiful."

Marcus regarded the view and nodded. "The garden is her joy. Down the right side, there is an herb garden, and there are steps that lead down to a private rocky beach. This is her sanctuary."

Observing Marcus as he spoke, nervous knots of tension and apprehension twisted in her gut. He had truly brought her to meet his mother, of all people. Was she an invalid? What made her different and why should she understand? The way he'd said that word made it seem as if it was laced with another meaning other than she was his mother. Words wouldn't form as he placed his hand on her hip and guided her toward the solid oak door of the white-washed cottage.

"For all intents and purposes, we're in a relationship, Ella. I never bring women here, never, and it will be too confusing to explain it all, so you'll just have to go along with it...."

Ella wanted to speak, to ask questions, but his phone buzzed and he instantly moved away and distanced himself from her. When he looked at the number on the phone, he cursed and signaled with his hand for her to wait. *So his mother was sick; now she felt totally out of her depth. Why did he bring her here?* Biting her lower lip, she watched as he paced back and forth across the garden, making an indent on the grass. Shouting and swearing into the phone, he briefly lifted his eyes toward Ella. He gave a halfhearted smile and turned away to stride off to the farthest edge of the garden, where he disappeared from view.

Damn him. Left adrift, Ella didn't know what to do. A sudden creaking behind her drew attention away from him and she swiveled around. On the doorstep of the cottage was a tall, if frail, lady with prominent cheekbones and hair swept elegantly back from her small face. Her wafer-slim body moved forward to greet her steadily, and she smiled. Her eyes were sharp and the color of roasted chestnuts, and her hair, mostly silver-gray, accentuated her beauty and warmth. Ella lifted her lips in a smile and extended a hand.

"You must be Ella. I've been waiting for you. Come along inside. My son shouldn't have left you standing here in the cold. You look frozen. Are you wet, dear?" The older woman arched her eyebrows and ran her gaze over Ella's damp clothes with a puzzled expression on her face.

She was dumbstruck and flicked her gaze back over her shoulder to look for Marcus. Had he phoned his mother? She was certain he hadn't and yet she knew her name. A million thoughts tumbled inside her brain, none of which she could easily translate. Ella knew when people weren't human by their unique odor. However, she could also detect humans who were *gifted*. There was a colorful glow about them, like a blinking neon sign. Most of the time this enabled her to sense whether they were good or evil. Upon seeing Marcus's mother, her cloud shone like a bright star or halo. Her whole being projected a light she hadn't seen since she was a child. Before she could think or speak, she found herself engulfed in the old lady's thin arms. The woman smoothed and patted her hair gently. Ella couldn't quite catch or understand the foreign words she said, but for a moment, she let the lady embrace her, feeling comforted beyond words as she rested her head on her shoulder. However, the heavy stomping of boots on the stone path signaled that Marcus was close, and she moved to break free.

"I'm sorry. I had to take that phone call—" Marcus stopped and stared at Ella, and then faced his mother, a serious, closed expression on his face, one that was hard to interpret.

Surely, the fact that he had brought her to his mother's meant that he had a good relationship with her? Ella shook her head. Something was odd about this reunion and she couldn't quite understand what was going on.

"It's good to see you, Mother." He stepped closer and leaned forward to brace his mother's shoulders with his hands, and kissed her formally on both cheeks before he secured his arm around Ella's waist and drew her against him.

"I see you've met Ella. This is my mother, Josephine Laurent. Shall we go inside? We're both soaking wet from an unexpected shower…"

He extended his hand to motion for his mother to enter first, but she remained where she was and stared at him from head to toe.

"I almost didn't recognize you, Marcus; it's been that long. You look tired and you need a shave but I'm glad you're here. I knew you both would come. I've been waiting for you. Come in and make yourselves at home." Josephine turned away and stepped into the cottage, pushing the door open. The smell of burning wood seeped out toward them in welcome. Marcus held Ella back as his mother walked inside.

"What did she say to you? And why were you hugging her?" he whispered.

Ella felt trapped, like a deer caught in the headlights; her eyes stared deep into his. Why on earth did he bring her here unless he wanted to reveal something of what he was keeping hidden? If his mother was the powerful seer that she suspected she was, then surely that would mean he would also have her gift. Or was there something else he hadn't told her? Maybe that would explain why his surname was different than hers? She frowned. She may have secrets but she wasn't the only one. Curiosity demanded she find out.

"Your mother said she knew I was coming. How is that possible? I know you didn't phone her while I was in the truck. Did you phone her beforehand? Marcus, come on, you're the one playing games now. Your mother's a seer, isn't she?"

As her words left her mouth, his olive complexion paled, and he raked his hand through his hair as a muscle in his cheek twitched. Ella knew it was a trigger and that he was angry with her words. For a moment, he simply narrowed his gaze and studied her in stony silence.

"For years, my mother would black out. No one knew what was happening, especially me. I'd rather not talk about that now." Moving in closer against Ella, he pulled her arms and gripped them, almost hoisting her off the ground.

"Ella, she said she knew *you* were coming. How? Do you know my mother? You need to tell me the truth or so help me…" he ground out, tormented by his mother's reception.

All her life, she'd been scared, fighting for her own survival, but studying Marcus, she couldn't help but wish that wasn't the case. That she had someone, someone she could trust, someone who would be there for her no matter what and she in turn would help. Placing her hands on her hips, she took a deep breath.

"Marcus, listen to me. I'm telling you, your mother is a seer. I can read people, people who are gifted. Your mother knew I was coming, that we were *both* coming. She must have seen it. Please, don't tell me you don't believe her. That you've closed your mind off to that possibility?" Ella knew she had raised her voice and now searched around in case anyone may have heard but the gentle rhythmic thrashing of the waves was the only background noise. "Why else did you bring me here if not because your mother can help?"

He eased his grip and bowed his head as if in submission. "I honestly don't know. I thought Josephine might be able to help. She has an understanding for all things that defy explanation and you remind me of her in a way. That look you have sometimes. Fear. I've seen that look in her eyes and I want to know if that was what my mother felt and why. For most of my childhood, she was locked up in a psychiatric unit. They told me she was schizophrenic. I didn't understand what that was, but it meant she wasn't around much. I went from one foster home to another. I've never felt close to her. But, lately, I wondered if I was wrong." His dark eyes bore into hers and they betrayed his utter turmoil and conflict as lines formed like waves across his forehead. Having revealed a secret part of himself, he shifted uncomfortably and raised himself up to his full height, breathing out and removing his gaze from her.

Ella realized he had exposed a piece of himself that he'd kept hidden, letting his control slip. She caught hold of one of his rough hands. "Let's go and find out."

As they both walked into the house, Josephine smiled.

"Come on in, you two. There's a lot to discuss, but first you both need a hot shower and some dry clothes."

They both stared at Josephine, who herded them into the warmth of the house as if they were sheep and gave out orders.

"Ella, the bathroom is at the top of the landing in front of you and across from there to your right is your bedroom; it overlooks the seas. I've put some clothes ready. Gracie, my helper, purchased them for me. I told you, I knew you were coming and I knew you would need my help. Now go."

Ella glanced over at Marcus, who nodded at her, and she did as she was told, leaving him alone with his mother.

As soon as Ella disappeared from view, Josephine turned to scrutinize her son. It had been well over a year since they had last seen each other. She stretched both her wrinkled and sun-kissed hands out toward him and he reached to hold her cold hands.

"I'm so glad you came. I know you still have reservations. You've always liked order and structure. I tried to enable you to have those things but I know I failed. Anyway, things have changed. Now you've met Ella...come and sit by the fire. I need to explain." Her voice was high-pitched and bubbly like a child. She led him to two cream velvet Queen Anne chairs that flanked the large stone fireplace, where a bright fire crackled.

"Mother, I believe there's a rational explanation for my concerns. I just need to figure it out. You addressed Ella by her name. Do you know her? What I mean is, have you met her before?" He couldn't settle in the chair and paced the length of the fireplace. The crackle of the wood made him pause and he stoked the fire to help it to regain its strength.

Josephine tutted, and sighed as she eased down into the comfortable chair, rubbing her legs as she did so. "You were always such a tightly coiled child, unwilling to accept anything that was different. I guess that's my fault. I never said so before, Marcus, but I am truly sorry I wasn't around when you were growing up. It was my biggest mistake. Sit, please sit...I need to tell you my story and it doesn't begin here in America. You see, I grew up in a village called Honfleur in Normandy, France. Everyone knew each other well; like any small town, you couldn't keep any secrets. My childhood was like any other until I began to see things that weren't actually there and my parents were frantic. They didn't know what to do. Everyone was leaving for the land of opportunity—America—so that's what we did. But nothing changed. You see, you cannot run away from your destiny; it will catch up with you eventually. Not long after we arrived in the States, my mother died in a car accident and after that, my father couldn't cope..." She looked away into the distance as the painful memories haunted her.

Marcus, seeing his mother's tears, sat down in the chair, wanting to hear the story that she had never shared before but unwilling to be caught up in any fantasy. He touched his mother's arm to encourage her to continue and watched her as she stared into the embers of the blazing fire, already lost in her memories.

She turned and faced him with tears in her eyes, and she reached for his hand.

"You were the light in a long, dark tunnel. There were days when I just couldn't reach that light, but I fought and struggled to reach it, for you. You see, when your mind is open, it gives you endless possibilities. My mind is not strong and it was easily corrupted in those early days. Marcus, I didn't understand as a child what I was, but as I grew into adulthood, I knew...I could see the future, things that had yet to pass..." She sat back in the chair and released his hand; her face twisted and lines of worry crossed over her brow and forehead.

"When I was young, I would play games with my friends, parlor games like betting on horses, to entice them and I won. I was showing off but I was playing with fire. I liked the feel of power and used it, but when others realized the power I held, it became dangerous. There are people out there who have great knowledge of this world and the world beyond. They seek out anything that defies logic with a desire to use it for their own purpose, for control. One supposed *friend* Simon realized my potential and used me. I had no choice—he was an evil man. Once you're known to these people, you are never free of them. For a while, I was. I met your father and we created you but the past crept up on us. Do you understand? I knew I would never be free and it was too dangerous to be around you. The people the man knew were crazy and even worse than he was. They would hurt and destroy you. Being locked away seemed a simple sacrifice if it meant you would come to no harm. Believe you me, in a world of demons, witches, vampires and shape-shifters, I'm of little importance really. Merely something that can be toyed with."

Josephine's body sighed, as if releasing a huge burden that left her exhausted.

Marcus knelt before her. "Witches, demons? Mother, what are you saying? I want to understand but you don't make it easy."

"Life is a battle, Marcus, and you must choose which side you're on because the evil is growing."

He reeled back from her words and stood up, more confused than ever. For a moment, he thought his mother would clear his mind. He pressed his fingers into his closed eyes. Confusion swirled around and he wondered why on earth he had come here. Only since meeting Ella, a deep need inside his gut for answers seemed to drag him here to his mother. His gut was telling him there was a connection but for the life of him, he couldn't see it. Leaning his arm against the cold stone wall, he stared out the rectangular window as the wind blew the flowers back and forth, turning his back on his mother. Coming here was a mistake. He should just grab Ella and leave.

Josephine left her seat to stand next to his side, just reaching his shoulders, and she crossed her arms. "Marcus, there is much in this world that defies rational explanation. Have you not sensed it? Even your dreams have meaning. Please, Marcus, you are the most precious thing in my life, you must know that. I was in trouble and we couldn't keep running from it. I made the drastic decision, the biggest regret of my life, but know this: it was because I believed I had no other option. I had to disappear from your life. You may never forgive me but I did it to keep you safe. In a masochistic way, I was relieved when you turned away from me, shutting off yourself to the belief in anything outside of the ordinary. You cannot believe how much I prayed for that. I didn't want you to face the pain or the disgust that I faced."

Josephine's rambling words stiffened his shoulders. She was talking about danger and keeping him safe, sacrificing herself to let him have a normal life. Now he knew she was crazy; nothing in his life had been normal. He'd been alone all his life, shipped from one home to another, each one worse than the last: beaten, starved, or worse. He turned to stare at her. "Face the pain from who? My father?"

She raised her head and smiled with a far-off look in her eyes. "Don't ever think that. Your father was a wonderful man, the only man who accepted me for who I was. Marcus, he loved us both with all his heart. He spent his life trying to protect us; you were just a baby when he died. His name was Mathew Drayton. He was an extraordinary man. He was a painter. I have some of his work stored safely. Maybe one day you'll get to see it, but for now it must stay hidden."

Marcus released his mother and pinched his nose. "Protect us, Mother? You have to be more specific. Who was he protecting us from? None of this makes sense. So you made some bad decisions when you were young—who doesn't? But why did we need to be protected? Why would anyone want to hurt us?" The vein at the side of his head throbbed and Josephine reached to smooth his hair that had flopped over his eyes.

"I don't know who killed your father but the people, the organization I was involved with are notorious and their reach without borders. I was placed in a private sanatorium and your father left with you in tow. It was a heartbreaking decision, but one we hoped wouldn't be forever. Your father was to take you and leave the country, but that never happened. I didn't know for a long time that he was dead and by then you were in the foster care system. It took years to be able to get custody of you, and by then, I knew what I had done was wrong. To hide was a mistake and I lost Mathew forever. You were all I had left but I'd lost you too...I'm tired, Marcus. These days, my body and mind are failing me."

He tried to dissect her words into something tangible but there were vital pieces of information she wasn't telling him. Staring at her creased and anxious face, he gently took her thin arm and helped her to sit by the fire, placing a thick woolen blanket over her legs.

"The Elusti are evil and merciless and even though I heard that Simon died, his legacy continues. They will stop at nothing to get what they want. I suspect they were behind your father's death, but I don't know. I couldn't see his future. I was told he suffered a heart attack, but he was only thirty-one when he died. I'm sorry it's such a mess. Mathew and I didn't get a lifetime together but the love we shared was more than most." She bowed her head.

The Elusti. That name almost brought him to his knees. They were always hovering in the background and they were responsible for his mother's terror all these years. He ground his teeth together. Possibly his father's death.

Something loosened inside his stiff heart as he looked at his mother and saw her for the first time. All those years, she had been carrying around so much guilt, and yet, she had in her own words, sacrificed her freedom to save him. A blinding rage filled his veins, hearing *the Elusti* come out of her mouth. He was more convinced than ever that they were

the enemy he must fight and defeat, not Ella. If they were
connected to his father's death and the reason his mother was
lost to him as a child, he would hunt each and every last one of
them down until they were all dead. He would extract his own
revenge, legal or not, but he needed specifics. Who? How
many? Where? What were their goals? Their contacts? Where
did they get their money from?

"What do you know of the Elusti?" he whispered as he
held his mother's shoulders and stared into her pale face.

"You *must* believe, Marcus. You have to reach deep
inside of yourself and open that door you've shut. Ella needs
you. She's neither witch nor shape-shifter. She has an old soul,
but it's a good one. A healing spirit hides within and she must
be protected. You are the only one; no more hiding. She's
your destiny and there's a child, but you must open your heart
and mind to all possibilities."

Instantly, as if punched in the belly, he shot backward
and removed his hands as if burned. He wanted to understand
and believe what his mother said but the more she spoke, the
more horrified he was. What did he know about destiny?
Healing spirit, old soul: it all sounded like the past and the
mumbo jumbo his mother used to talk about, added to her
statement that there were witches and shifters. He truly felt as
if he'd walked into the twilight zone. His brain would explode.
In one brief sweep, his mother had tried to bridge a gap that
spanned thirty-five years of his life and now she predicted a
child. Marcus could deal with the cold, hard facts about the
Elusti but the rest, he couldn't or wouldn't accept. It wasn't
possible.

A child? His and Ella's?

Sweeping a hand across his forehead, he pressed the
temple, trying to arrange his thoughts into some kind of
logical order, but they wandered toward Ella. There was an
unmistakable and dangerous chemistry between the two of
them…but a *child*? He'd never wanted that kind of
responsibility or commitment. Hell, he didn't know what
being a father entailed. His memory of his own was vague to
say the least and any father figure since wasn't fit to bear that

title. He didn't have relationships. Eventually some of the women he dated hinted at commitment, and that's when he ended the affair. He didn't know how to play happy families. He'd never had one and it terrified him that he would end up like his mother. But that had all been a lie?

A heavy weight pulled on his insides. Was his mother delusional or did what she say have some truth to it? He'd believed for most of his life that she had been mentally ill, and he'd tried to remain impartial and not blame her but part of him had hated her, blamed her for all the bad stuff in his life. Was the truth worse: that she had loved him so much, and feared for his life, that she had sacrificed hers to keep him safe? Although her words tightened his belly, they scratched at his heart, wanting to know the truth. He placed his arm around his mother's shoulders and cuddled her, soaking in her delicate scent of jasmine. She was his mother, his only living family.

"Mother, I'm trying to keep track of what you're saying. How do you know these things, for a start? As for protecting Ella, she's the most infuriating, stubborn, willful, headstrong woman I've ever met, who doesn't listen to a damn thing I tell her. Protect her? I may well end up killing her or vice versa."

Josephine smiled at Marcus and nodded her head. "She's certainly got you in a tizzy, and she's definitely not like the girls you normally date, I know, but she brought you to my door. That must tell you something. There's so much to explain and as usual, I jump from place to place like an excited child. I fear we don't have time to go over the details and that soon you'll be leaving. You see, Marcus, dear boy, from the minute you were born, your father and I knew you'd inherited my abilities. Don't frown. Listen with your heart, not your mind. You'd stared off into space, as if you were watching a movie. Just like I used to, you were entranced by something no one else could see. Do you remember about Princess Lia, the friend who visited you? You used to tell us about her, how she looked and where you went. You said she visited you in your dreams, do you remember, Marcus? You must know that Princess Lia is Ella..."

The corner of his mouth lifted and he slumped into the chair across from his mother, defeated with the secrets his mother was exposing, some of which—although he wouldn't admit—he had no choice but to accept as the shocking truth. Of course, he remembered Princess Lia, although he still didn't entirely believe it was Ella. The hair color was different but her eyes—they were striking, unique and exactly the same. A sinking sensation pulled his gut as he saw flickering images of the girl who appeared in his dreams. If her hair was blonde, she would be the spitting image. How could he not believe it? "I... Don't say anything to Ella. Don't you dare tell her one word."

Lavender filled the air, and Marcus whisked around.

Ella stepped into the room, casually rubbing her damp hair with a towel. "Tell her what?"

CHAPTER SEVEN

Ella stood barefoot in a new pair of tight-fitting boyfriend jeans that left an expanse of bare, creamy skin that peeked at him as she dried her hair. Her top was a black silky blouse that plunged in a deep v at the front. Marcus instantly felt his body react as his gaze strolled over the two buttons that held the blouse together and the valley of exposed rounded curves that he knew led to ample breasts. His mouth watered and he sucked air in to breathe as if he had been starved of oxygen. He glanced upward and stared at the loose curls that framed her face. Her hair looked lighter and longer.

Was that possible?

He shook his head as if to dispel the trance he was under. A hot, pulsating sensation raced through his veins, arousing him. Of all the women in the world, why did it have to be the one he was meant to bring in before the FBI and wanted for murder? How did she have this power over him that no one else had and made him feel utterly powerless to resist her? Wave after wave of desire flooded him; his nerves tingled as each muscle flexed and his manhood stirred to life, wanting her. She was breathtaking and utterly sexy. In order to cool his emotions, he rose and stood behind the chair to hide his body's passionate response.

"I used to dream as a child and it seems there may be more to it than that." Straightening his back, he reined in control and carefully watched her reaction while he flicked his narrowed eyes on his mother's. He wouldn't put it past Josephine to blurt out his secret and make it more awkward than it already was. He needed some time to sift through all that information and make up his own mind.

"Stop trying to analyze it all, Marcus. Just listen to your heart!"

Marcus glared at his mother and shook his head. Ella watched the exchange and having finished drying her hair, dropped the towel on the side of the empty chair opposite the yawning Josephine. Raising his hand, he curled his finger to signal Ella to follow him as he left the cozy room and marched into a smaller side room, which opened into the back garden. He walked until he stood in front of the two long glass doors that led outside.

"What kind of dreams?" she said, behind him.

"This is something I don't talk about, but since meeting you and now talking with Josephine, it's opening that door I closed long ago. When I was a child, I used to dream about a girl with long wavy hair and big blue eyes. She was my friend. I believed she was real, but I knew she wasn't because it simply wasn't possible. Anyway, Mother's convinced that you're her." He stared over at the door that led into the next room. "Josephine used to see events that hadn't happened. I didn't believe it. I'm not sure that I believe it now, but as a child, I didn't know what it really meant and when she disappeared, I was told it was for my safety. I hated my mother, thinking the worst of her, but it seems there's more to the story than I realized. You said my mother was gifted; she says she has abilities to see the future. She predicted you. She also says that I have her abilities too. A second sight, she calls it. I was led here looking for answers, which I have, but it leaves me with a hell of a lot more than I bargained with."

Marcus couldn't move. He'd been strong all his life; even when he knew others couldn't, he held up. He faced the death and chaos as it numbed part of his brain that he wanted shut off, but hearing his mother's words, it was like the polar ice caps melting: inside, he drowned with confusion and emotions he couldn't ignore.

Ella bridged the gap between them and stroked his arm tenderly as his heart hammered in his chest. "Wow, that's some heavy-duty conversation."

He stretched his hand out and wove his fingers with hers. Holding the small, warm hand, he rubbed the lines that were imprinted on her palm with his rough thumb in a lazy circle. A small intake of breath from her and he met her gaze. His eyes bored deeply into hers and an undeniable need and thirst swam through him.

"I don't know what you are. My mother says you have an old soul. What does she mean? No, don't answer that yet—all I know is that I won't let anything bad happen to you. I want to help you. I gave my boss some cock and bull story and we have another twelve hours. He thinks you're about to give me a full confession and that will make his job a lot easier…" His face was pinched and serious as he ran over the possibilities of what he was doing. Shaking his head as if to erase any concern, his focus was back on Ella and figuring out her connection and involvement with the Elusti. He was going to bring this organization down.

"I need a drink." Marcus let go of Ella, needing some space and a clear head. He walked over to a glass and metal cabinet in the corner filled with an assortment of liquor. Lifting up a fine crystal decanter, he poured a large measure of an amber liquid into a glass tumbler and knocked it back immediately. The rich whiskey burned the back of his mouth. "Our best bet is to discover who really killed the professor and clear your name, which is easier said than done. Why are you on the FBI's Watchlist? Ella, what have you done? I couldn't find any prior arrests, no grounds for concerns that you're a terrorist. I was told you were a national security threat."

Ella stared around the room filled with antiques on the shelves and books on another before she let her gaze wander toward the outside and the garden. "Marcus, I've been hunted all my life, so it doesn't seem too farfetched to believe I'm on their radar. As for why, I don't know. At this moment, I honestly don't know if I killed Aidan or not. I'm being as honest as I can with you. My life is complicated. I tried to explain, maybe not clearly, but it isn't easy. Anyway, there are parts of that night I don't remember at all. All I know is that once again, I was deceived and Aidan knew who I was, all along. Just like you. Somehow, Aidan is connected with the Elusti. I don't know if it was out of choice or because they found me and he was trapped. I know now that I was nothing more than a curiosity to him, some unique treasure.

"As for the FBI watching me, I cannot answer that. I didn't know they were, let alone that I was on any list. I'm not a terrorist. I'm not an assassin; my only crime is that I'm different. What I do know is that the Elusti are all-seeing and it's why I have a hard time trusting anyone because usually anyone I get to close to lets me down and betrays me. I told you that. Marcus, you're…" She walked over to him and placed both her hands on his chest.

"What, Ella? I'm what?" He dipped his head closer to her. His eyes washed over hers as her long lashes swept against her snowy skin and then lifted. Her deep blue eyes stared into his, and he saw the pupils flare with expectation. A longing to possess those sweet rose-bud lips coursed through him. Moments ticked by as the wall clock chimed and burning desire laced the air between them.

"Don't deny it, Ella. There's a connection between us. I want you as much as you want me, but it will only *complicate* things," he whispered against her ear. Remembering his mother's prediction of a child made him step away and walk out the French doors as he reached in his pocket for his cell phone. At one time, a quick romp with Ella would have been fine: his morals were his, and he answered to no one. He gave in to the needs of his body. It made him feel better about other parts of his life that he couldn't handle. But now, he was terrified his life would change and that once with Ella wouldn't satisfy his growing desire. After what his mother said, he needed to ensure they remained distant from each other and ignored any chemistry, even though he wasn't sure that was possible any more. The need to protect her was driving him to distraction and any thoughts of his career would soon be up in flames.

It wasn't simply his body that yearned to make her his; there was a stirring in his cold heart that begged for release. It was out of the question to abandon her and it was out of the question to hand her over to the authorities—there was no one he trusted there. She would get eaten alive. For some reason— and he couldn't begin to explain why—he trusted and believed her; that didn't happen to him easily. He trusted her as though she was a member of his team—hell, she could be. No, his damn gut was telling him—no, urging him—to do whatever it took to keep her safe and by his side. *What a mess.* None of this was part of his plan. His fingers busily tapped away on his phone, which vibrated with a call. Lifting it to his ear, he listened and hoped for a miracle.

"Jake, buddy, tell me you have some good news. I could do with some." He walked through the garden, needing the fresh air to cool his heated blood and lessen his desire. Smelling her perfume, seeing her washed and dressed in jeans and that sexy top had turned him on more than when she was practically naked on the bed. He knew just looking at her that he wasn't alone in this mutual madness. Try as she might to deny it, he knew that Ella desired him. It was there in her smoking eyes, beckoning him. Hell, he couldn't even think straight. Maybe he should just put them both out of their misery and be done with it. Maybe the fizzle would burn out.

Whatever was going on, whether he liked it or not, somehow there was a bond between them. Hell, perhaps there always had been. Perhaps he'd been waiting for her all his life. He ran his hand through his hair. Ella was the unknown. Life would never be ordinary or boring with her. But she was the epitome of what he grew up hating, and if his mother was telling the truth, would they spend the rest of their lives being hunted and persecuted? If Ella was as different as his mother or worse, they would never have a normal life. No matter what the dreams predicted or his mother said. It would be better for them both if they stayed apart from each other. He would help Ella, and get to the bottom of the professor's murder, but then he would set her free.

"Marcus, are you there, boss…"

"Sorry, what's the news?" He shook himself out of his daydreams and listened to Jake as he rattled on about files being encrypted and codes not being the usual. He was stressed but Marcus knew if anyone could get the information, it would be Jake.

"I need more time, man. This isn't some run-of-the-mill computer system I'm breaking into. There are many layers to their security. I keep coming up against new firewalls. I have managed to place a tap on your boss's phone so we can see who he's chatting to, if that helps?"

It wasn't the news he'd hoped for. If Jake had managed to get into the FBI's system, that might have given him knowledge of their involvement with the Elusti. Although he knew getting outright confirmation would be damn near impossible. They wouldn't identify themselves; it would all be in code. He knew it would be like looking for a needle in a haystack.

"Yes. Have you put a tail on him?"

"Bear and…shit, I wasn't meant…" They were part of his team, Bear and Shadow—they came as a package and he knew if Bear was working on this, so would Shadow.

"I appreciate it. Tell them I said hi and to stay out of sight. I don't know what I'm getting into here but if the Elusti are at the root of this, I have to take it as far as I can. Do you understand what I'm saying? It doesn't mean you guys have to be involved. This is my mission. It isn't sanctioned by any agency. I'm alone."

There were several deep breaths and about a minute's pause. "That's bullshit, boss. You're not alone—never have been, never will be. We all made a decision while you were out chasing the skirt that this is payback. Do you understand me? Maybe we need to set up our own agency?"

Deep down, he hadn't expected anything less and if the roles were reversed, those would be his words. He nodded, even though Jake wouldn't see him, and let out a deep breath. Setting up his own crew, his own agency was the stuff dreams were made of but it took money. But after this, he would need a complete rethink of his future for sure. If he managed to stay alive.

"Gotcha. I appreciate it but don't take any unnecessary risks. Keep me informed on any news because we'll need to move soon. We cannot stay here forever." The phone clicked. A twig snapped behind him as a rush of air touched him and he spun around, ready. He lifted his fully loaded Sig and aimed it in the same direction, fearing an intruder or worse. Instead, Ella stood there; her hair blew wildly, her blue eyes sparkled and her raspberry lips beckoned to him. He released his hold on the trigger and replaced his gun into his holster.

"It's only me," she said, frozen to the spot.

"Damn it, Ella. I could've killed you. Don't ever creep up on an armed man, especially me." Deep trenches formed across his lightly tanned forehead. He was on edge and she was the reason. She moved closer and stood inches from his side, so close he could feel the heat emanate from her.

"You left me and I wanted—" She reached her hand up and let her fingertips smooth across his jaw until they stopped at the border of his lips. Standing on tiptoes, she stretched her arms around the back of his neck and pulled him toward her. "Kiss me."

The wind rustled through the amber and yellow leaves left scattered in the garden, the sweet scent of the flowers running havoc with his overloaded senses. Marcus wrapped his arms around her waist and held her against his heaving chest. This was the last thing they should be doing—they didn't have time and it was more than a little complicated—but his heart responded nonetheless. The fact Ella was melting against him increased a wild need to take, to possess, that he couldn't explain or fight. He wanted her.

He lowered his head and nibbled at her soft lower lip as she parted her mouth for him. It didn't matter that they were outside; he moved his hand from her back and slipped it underneath her barely there blouse to caress her warm, silky skin, making her tremble. Roaming it across her ribs and continuing its journey upwards, his hand sought her round, pert breast. As his fingers reached her nipple, his thumb stroked through the lacy material; Ella shuddered against him and a moan escaped. His thumb rubbed the sensitive tip and he squeezed gently; her pupils dilated, leaving only a sliver of blue around them.

"I need you to kiss me." Her voice was hoarse and demanding. Her skin was so soft like a flower petal, and he longed to explore all her delicate curves and discover all the places she liked to be touched while he watched her as he sent her over the precipice, hurtling toward ecstasy. An overwhelming need to please her drove him.

However, if he took that step, he wasn't sure he would be able to recover or walk away. The growing intense need to claim and brand her in some way made no sense to him because he had never felt this way ever about a woman. If only she knew the power she held over him. That startling revelation made him snatch his hand away as if burned. He needed to stop. There was no future for them, and he couldn't bring a child into a world that was as messed up as this. No way. Marcus kissed the tip of her nose and backed away, watching her face crumple with disappointment. He walked a short distance away.

"I don't have relationships, Ella. I have sex. I love sex, but that's all it is to me. If that's what you're looking for, then I'm your man. I cannot give you any more. You need to know that before…" he said more harshly than he meant. Staring at her eyes still wide with desire, he stalked toward her but she stumbled back. Ella's eyes glazed over with what he thought was confusion and hurt. He wasn't sure but she swept her arms up to cross her chest protectively and he stopped.

"I'll help you, but don't mistake that for anything more. My mother, the dreams—they stay out of this mess. Do you understand?" He pushed his face right into hers, clenching his neat row of white teeth tightly and a wall of stone faced her, making her flinch.

"Marcus, I…I'm sorry, you're right. I don't know what came over me. The last thing I need is to get involved with some guy who's only going to hand me over to the FBI."

A muscle in his cheek twitched as he heard her words and watched as she tried to be strong. She was vulnerable despite all her bravado. Ella deserved a warrior but it wasn't him. He was no hero. He would only end up letting her down. Ella turned and walked toward the house.

"When I caught you at the bank, you said you were going home to Wales. Why?" Marcus called to her back. Ella swiped her cheeks with her hand before she faced him. A pasty-looking Ella stared at him, and then her gaze stared off at the sea.

"I need to go back to where it started, to where my first life began. I know you don't want to accept who I am or who your mother is or who you are for that matter, but sooner or later you'll have to face it. I'm a soul-shifter, Marcus. In the sixteenth century, when Elizabeth I sat on the throne, ruling the land by Divine Right, I was murdered for a crime I didn't commit. My name was Gwendolyn Smythe. I was sentenced as a witch and hung. It seems in each of my lives, there are a few common elements. I've always had some connection to helping others, as a healer, a nurse, or teacher but the desire to help is strong. Another factor is the men in my life always let me down. I was a widow but left with a small property in a village outside of Carmarthen called Twi. I helped the villagers, mainly mothers with their babes, but anyone who suffered an ailment came knocking on my door. I *helped* people. One such man called Charles Mostyn was a patient and I treated him for his ailments with my herbs and lotions. He was a powerful man, a justice of the peace."

Marcus put his hand up. "What, you expect me to believe you're five hundred years old? You don't look old enough!" He scoffed and smiled but it was flat on his face, disbelieving her words.

"Marcus, I'm not physically that old. My soul—oh, just listen, will you? I'm a healer. I care for people and animals; that has never changed in all my lives. There was a woman called Lisa Way; she was my friend, at least I thought so. Anyway, she was having secret liaisons with this man but he was married. I hasten to add, I knew none of this. When he wouldn't leave his wife, things turned nasty. When I discovered what was going on, my fate was sealed...."

Ella inhaled the salty air and walked to the edge of the garden where the roar of the ocean uplifted her. Memories of the screams of the waiting eager crowds who watched as she was hung surfaced as the seagulls screeched and she gasped. Hangings were a dime a dozen in those days, where an evil man named Rowland Lee was put in charge of ruling over

Wales. He was a cruel man who hung over five thousand criminals in nine years and he worked for King Henry VII. Hearing a low growl, she turned around as Marcus grabbed her arms and pulled on them.

"You said all the men in your life betrayed you. That time it was a woman?" His thick brows dipped, forming a v shape as he held her shoulders in a bruising grip as he spat the words out. Marcus stood by her side and stared at her as his nostrils flared in anger. The silvery gray waves beat ferociously against the rocks, sending the spray up toward their faces and her heart stampeded inside her ribs. She'd faced worse. She wasn't afraid of Marcus; she was used to rejection, humiliation, and disgust, all the emotions that mirrored on his stern face.

"True, Lisa lied, plotted, and murdered, but it was the men who sentenced me to death. It was the local vicar who swore I'd charmed a child into madness and it was a mostly male jury that found me guilty of witchcraft, which I might add, I've been found guilty of twice and hung twice. I'm not a witch. I'm a soul-shifter, born into the clan of Ariana. Here's my birthmark—the crescent moon. I didn't choose this life. This is who I am. I don't die—well, I die, but my soul is born again into another life. I didn't know that Lisa was planning to kill Charles. I gave him the herbs to help with the headaches he suffered. Anyway, I made my usual mixture of crushed feverfew leaves, which taste slightly bitter so I added some honey, but it was good for headaches. It was not a harmful substance. It was not poison. On the day in question, I was called away to tend to a sick child. When Lisa offered to take the medicine to him, I didn't think twice. I agreed and let her go. I thought nothing more about it. The next day, he was dead. They said I poisoned him, that I was a witch. I would never do that. Our people believe life is sacred."

Marcus couldn't breathe or swallow. She was a witch—no, not a witch: a soul-shifter. She had been sentenced to death and hung. He massaged his neck; the air around him swirled fast. His heart charged along and the pulse in his neck ached. A fiery storm of anger and rage frothed from inside like a volcano. He was furious but he wasn't sure at who: her or those who had hurt her. She stood before him wide-eyed with her flowing locks and blue eyes, as if butter wouldn't melt in her mouth. Utterly convinced of her words, surely she was delusional. "You remember the past but you cannot remember the night of the fight or whether you killed Aidan?" He pulled her small hands into his roughly and held them, frowning and trying to focus on the present.

"I don't know. He was torturing me, and then I was dumped in the forest. Why? When I died that first time, Marcus, I didn't know who I was, and I didn't know I would be reborn. When I awoke in my fourth life, I thought I was going mad. I had new memories but the old ones kept interfering and haunting me. I had nightmares as a child and no one knew how to stop them. When I'm reborn, it's like I've been in a deep sleep for centuries. Everything aches and feels strange, awkward. When I stare at myself in the mirror, I don't recognize the face. It's not me and yet it is. Do you understand the madness one feels? In my fourth life, my mother died giving birth to me and my father was never around. When I moved to Tregowen House, there was a magic to the estate that I had never experienced before. There I met Barnaby, a mysterious but kind man, a laborer who knew what I was the minute he laid eyes on me and my mark. He introduced me to others like myself. It was the first time in all my lives I felt at peace with who I was." The wind blew her hair around her small face as pale as the milky moon.

Marcus stared, unblinking, absorbing her story and grasping the meaning.

"How did Barnaby know what you were? Was he the same?" The ocean roared as loud as Marcus's heart pounded in his chest.

"Barnaby was a Romanian gypsy…he saw my crescent moon-shaped birthmark. He'd seen it before and knew I belonged to the clan of Ariana. The moon goddess. There's a legend that says Ariana, the moon and fertility goddess, was lonely in the heavens above and one day a man from the earth below called out to her. Hearing her name, she descended to the earth in search of the one who had uttered her name but she couldn't find him. As lonely as she was, she sought out many human lovers and for centuries roamed the earth, bearing many offspring and thus creating her own race, her own clan. Finally, she discovered the one who was her true love but he was old and dying. To save him, she took him back with her to the heavens, where they lived forever. Every now and then, Ariana is said to interfere in the lives of her descendants as the gods were not happy with her journey into the human realm, and they cursed her descendants who are now half-gods and half-humans. The curse allows each soul-shifter to be reborn up to five times as Arianna roamed the earth for five centuries until they find their true love or their existence ends." Ella moved her amulet up her wrist to reveal a pale indent on her wrist and he traced the outline with his finger.

"Maybe Aidan knew that story from one of his ancient scrolls, I don't know. Maybe, he was involved with the Elusti or drawn into it by association. But they won't stop. They realize I'm not completely human and that I can become immortal. They will hunt me forever until they have what they want, which is me. Only now, they don't want to kill me but use me."

"Now, hang on—immortal? How?" Marcus eased his stance and sucked in the air around him. He needed answers and although he didn't quite buy this five-hundred-year-old soul-shifter story, he wouldn't dismiss it yet either. How could someone go through one life after another, remembering the previous lives and how they died without going insane? His ghosts haunted him but Ella...he shook his head and stared at her as he waited for her to speak.

"That's another story but I'm not immortal now and it's..."

"Complicated," they said in unison.

"I need to go home to Wales." Ella stared back at him and nodded. "I need to go. It's where I first learned who I was and something is pulling inside of me, calling me back. I think it's Ariana. And besides, I have to go. Something's wrong

with me, and I need to find out what." She scrunched her face
and let out a low moan.

"Ella, what is it?" He caught her in his arms as she
slouched against him weakly.

"I think I'm dying."

Absorbing the story, he watched the light in her eyes
flicker with a bright spark and then wane. The image of the
girl in his dreams rose sharply; it was her, he could sense it,
and here he was holding her in his arms. She had reached out
to him in those dreams, helping him when he was sad and
alone. He couldn't deny her. Who had killed the professor and
why? Ella was the innocent in this, he was certain, but why
was the FBI entangled in this mess? If he could find
something that proved they were working with the Elusti, that
would confirm his suspicions and what he was doing would
make more sense. He feared Ella was simply a pawn in a
much bigger game. His body tensed as the wind moaned and
his heart raced with fear for Ella. He wanted to reassure her
that everything would be all right, but as he opened his mouth,
the words became trapped as another image flashed into his
head, which showed Ella lying in a puddle of her own blood.

"You're not dying, Ella. I'll be honest: I don't buy
your story, but I'm a pretty good judge of character and I don't
believe you killed the professor, so until I know exactly what
is going on, I'm sticking to you like peanut butter and jelly.
Work with me. If you need to go to Wales, we'll figure out a
way to get there. This is all part of the mission and when this
is over, I will walk away but you will have your freedom."

****

Philip Jackson peered out through his third-story
window and watched the early evening traffic below build up
along Pennsylvania Avenue. Someone honked their horn, and
the elderly man crossing the road gave the taxi driver
responsible the finger. *Little people with little minds*, he told
himself. He grimaced. The average person had no idea what
went on inside the walls of the J. Edgar Hoover Building.
There was a war being fought, where life-and-death decisions
were made every day. And he was determined that America

would win that war. He pulled open the drawer in the middle of his large cherry veneer desk and snatched up a small bottle of pills. He popped one oval-shaped Xanax into his mouth and swallowed. His hand massaged his temple to ease the persistent throb. He'd been popping these pills like Tic Tacs, but they eased some of the burden of his job. A sudden gut-wrenching twist of fiery pain made him clutch his chest and he reached for the water on his desk to dampen the flames of heartburn. Loosening his tie and opening the top button of his white shirt, he plopped into his large black leather chair with a heavy sigh. Thirty minutes and then he'd find his release.

Jackson was just so goddamn tired. He was tired of his job, the bureaucracy, and all the political bullshit that hampered any progress in putting the criminals away. Action, not words, put an end to evil. The war had become a personal agenda for him after he'd lost his wife. For a second, he closed his weary eyes, and the face that was covered in deep valleys smoothed away. Since Martha had died, his hair had thinned and turned gray almost overnight. His cell phone beeped.

"I told you not to call me on this number. Have you completely lost your mind? I know they fucking escaped. Drayton is out playing super-agent..." Jackson stared across at the pictures of his wife, who died several years ago and although he missed her, he was grateful that she was no longer alive to see the evil that lurked in the world or the part he played in bringing those responsible to justice.

"Look, I want her alive—do you understand? Drayton is expendable—do you hear me? Make it look like she killed him, too. Nobody will care what happens to her then. But if she's not in custody within twenty-four hours, we're going to do this my way and fuck all this bullshit," the gravelly voice at the end of the phone hissed.

"Drayton's a threat, and I'd gladly get rid of him but he's no idiot. He knows about the Elusti and he's putting two and two together. I don't know how he knows about the group or what he knows, for that matter, but he's asking questions. His death will tie that up neatly. That's not the problem, but if the girl is who you say she is, how will we be able to restrain her? I mean, there was a fire at her house. Markov, the agent who witnessed it, said she started it." He swiveled his chair to look out at the early evening sky. The face of the enemy was changing and it wasn't even human anymore.

"Don't worry about that. I have been working on something that will restrain her. Just set it up. Somewhere out in the open."

There was silence, and the caller who he only knew as Master was gone. Jackson replaced his cell back on the desk. He didn't like some of the rumored methods that the Elusti used but they achieved results. When he'd agreed to join the covert group that was embedded deep in the government and many security agencies, he'd had his qualms. Now, several years later, and after his own wife had died on board Flight 77 that had crashed into the Pentagon on September 11, 2001, he knew he'd made the right decision. Evil had many faces. The Elusti was ruthless in their hunt for the so-called soul-shifters and yes, innocent people had been killed. But this was war and that's what happened. Sparing a few for the greater good had always been his belief. His duty now was to his country and he intended that America would lead the world with the perfect killing machine. The Elusti was devoted entirely to developing the ultimate weapon. A soldier with incredible strength and resilience. One that could heal itself and was immortal. Imagine that. No one would be able to defeat them in battle. No one.

CHAPTER EIGHT

Seeing fear etched across Ella's face twisted Marcus's heart, which, until she had been around, had been cold and detached. Could she really be ill? After the talk in the garden, he helped her to walk inside as she wobbled walking on her own and he sensed an incredible weakness that hadn't been there before. This was all they needed. Could it get any weirder? Lifting her gently into his arms, he carried her upstairs and prayed it was merely fatigue catching up with her. He placed her down on the bed and left her to rest. Maybe it was just exhaustion. The past couple of days had been grueling to say the least. Now, he couldn't stop worrying about their next move, and whether she would be strong enough to go anywhere. *Wales*!

Who was he kidding? Less than twenty-four hours ago, nothing would have come between him and his promotion. Now he wasn't sure whether he would survive whatever was going on. He sucked a deep breath in and swore out loud. When he didn't know the answer to a problem, he cooked, and that was why he dressed in his mother's pink checkered apron in the kitchen and gathered all manner of ingredients from her well-stocked shelves. Twenty minutes later, he sliced onions as Ella approached but remained in the doorway to watch him. The smell of her perfume greeted him above the sting of the onions and he turned to study her more intently. A little more color filled her pale cheeks but something was off.

"Feeling any better?" Her hair was tousled and damn if it wasn't reaching below her shoulder blades. He tilted his head to the side and stared at the curls. The blue of her eyes were mixed with a streak of violet and she stared, wide awake, as she pouted and sucked on the end of her hair.

"Depends what you mean by better. I feel strange, not myself at all but good."

As the words left her mouth, she waltzed into the kitchen and a rush of need made him turn away from her and face the stove. The pan sizzled with hot spitting oil. He threw the onions into the pan and steam rose as they hit the oil and hissed. There was a raspy sound to her voice, and he knew without glancing at her she was aroused. Jeez, he was only human. A low laugh escaped his lips, and finally he turned to face Ella, who hovered closely. She observed every move he made and the hairs along his neck stood up. He coughed to loosen his vocal cords, which were tight and dry.

"Why don't you sit down? It won't be long; it's only chicken and noodles. Josephine's gone to bed, so it'll be just us." He tried to keep his words and tone calm and ordinary, not showing any hint of the emotions he was wrestling with but as the words left his mouth, Ella sidled up behind him and leaned into him. She crushed her breasts into his back, and spread her arms over his broad shoulders, rubbing them down his arms and clasping his hands.

"Ella…" He kept his voice low but firm.

"I know, I know. You only do sex. Well, that's all I need. I need you. I cannot stop this feeling, and I need you. It's building and building, until I want to scream and it's driving me crazy. You're driving me crazy." Her voice pleaded with him. She pushed against his back, kissing his shoulder blade and moaning against him.

His cock jerked to life with a fierce need of its own. Marcus swiveled around, and easily lifted Ella off the ground. She immediately wrapped her long legs around his waist tightly, coiling her body against his. He groaned low and it sounded feral to his own ears as he pushed her back against the white-washed stone wall and nestled his lips against the hot pulse that throbbed in her neck. She arched her body into his and made a sound like a cat purring. Waves of pure animalistic need shot through him and his hands roughly shoved the thin satin nightgown out of the way to expose a sea of unmarked silky skin. Ella wore a pink lacy bra and a barely there matching thong that dangled a diamanté in the middle. Studying her body, Marcus wet his lips, mesmerized by her sheer beauty. He met her pleading gaze, and devoured her pink lips, plunging his tongue inside to tangle with hers.

Marcus knew he should pull back, he knew this was wrong, but his body reacted to hers as if under someone else's control. Any rational thought evaporated. Taking his lips away from her mouth, he swiveled Ella around and laid her across the wooden kitchen table. Leaning over her, he watched as her hands snaked their way around his back to untie the apron and then they tugged his shirt out of his jeans. Ella was on fire; her skin was flushed and hot to the touch. She swiped her tongue across her plump lips and arched her body up to meet him. Marcus stared into the liquid depth of her eyes, mesmerized by the swirling pools of desire. God, she was the most beautiful woman he'd ever encountered, and hot. So damn hot.

She sat forward impatiently and practically tore his shirt off and gasped as she stretched her hands over his abdomen and bare chest. The velvet touch of her fingers over his skin drove him wild and he couldn't hold back much longer. Ella twisted her hands around his neck to pull him down so their bodies met and rubbed against each other, causing a delightful friction.

Skin touched skin and a fire ripped through him. He licked his way across her collarbone and headed downward between her soft, round breasts. Quickly, he unclipped her bra as she lifted her back for him. A shiver of excitement and need gripped him as he stared at her pink, hardened nipples. He rubbed his thumb over the right hardened nub first and tweaked it, which caused Ella to let out a whimper.

She was so responsive to his touch and he loved it. Lowering his head, he captured her nipple in his mouth and sucked it. Her skin was blazing with heat. Ella wriggled and moved her hands downward to pull at the zipper in his jeans. This was moving fast, faster than he wanted. If they were going to have sex, he wanted to savor his time with Ella because he knew he would still walk away. He would have to.

A waft of burning onions made him lift his head. A loud ringing sounded in the kitchen and smoke billowed from the stove.

Shit.

Marcus jumped away from Ella, leaving her exposed and lying on the table. He raced toward the burning pan and threw it in the sink, turning the faucet on, and opened the window. With a glance back at Ella, he saw she hadn't moved. In fact, she was still writhing on the kitchen table and her hands stroked her inner thighs, skimming the skin upward and touching herself intimately. Something wasn't right.

Dammit.

He could hear footsteps run down the stairs and he charged over to Ella.

"Ella, Ella! Come on, get dressed. Ella." He pulled her arm and shook her, as if to wake her from the stupor she was in. As he yanked her forward, his mother walked in, wrapped in a long cream chenille nightgown, frowning.

Josephine took one look at Ella and then Marcus, and moved quickly to Ella's side. She lifted her hand to touch her forehead.

"She's burning up. We need to get her to bed. I have something that will help."

He wasn't close to his mother, and at times thought he hated her, but watching her now, he was amazed at her control and the fact that he knew he trusted her. There was only so much weird he could ignore. Ella was not herself, and something was going on. If his mother could help, then he had no choice but to let her intervene. Covering Ella in her dressing gown, he lifted her body and cradled her against his chest. She didn't resist or even seem to acknowledge his presence. He nodded at his mother and then strode out of the room, headed directly upstairs to his bedroom. He could've put Ella in her room but feared he would be watching over her anyway and his bed was bigger. His mother followed right behind him. Using one arm, he swept the dark-gray comforter back and lay her down against the mattress. She didn't rouse from her semi-conscious state. His mother stepped closer and rested her hand on his shoulder and he looked at her.

"What the hell is wrong with her?" He crouched down low and smoothed her damp hair away from her face as she twisted and thrashed about on the bed as if possessed. Her body was bathed in a thin film of sweat.

"You mean you don't know?"

Marcus stood up and walked closer to his mother, who moved several feet away from the bed. A smile widened across Josephine's face and her eyes twinkled.

"I don't know anything anymore, except I'm fired for sure, and in twenty-four hours, the FBI and a whole truckload of shit is going to come bursting through those doors." His powerful frame dominated the room and his mother shook her head.

"Marcus, there's no need for such language. Ella is your mate, and she's in her cycle. She needs you." His mother's willowy frame nudged him closer to the bed.

"Run that by me again. She's my mate, and she's what?" A long sigh blew out from his clenched teeth.

"Look, I'll go and get you a stiff drink if it'll help, but Ella's been calling to you since you were a child. You two are bound together. I've always known that. I just wasn't sure any of us would live to see it actually happen. You belong to her and she to you. Ella's special. She's lived many lives, waiting to meet her true love and being of the clan of Ariana—not only the moon goddess but the goddess of fertility—she's effected by the cycle of the moon. Look..." Josephine pointed outside at the glowing yellow moon.

"What?" He stared back at his mother, totally perplexed.

"The moon is in its waxing phase and this has an effect on the lovely Ella that will reach its peak when the moon is full. It's part of the mating cycle and not under Ella's control. She probably has no clue either, as I doubt she has experienced this before as *you're* her mate. You're the trigger."

For a moment, the room shifted and spun. He couldn't respond or form any logical words at all. Was this yet more babble from his mother? And yet as he glanced over at the still and silent Ella, he didn't have a clue how to proceed.

"How? Why now in among all this sh—sorry—mess? At the coffee shop, there was nothing. I never felt so much as a spark." Part of him was lying; there had always been something, but he was freaking out.

Josephine rummaged around in her nightgown pocket and held up a syringe.

"Give her this, in her thigh. It will help for tonight. I don't have all the answers. Have you two grown closer lately, kissed perhaps? Anything that would start the cycle? Getting intimate with her mate will produce a heightened awareness and a strong, almost impossible compulsion to have sex. I know this because your father was a soul-shifter, Marcus."

****

Different faces—she saw images of her previous lives like a movie: Gwendolyn with her motherly hips, tied-back auburn hair and broad smile, always holding a bunch of herbs like thyme or some medicinal flower. Isabella was taller and much thinner, with shiny raven hair, pale and innocent, full of hope. A flash of a screaming baby—Meg coughing and making a whooping noise; she only lived fourth months. And perfect Lady Elizabeth Dempsey, with her coiffed and tightly curled hair, dressed in her beautiful pale satin gowns and riding on her beloved Arabian Spirit was like a lamb being led to the slaughter, a fate she had accepted and had little power to change. All these images converged, swimming together, crying and clawing for life. Ella twisted as she felt her neck squeezed, her back burn, her arms in agony. Gasping for air. Gasping for the pain to end as her body couldn't take any more agony. The noise of the whip as it slashed against her skin, tearing the soft layers apart—stinging and burning. Her eyes bulging as the noose tightened. Twisted and turning, she screamed and writhed in pain and the horrific memories of all that she had endured.

"Ella! Dear God, Ella! Wake up—it's only a nightmare. Wake up."

The voice itched in the distance, calling for her but it was far away and the water was pulling and dragging her down; water filled her mouth and lungs till they burned.

Screaming was useless—they were killing her. A rough hand shook her forcefully and a heat touched her shoulder, not a burning heat like a poker or branding iron, but a soothing touch and she twitched at the smell of patchouli and mint. Her body responded to the scent and she bolted up.

Marcus was next to the bed, leaning over closely, touching her forehead and lifting a glass tumbler to her lips.

"Nightmares?"

Ella blinked. She hadn't had the recurring horrific memories for a while but now and again, one or all of her ghosts would visit, as if warning her of what was to come. *Death.* She accepted the liquid and gulped down the cold water, choking and spluttering it all over her.

"Slowly, Ella. Take it easy."

She wiped her mouth and swallowed again, blotting out the image on the horizon of herself tied to a wooden ducking stool, being submerged in front of the enthusiastic crowds. The word witch had followed her around like a curse and now she was being hunted by the FBI as *the Witch.* She laughed hysterically and rubbed her head. Each life she had lived, the men had so easily offered her up when their own mortality was in question. Young Robbie, so full of promises he never intended to keep but to let them take her away, knowing she would be killed. How could they betray her so? Glancing at Marcus, she studied the room and waited for something to alert her to his betrayal. Where were the big guns?

"Are you all right now?"

She took a deep breath. She was muggy and dizzy but a shower would help with that, she hoped.

"I'm sorry if I woke you. They don't happen often."

Marcus stood partly dressed in a crumpled gray T-shirt and tight black boxers that hugged his bottom and hairy thighs. Ella swallowed and wondered why she wasn't in her room. She swiftly peered back at him and took in his wayward hair and dark shadows that mirrored his eyes. He looked exhausted. Had he been looking after her through the night? But why? Feeling her chest, she wanted to ask the question that plagued her mind—had they shared a bed?—but she couldn't bring herself to say the words, staring at him instead.

"Ella, no. Whatever you're thinking—and I can guess what it is—the answer is no. Now, go and have a shower because we're leaving."

Ella swallowed, not wanting to hear anything more and needing to wake herself up. She pushed herself off the bed and the world tilted as she swooned. That was odd. Her hand rose to her head as she sucked in the air to steady her balance and walked into the en suite without looking back or saying anything to Marcus. Twenty minutes later, Ella was wide awake and dressed in a short woolen skirt, another chiffon almost transparent shirt, and thigh-length boots.

Marcus gathered his belongings from the side table.

"Look, I'm sorry about the kiss." Ella moved away from the door and folded her arms. She leaned back against the wall, wanting to clear the air, and it was the last thing she could remember about yesterday.

Marcus stared at the clock, which read six thirty. He shook his head and glared toward Ella.

"The kiss—you're worried about the kiss? Do you remember any of last night?" He grabbed his phone and scrolled through for messages.

Ella pushed away from the wall and her cheeks flushed a bright pink. "Not really." Faint lines creased her forehead and she frowned as she stared over at the watercolor of the ocean on the wall.

"Well, we can't talk about it now—we have to move—but there was more than kissing, I can tell you that much, and we will talk about it later. For now, we're leaving."

"What about Josephine?"

"She's gone."

"Where did she go this early?" Ella took a step closer and studied him closely.

Marcus put his hand up to stop her moving; he couldn't afford for her to end up like she did last night, if what his mother had said was true. He shook his head.

"Don't come any closer. And she hasn't just gone out—she's gone. Jake came and took her in the night. It isn't safe here anymore. Give me two minutes and I'll be ready."

Ella clamped her arms around herself. *Did she smell or something?* He couldn't make it plainer that she repulsed him if he tried. She bowed her head low. Why was the way he reacted affecting her so? His words were a slap in the face, because without even knowing why, she was about to follow him into the shower to get some answers. Biting her lip, she cursed, and her body trembled. This wasn't her. Ella was never the one to make the first move, ever. But her body and senses were overthrowing her mind. A terrible need was climbing inside her blood, and when she saw Marcus, the need to touch him increased. God help her. He was the last thing she needed.

Every man eventually let her down, and there was no way she was going to succumb to another man, only to be betrayed, no matter what. She knew now was her chance to flee, but something had changed between them in the past twenty-four hours. True, she seemed to repulse him, but he wasn't outright rejecting her either. He'd responded to her kiss. He was weighing up all the odds, plus trying to convince himself that she wasn't a total nutcase. There was a vulnerable side to Marcus and she'd seen it. He'd exposed that to her by bringing her to visit his mother, as if perhaps he wanted to show her that he, too, was different.

There was a connection between them. An undeniable thread. With that in mind, she decided she would stand a better chance with Marcus. When he came out of the shower, dressed in Italian tailored black slacks and a navy shirt, she sat patiently waiting for him. And what was happening with her hair? It was growing an inch day by day, and the dye fading fast. It was turning back to her own natural shade. She pulled a strand and sucked the end, frowning at Marcus as he stood before her, buttoning his shirt and fixing a matching navy tie. His dark hair was wet and sleeked back. His face was free of stubble after a shave and he glared toward Ella as he picked up his jacket, looking once again like a male model. She stared at him.

"Is your hair getting longer?" He pulled his arms through the fitted jacket sleeves and pulled his shirt forward, straightening himself. After he grabbed his wallet from the bedside table, he marched toward Ella and lifted up strands of her hair, studying them as he rubbed them between his fingers.

"Yes. I don't know why. It's never happened before, but the hair color is fading and I'm going back to…"

"Blonde."

They stared at each other for a second, and then he shook his head and walked out the door, taking the steps two at a time as she followed him. He picked up his brown leather luggage case and gathered up Ella's bag, which she reached for but he carried. His eyes stared at her in a challenge she couldn't be bothered to start.

"We're heading for the airport. I have two tickets to London Heathrow. From there we'll go by train to Wales. Where in Wales do you need to go?"

Marcus talked as he walked out the door of the cottage, and as Ella exited, he turned around and locked the door, pocketing the key. He took long strides and Ella trotted at a pace to keep up with him. The old truck was still parked where he'd left it, and after a quick glance around, he opened the door and Ella jumped in. He then walked around, opened his door and got in. Moments later, he started the engine and headed toward the interstate.

"Cardiff."

"Ella, my boss thinks I'm bringing you in at ten o'clock this morning. When that doesn't happen, anything is possible. He may already suspect something isn't right; he may have eyes on us now. Either way, we need to be prepared for any likelihood. I also have a request, and you may think it's strange but it's for your own good. I'll explain when we're on the plane."

Ella turned her head a fraction. "What request?"

Marcus didn't take his eyes off the road but gripped the wheel tighter. "No touching. I'll explain but until then keep your distance from me, understand?"

Ella was speechless. She wasn't sure what scared her more: knowing the FBI would soon realize that Marcus hadn't brought her in as planned or whether she would be stopped at security when her face was plastered all over the news or hearing Marcus's words. Her stomach dropped like a stone and she clamped her arms across her belly as if thumped.

"Sure, I can do that."

CHAPTER NINE

Ella willed her nerves to settle. Getting into a panic would set the alarms off immediately. Marcus had booked her a ticket as Juliet Jones, a British girl, and one of the identities from her fake passports. Her hair was longer than in the picture and a dirty blonde, but she stared confidently as Marcus had explained he had booked them on board a private jet belonging to a friend and apart from waiting a short while alone, he would be back to escort her directly to the plane. This way, they were excused from the main throngs of security, although it didn't lessen her anxiety. A buzzer sounded behind her and her hackles rose, fearing that she had been discovered. Two heavy-set airport security men passed her by, grunting and staring at her, but they carried on walking. She touched her purse where her forged documentation and wallet lay hidden and moved around. Her glance darted around the large waiting area to check for Marcus but she couldn't spot him.

Ella checked her watch, but knew he'd been gone more than twenty minutes. Maybe there was a problem. Marcus had told her to keep a distance from him, and to be patient while he contacted his friend. Taking a deep breath, she had no choice but to remain calm and hope he was being honest and that this wasn't some kind of setup or trap. With one more glance over her shoulder to see whether Marcus was around, she let out a sigh. She stood there idly, as if waiting for something to happen, and she needed a distraction. The airport was busy with visitors to Boston and travelers leaving to either return home or fly away on vacation, pulling their luggage behind them.

She wished she was one of them and that her life was ordinary and carefree. She stared at each man, woman, and child scurrying around and imagined their destination and their story. Searching the vicinity for a place to sit, she gazed up at the overhead television screen. Ella froze as she caught sight of the news report giving the day's headlines. Her heart stumbled, and moisture trickled down between her shoulder blades. Nervously, she gazed around as she waited for the news to flash her picture; the fine hairs along her neck told her it was coming. Watching the crowd, she flicked her gaze back at the screen. The channel changed from the news report to a repeat of *Friends*. A smile lit across her face, and sighing, she moved away. As she strolled toward the end of the airport and headed for the restrooms, an icy shiver touched her shoulder and she inhaled a deep breath. A gruesome specter dressed in a long black hood and cloak danced several feet off the ground in front of her. It was a soul-catcher.

"I told you last time—your time is running out, and I will be waiting." A deep monotone voice bellowed from inside the hood, as a long-nailed finger pulled Ella's chin up.

"You'll never own my soul, never."

A hiss emitted from the soul-catcher's mouth, and he spirited away. A scream rent out in the opposite direction of where she stood and Ella swung around. Several people gathered around an inert body lying on the ground. It was pointless; the soul-collector was there and he was busy at work. His skeletal hands reached inside the unconscious man's chest and ripped his soul forward. It was like a translucent outline of the man himself, and the specter opened his mouth to suck and draw the soul inwards, snapping his long, needle-like teeth shut tight.

Ella watched the gruesome scene. Without thinking, she lifted her hands, spread her fingers out flat and aimed at the ghoul, summoning her fury into a ball of heat that shot out and fired directly into his belly.

The ghoul lifted his head and gazed directly at her with missing eyeballs. An unearthly screech filled the air as the specter twisted and shriveled. His arms flailed outward. The hood that shaded his face flew backward, and a long mass of white hair flew behind his shoulders. Of course, his ghostly appearance was just that and no human eye was able to see the ghoul or his intentions.

None of this frightened Ella, and she continued to pummel more energy into the evil spirit, until his bloodcurdling howl fizzled and died. His mouth squeaked open and released the newly captured soul, which floated back toward the man. Ella watched the unconscious figure as he lay still on the ground. The man's heart had stopped beating, and after a quick jolt of electricity from Ella's fingertips, she restarted his heart into a sinus rhythm. A slim woman in a security uniform was performing CPR, and within seconds, the man's eyes opened. The crowd moved as the paramedics arrived on scene and after administering some oxygen, they carried him away.

She looked around; the specter had vanished, but she felt the burn of someone's stare. Turning around she caught Marcus's gaze upon her from across the airport lounge. His dark eyes bored into hers like steel pins. He was furious. *Damn him.* Pushing her way through the throngs of people, she passed demons and vampires, who glared at her as they recognized another otherworldly soul. None of them were her enemy, but they weren't her friends either, and bringing unwanted attention to *their* kind was frowned upon big time. Holding her chin up high, she swiftly made her way, and didn't clap eyes on Marcus again until the crowd dispersed and he caught hold of her elbow roughly.

"I distinctly remember saying to stay out of sight. I said be patient and not draw attention to yourself."

Without another word, they passed through the check-in for the private jet, showing their passports and tickets, and they were escorted by a well-dressed man in an immaculate navy uniform with a gold badge in the shape of wings with the name Steel engraved on it. Ella smiled at the young man, who smiled back and took their cases but didn't say a word. Marcus stared at her, grabbed her hand and they followed the man to a private elevator that took them below to one of the airport hangars. A loud droning noise greeted them, along with the overwhelming smell of jet fuel.

"Have a good flight, Commander." The pleasant young man stood to attention to salute Marcus and he saluted him back.

"At ease, Lieutenant." Once the man had walked far enough away, Marcus turned to a wide-eyed Ella. "We're flying on my friend's plane and he's ex-Navy. He owes me a favor and I'm collecting it."

"*Commander*? Now I understand why you're so bossy."

Marcus assisted her up the narrow steps that led onto the plane and an attractive brunette flight attendant showed them to their seats. They were the only passengers. The small private jet held several plush cream leather seats, a long stretched-out sofa along the one side of the plane, and a moderately sized desk with a computer screen on the other. She studied the plane's interior as she placed her small duffel bag in the overhead compartment, noticing the attention the young woman with smoky eyes gave to Marcus. He barely acknowledged her existence, giving a curt smile before he stored his own bag.

The flight attendant's scrutiny didn't leave him and it irritated the hell out of Ella. Wherever they went, he drew the attention of women like bees to the honey pot. She slumped down in her window seat and yawned as she stared out as several men in the hangar loaded boxes and boxes of supplies. Ella was exhausted and waved her hand across her face to keep herself awake. She risked one more view of Marcus, who chatted easily with the pretty and chatty woman as he removed his jacket and stowed it in the overhead. His size dwarfed the air hostess, whose cheeks flushed easily in his presence.

The conversation reached her ears. They were talking about the flight time and the weather in London. Ella watched the woman smile and imagined her asking him for a date, her attraction to him evident by the heightened color in her cheeks and the close proximity. Ella groaned loudly and lifted her eyes to the ceiling to blank out the scene. Minutes later, Marcus sat down as the cabin crew took their seats and he clicked his seat belt. She closed her eyes, shutting off the world around her and willing the jealousy to fade away. It was crazy.

"I was merely being polite, Ella, and checking on the time of arrival. Anyway, I have a bone to pick with you. What was going on in the departure lounge? Did you have anything to do with the man who collapsed?" Marcus spoke in a hushed voice.

Ella didn't open her eyes. The scent of his musky aftershave made her body tremble all over, causing an exquisite but painful need. All of a sudden, her mind imagined his hands caressing her body in all sorts of secret places and delivering such pleasure, she squealed in delight. His voice was a distant hum that she ignored as she enjoyed the sensations that coursed through her body.

"Ella." His demanding voice scratched against her neck, and her whole body shivered. Desire for his touch roared and she was going to explode. Why was she like this? At a distance, she'd managed but here up close and personal, it was torture and she knew torture. Her insides burned like lava and she clamped her legs together as a growing throbbing increased her need.

"Ah." Ella couldn't help letting a moan escape her lips and realizing this made her push forward and open her eyes. This couldn't be happening. She was on a plane and her body was pulsing with arousal. She wanted to strip her clothes off and climb on the delectable hunk of toned maleness that sat next to her. Her hand automatically reached up to stroke her throat, as if dying of thirst. She threw back a glance at Marcus, whose face held in a tight pose. As she stared at him, her tongue did a slow lick of her lips and she edged closer to him, sniffing his neck.

He grabbed her hand, and jerked her closer to his mouth.

"You need to listen closely to me, Ella, and you need to swallow this. It'll make you feel better."

Ella clearly heard his words and knew he understood what was happening to her.

"What's wrong with me?" she whispered. Her head moved back against the seat and she shut her eyes, demanding her raging heart to slow as she took short pants to steady her erratic breathing.

"Look, you're feeling—there's no better way than to just say it. You're feeling aroused, am I right?"

She couldn't bring herself to look at him; this was embarrassing. She simply nodded and squirmed in her seat. He pushed a plastic cup into her hand and lifted it to her mouth. Without opening her eyes, she swallowed the liquid down without giving it a second thought, praying that he was helping her, not leading her into danger.

"Apparently, your body is craving sex. Not just random sex with anyone, but with your *mate*. When you're close to him, your body responds and it triggers a surge of hormones. You get hot and well, you end up feeling the way you do. You need to have sex or achieve an orgasm and then you'll feel better. I'm sorry."

Ella listened to each word he spoke and was about to nod off, but knew that Marcus's tone was off. He sounded unsure, and there was a bite to his words, especially when he said *mate*. However, his final statement, *I'm sorry,* woke her up. A sleepy Ella blinked at him, startled, frustrated, and shocked. Her cheeks flushed and her mouth opened.

"*No*, you cannot be…it's not possible," she quietly hissed. She wanted to scream. "You've had me in shackles for most of the time I've been with you. You are working for the FBI, and you're meant to be bringing me in. I'm not falling for the 'I'm your mate' thing, so go to hell, Armani."

A smirk lifted across his face, and he touched Ella's hand, which waved furiously around to illustrate her point. Marcus grabbed her wrist and rubbed his thumb in a sweeping and mesmerizing rhythm.

A gasp of pleasure involuntarily escaped her lips and she jerked her head around to peer at him. She bit into her lip and tasted the metallic saltiness of blood in her mouth. *Dear God!*

"Believe you me, I'm still trying to process it all, but I'm willing to ease your suffering."

His mischievous smirk had her heart pounding—not from desire but molten anger. Ella shook her head and pulled her hand away from his. Turning away so her back faced him, she coiled herself into a ball and stared out at the cloud-filled sky. Her eyelids were heavy and she could no longer stay awake. It was all too much.

Marcus settled back into his seat, the easy smirk dissolving. He knew Ella was exhausted from the past couple of days and yet still she managed to get herself involved in whatever was going on at the airport. He blew out a sigh of exasperation, and glanced over at the now sleeping Ella. Sweeping his gaze over her lovely and perfect features was like receiving an electric shock to his heart and it raced irregularly. As he stared at her, he held his breath inside his lungs; a million thoughts pounded inside his brain. He had never cared for someone, and no one had ever cared truly for him. Women wanted him, mostly because he was a SEAL. No one truly wanted the baggage that came with that: the nightmares, the deep scars, the broken and terrifying parts of him that he didn't share with anyone. What would Ella make of them? He had never allowed anyone to get close, and couldn't begin to understand what belonging to someone would be like. He'd rejected a long time ago anything that defied logic and yet gazing at this extraordinary woman, he couldn't bring himself to deny her. Could he? She had nightmares of her own; maybe they could heal each other? But his mother's words chilled him.

Mate. Father was a soul-shifter.

His mother's confession about his father compounded his confusion. And the words kept bashing inside his brain until he was dizzy. His head was about to detonate with the news his mother had dropped in his lap. Before she had left, she kindly informed him that until Ella fulfilled her need, she would get weaker. *No pressure.* He yawned. All his resolutions about leaving her alone since then had flown out the window. The sedative he had given her would settle her for tonight but as the moon grew larger, so would her need for him. And as long as they could keep their hands off each other, she would be fine. At least, until they could talk about what was happening to her. Marcus had a sick feeling in the pit of his stomach that she didn't know.

Marcus. Marcus.

She looked no more than a child curled up the way she did. *His mate. His. Hell.* Allowing his gaze to sweep over her sleeping form, he ripped open the plastic packet containing the thick red blanket and placed it over her. At any other time, he would have gladly jumped at what she desperately needed without another thought, but it was different now. This was Ella and she was his blasted mate! If he accepted this fact, it would mean he would have to accept everything, including the fact that he, too, was different. That he'd lost his childhood because of all that came with that fact. His mother had given him the quick idiot's guide to being a mate and his stomach clenched.

According to Josephine, a mate is a lifelong commitment and to find your mate was a once-in-a-lifetime kind of event. Having sex was part of the bonding but to complete the joining, there was more and once the steps were completed, it was forever. He couldn't swallow or breathe as he recalled his mother's weighted words. A tight twist in his gut caught him as his mind tossed that idea over and over. It explained the need to protect her, which overrode his need to stay alive or do his job, which he seemed to have forgotten. Ella may be suffering, but she wasn't the only one.

He adjusted his position to ease the growing strain and discomfort in his pants. Marcus ran his hand across his forehead and signaled the air hostess for a drink. The idea of commitment, of family and all that entailed, brought on a cold sweat. However, as Marcus swallowed his drink, he acknowledged the decision he had made as he sat next to Ella, flying across the Atlantic Ocean on some wild-goose chase. His career with the FBI was up in flames. As the cold liquid slipped easily down his throat and burned at the back, he grimaced at his mother's words.

"Your destiny is intertwined. I see a child, but you must make the right decision. Ella is your mate, and she needs you."

Closing his eyes, a clear image of a smiling boy with blond locks faced him. The child was no more than three years old, but he smiled, a carefree smile, and his face lit up. He was in a garden edged with hedges and flowers. Laughter filled the air, and his heart ached with love. Gasping, Marcus shook himself awake. There was no mistake that child was the spitting image of Ella, but before he jerked himself awake, he caught sight of Ella running toward the little boy, sweeping him up in her arms and swinging him around. It was a beautiful sight. His heart beat loudly in his ears and he swept his vision over the sleeping woman next to him. Whatever she was, there was a future out there for them—if he had the balls to grab it.

CHAPTER TEN

Marcus hadn't managed any sleep on the plane or the train that took them from Heathrow and left them in the bustling Cardiff Central station. Standing outside the station as people passed him by, thick plumes of cigarette smoke made him want one badly. An old habit and one he had kicked a long time ago but the smell was enticing. It was a gray day, and the start of drizzle didn't improve the tension in his body. Everything had been so easy: as soon as he spoke with Jake late last night, the plan had been put into supersonic action. Ben Steel, his old captain, who had left the SEALs around the same time as him, had set up his own elite security company and was doing extremely well working for wealthy clients around the world, where money was no object. Jake was in contact with him and after Marcus had discussed his plans, the tickets were arranged, along with the use of Ben Steel's private jet. It made him nervous to accept help, even if it was from an old friend who owed him big-time.

Going through mainstream security would have been impossible to pull off without one of them getting flagged. He was nearly always stopped and searched each time he entered an airport anywhere; it was a given. His colorful passport had so many stamps from countries that were constantly in the news for some type of terrorist attack or civil unrest. He rubbed the back of his stiff neck and squinted at the sudden appearance of sun between the thick rolling clouds. Ella was quiet and as subdued as a church mouse after sleeping through the flight and the train journey. He actually missed the sound of her voice, but knew, like him, she must be swamped with all that he'd said, and the drug he gave her made her sleepy.

"I've booked us into a hotel right in the heart of the city center. I thought we'd go and check in, have a shower and get something to eat before we head off. Where are we heading to?" Marcus stood and twisted his shoulder to ease some of his knots and placed his sunglasses on his face. The sunshine was evaporating the clouds, and warmth spread across his back. He lifted his gaze toward Ella, who pulled her short skirt down, which was impossible as there was only so much material. Eventually, she gave up and shoved her bag over her shoulder, glancing around as she shielded her eyes from the sun with her hand. Finally, she looked over at him.

"Sorry?"

"Ella, have you been listening to anything I've been saying?"

"Yes, no, sorry. I'm feeling hot and…" She drew her lips into a tight line. Her words hung awkwardly in the air as she looked away.

Marcus knew exactly what she was about to say. What was happening to her never left his mind, and he knew it made her uncomfortable. It had the same effect on him and knowing he was responsible didn't help. For a second, he was speechless. People were glancing at them and nodding. Marcus politely nodded back and noticed when the clock chimed, it was already two o'clock. "I know how you're feeling. None of this is easy, but I promise we'll figure it out." They were his words, but he couldn't believe he was saying them. He was making a promise, one he wasn't sure he could keep.

What the hell was he doing? He was trying to gain her trust because after fleeing the country with Ella, they were in this together. His time with the FBI was most certainly done. Did he even care? Marcus caught hold of her hand and squeezed it tightly in his. If he choose to believe his mother, then he was responsible for the way Ella was behaving. *If.* She was his responsibility and he needed to help her. Ella gave him a startled look at the unexpected touch, and her cheeks erupted with red blotches on them.

"I can't seem to think straight when you're around. You're messing with my head."

He stepped closer and his finger tapped the end of her nose. "You're having the same effect on me, you know."

Ella's body swayed toward his like a flower toward the sun, and as his hand touched the skin on her cheek, she blinked. Marcus lowered his head and kissed her moist, soft lips that begged for his touch and his alone. That knowledge alone was intoxicating. She tasted so sweet, and soon his tongue teased her lips open so he could explore her mouth, possessing her. Ella's tongue dueled with his, and instantly he pulled her against his strong body, leaving no space between them.

"Get a room!" Someone walking by shouted.

Marcus lifted his head, but didn't release her; he cupped her cheek and stroked his thumb across tenderly. He smiled down at her and kissed the tip of her nose.

"Come on, they're right. We can check in—it's past two o'clock." He pulled her to the side of the road but she pulled away, unwilling to move.

"Hang on. I thought you said no touching? What's changed?"

"A lot. Now come on." Marcus grabbed her hand and pulled her to the edge of the road to flag a taxi. He swept his hand into the air; a taxi pulled up and the two of them jumped in. The taxi-man collected their bags, and Marcus gave the man the address of their hotel. A short while later, the large black taxi-cab pulled up outside the Hilton. It was opposite Cardiff Castle, right in the center of the city. Stepping out of the taxi, Marcus reached for Ella's hand to help her out.

"Thank you." Ella stood up, adjusted her crumpled top and yawned.

"I've booked the honeymoon suite, and I fully intend to use it." Marcus spoke to the driver as he handed over a fist full of notes, and the man grinned as he glanced back at Ella. Their bags were already loaded onto a brass trolley and were being taken into the large glass encased hotel. Following on the heels of the hotel doorman, they walked in on an elegant and shiny granite tiled floor across an expansive foyer full of large golden mirrors, crystal chandeliers, and pale marble columns. Beautiful fresh flower arrangements adorned the glass and golden hall tables. Modern striped art decked the walls and sumptuous cerise velvet armchairs added splashes of colors to the luxurious interior.

"Marcus, are you joking?" Ella whispered against his shoulder. When she looked at him with those big luminous eyes large enough that you could swim in them, he wanted to sweep her off her feet and not worry about later or tomorrow. "About what, Ella—the fact that I said I've booked the honeymoon suite, or that I intend to use it?"

She had the habit of tugging on her lower lip when she was nervous, and he couldn't shake his gaze off it. He inched closer.

"Both." She stared at the ground.

"Ella, I'm not sure how much longer you can keep going without some release and damn it, there's only so much a man can take, and I am very much a man."

He moved against her, as if proving it was as uncomfortable for him as it was for her. Marcus saw her look of understanding and walked faster toward the glamorous lady at reception, who checked them in. The woman gave him more than the once-over. Her eyes rested on Ella's briefly as she handed over the key card. Marcus smiled politely, and placed a protective arm around Ella's waist to guide her toward the elevators. There was only one woman he was interested in, even though she was wanted by the FBI and the Elusti, and her soul had been around for five hundred years—if he believed her story. In spite of all of that, she was the most intoxicating woman in the world, and as much as he should stay away, he was way past that now.

"I need to tell you something, Marcus. I need to explain…"

The doors to the elevator clanked opened and a group of people spilled out around them.

Marcus strode in and she hesitated before she followed him. He knew although her body desired him with a desperate need, her mind was a different matter. When he stared down at her delicate heart-shaped face, he saw her terrified look. He stepped forward and tugged her inside as the doors closed.

"I know all about the mating thing, and I think I have the answer. I can relieve some of your need. I know how to please women; trust me. You'll be stronger, you'll feel better, and we don't need to have sex. Then, we'll go wherever you need to go," he said, so matter-of-fact that he managed to convince himself that would be enough.

"Marcus, it doesn't work that way. For a while, the need will recede but it won't dissolve and if we have sex, it won't end. I will always want you. Only you and it will be the same for you. It is a powerful bonding and not one that can be undone unless one of us dies. You're right—it will make me stronger, but it will also make you stronger and your insight will not be hidden any longer. Are you prepared for all that?"

"There are steps to the bonding, steps that we don't have to take. This, I know. I can help you without us bonding, if you want?"

He gazed at her beautiful face and let his words sink in. If they did have sex, she would be his but they could still walk away from each other if they didn't completely bond. His mother had mentioned that she had decided not to bond with his father for personal reasons. There were tears in her eyes when she revealed this. He still couldn't quite wrap his head around all of this, to be honest. Try as he might to deny his feelings toward Ella, if she kept wiggling her tiny butt any longer he was going to push the emergency button and he would take her right here in the elevator despite his declaration that he would help her without sex. She was his undoing.

The elevator came to a jolting stop and the doors slowly heaved opened. It pinged, letting them off on the top floor to the honeymoon suite. Marcus cupped the side of Ella's face and drew her lips to his in a soft, urgent kiss while his arms held the doors open.

"Let's take one step at a time," he whispered against her neck; she shivered against him and stroked his chest with her hand. With that, he stepped back from her and waved her out of the elevator before slowly walking behind her.

Ella kept looking over her shoulder to check that Marcus was actually there, thinking that maybe he had decided to make a quick escape. She couldn't blame him. It wasn't every day the person who was your target, a suspected murderer, turned out to be your mate who needed sex in order to be able to function normally. But his words *trust him* twisted inside herself. Could she trust him? In all her lives, she had never met her mate. She had given up believing he even existed. The fact that it was Marcus was absurd, ironic, and yet deliciously sinfully perfect. She couldn't help but laugh out loud. A hand grabbed her shoulder and twisted her sharply around.

"Just exactly which part of this is funny, Ella?" Marcus scowled.

His obsidian eyes and his face, all angles and planes, studied her intently. She sucked in the air and stared at his handsome face. He was beautiful in a lethal way. Her arms automatically reached and stroked his bulging biceps, feeling the hard, tight muscle under his shirt.

The touch made him gather her up by her waist and he threw her over his shoulders as she screeched. Marcus slid the room key through the slot; the green light came on and the door beeped. He strode through the living room and kicked the bedroom door open. He didn't stop walking until he nudged up against the massive king-sized bed dressed in luxurious white bedding. A huge bouquet of delicate pink roses filled a large crystal vase on the dresser and rose petals were scattered on the bed. Lifting Ella's petite frame off his shoulders, he tossed her onto the flower-strewn bed and she giggled nervously.

"There's champagne chilling in the fridge, as well as chocolate-covered strawberries. Why don't you take a shower and then I will." He watched her for a moment before he turned away and left her alone in the room.

Ella was muddled and confused. Sparks fired in her belly and the last thing she wanted right now was a shower. She wanted him. For a second, she lay back on the mattress, wondering what exactly they were doing. Did he really want her? He said he would help her, and maybe he thought that was what this was, but nothing more. He didn't really want her, otherwise why would he just up and leave her in here alone? If he really was her mate, then why was he fighting her need to have sex? Any other man would surely leap at the chance. Was he nervous? Hell, she was on fire and was sure that whatever happened between them, she would enjoy it because just the touch of his hand was like electricity, and she was about to explode. Her fingers touched and smoothed the dusty rose petals. Was she really all right simply having sex with no strings? What would that truly entail?

As her mind sorted through the myriad emotions, it occurred to her that maybe he was giving her some space to get herself ready. Hell, she was more than ready. Even if she was inexperienced as Ella, she had vivid memories of her other lives and her body instinctively knew what she wanted and what she wanted to do to Marcus. Even so, she walked into the bathroom, thinking a shower might ease her need.

CHAPTER ELEVEN

Ella stood naked under the powerful jets of steaming water; her hands rested against the white tiles, while she relished the feel of the stinging heat against her skin. Steam swirled around the floor-to-ceiling glass enclosure. A sudden draft sucked the steam away and a clicking noise made her snap her head around in the direction of the door. She was no longer alone. Quivers of awareness trembled from the center of her core up her belly and spread outward. Her heart hammered against her ribs as she covered her nakedness with her arms shielding her body.

Standing there, studying her outside the sliding steamy glass, was a completely naked and intense-looking Marcus, who looked like the devil himself.

He stared at her confidently and proud, like some ancient Roman statue: still, silent, and broody. He slid the door open, not taking his gaze off her.

She clutched her arms and dug her nails in the skin. Marcus was the most beautiful man she had ever set eyes on, and he stared at her with undeniable desire. Licking her lips, she stared into his dark, almost charcoal eyes for some kind of sign that there was more than simply passion. Was this just sex? Did it matter? A burning need to reach out and touch the ripples of muscle in his taut body consumed her. He didn't have an inch of fat to spare anywhere. She held her breath as Marcus stepped in and stood directly behind her quivering body.

Looking over her shoulder, her gaze ran over his broad shoulders, down his tight, sinewy arms, his wide chest, and sculptured abdomen toward a fine spatter of dark hair shaped like a *T* that led to narrow hips and long, powerful legs. Ella swallowed as she raised her gaze back up toward his hips and groaned as she stared at his pronounced arousal. Shocked and yet fully turned on, she turned her head away to face the water, letting it wash over her. Butterflies erupted and desire thrummed throughout her trembling body.

"Don't hide yourself from me, Ella. You have the body
of an angel and I'm going to kiss every soft curve and crevice
of you."

Water sprayed across her face and she jumped when
firm hands braced her shoulders and kneaded her tense
muscles. Ella didn't turn around; she simply let her head fall
back against his chest. Marcus smoothed his warm and hard
body up against hers and his cock nudged against the cheeks
of her bottom. Kisses descended alongside her neck and she
pressed her back against his chest, moaning as wave after
wave of pleasure erupted inside her body.

"That's it. Relax. Let it out—let the sensations fill you
and let go of your body, Ella." Marcus's deep, husky voice
was laced with a command that resonated deep within her as
he nibbled and sucked on her neck. Ella was sure she would
burst into flames and drop to the ground. She dissolved into
his hands and gave in to his expert touch as he stroked and
built her fire. Her pulse raced and her heart thudded out of
control. Instinctively and unable to ask, she trailed her hand
down over her flat belly, savoring the feel of it over her
sensitive skin until she cupped her sex. Tentatively, she
inserted one finger into her hot and wet core.

At the intimate invasion, she jerked her body and
tingles coiled inside. She pressed her head deeper into his
chest, closing her mouth as the need to scream rose. Her legs
bucked and Marcus grabbed her around the waist to prevent
her from sliding to the ground. He moved his hand over her
right breast to cup the plump, soft mound and pinched her rosy
nipple, which resulted in her throaty moan. She couldn't help
it any longer; she was at his mercy. As Ella leaned on him for
support and pushed against his rigid cock, he moved his hand
lower over her belly button and down, cupping her sex and
stroking lazy circles as he moved closer and closer to her silky
folds. Ella was going to explode if he didn't touch her; she
pushed her own finger in again but couldn't find the release
she desperately needed.

"Marcus, I cannot take it any longer. I need you."

Marcus kissed Ella's cheek and the side of her mouth; his hand clasped Ella's as she tried to reach her orgasm. "You only had to say." He thrust his finger deep inside her wet heat and Ella's inside clenched together as the gathering sparks erupted. When he inserted a second finger, the rising euphoria exploded and she screamed. All she could feel was the waves of bliss and her body rocked with the throes of ecstasy. She couldn't feel her mouth as she gasped and held his hand deep inside her, quivering as he moved it back and forth.

"Marcus." She lifted her other hand and stroked his face in a lazy, totally slumberous way, her body still suffering the after quakes. She felt extremely guilty as he had pleasured and totally satisfied her, but she hadn't relieved his obvious arousal, which nudged her. "I want you," she breathed.

"And I want you, like I've never wanted anyone else before, Ella. But it doesn't change anything. Tell me you understand. Tell me." Marcus spoke so forcefully he sounded angry.

She moved away slightly, but her body was in control and any last-minute indecision was lost as a gigantic wave of need overwhelmed her. Ella swiveled around to kiss his lips and slid her body against him, leaving him in no doubt as to what she wanted from him.

"It's just sex," she whispered against his mouth.

As the words left Ella's mouth, Marcus hoisted her up, and she wrapped her long, slim legs around his waist as he shut off the shower and nipped her neck with his teeth.

"When I take you, Ella, I want to savor the feel of you wrapped around me and that requires a bed." He carried her in his arms as he pushed the glass door open and navigated his way into the other room. He stood next to the impressive king-sized bed and kissed her lips gently; he lowered her wet body onto the mattress. He stood back and gazed at her slim, firm body as she writhed against the sheets, her eyes full of desire, her body hot and ready for him. He could not deny the rising need to possess her any longer. She was his and waiting for him. He knelt on the bed and crawled toward her, grasping her ankles and pulling them apart to reveal her plump, silky folds coated in her essence.

"Ella, you're so beautiful like this, spread out, waiting for me. I'm going to devour your body until I know it like my own but I'm not sure how long I can wait."

Leaning forward, he smoothed his hands up across the soft inside of her thighs and lowered his head to lick the wetness that escaped her pulsating heat and groaned as his hands clenched on her legs. Desire hit him straight in the chest and all rational thought evaporated as his need for her overtook him. When he flicked his tongue over her quivering entrance, she bucked wildly and he adjusted his hand to hold her hips and keep her in place. His tongue invaded her entrance, pushing and probing right between her folds as he lapped up her creamy moisture.

Her hands gripped his head, pulling on his hair as she pushed her core closer to him. "Yes, oh God, yes, but I need more. I need you." Her voice strained as her belly lifted off the mattress. She tried to clamp her thighs closed, but Marcus pushed her legs wider and grunted as he pulled his body upward, kissing her abdomen and licking her skin as he tasted her. He stretched his hand over to the side table, pulled open the drawer and lifted out a foil packet. *Take her. Take her. She's yours—make her yours.*

He sat back and watched her as she glared at him, speechless but waiting for him; her gaze fixed on his hands as he ripped the wrapper open and placed the condom on his penis. She sat up and while staring at him, rolled the sheath down his hard, erect sex. Any argument disappeared. He pushed her back against the bed and he nipped her nipples, making her squeal with delight. God, she was delectable and pushing him over the edge as her aroma invaded his nostrils.

Marcus prowled over her body like a hunter stalking its prey, with slowness and yet fixed determination to capture his prize. As he squeezed and cupped her left breast, he raised his head and devoured her lips, mixing their juices and pushing his tongue until she opened her mouth and allowed him full entry. Ella was in a wild frenzy as he darted his tongue in and out, mimicking what he planned to do to the rest of her body. As his cock nudged her entrance, she pulled against his shoulders to drive herself into him and his body stilled as a quiver of excitement rippled through her.

"Marcus—Marcus, please," she begged.

Marcus lifted his head away from her, pushing on his hands as he stared at her glazed sapphire eyes, flushed cheeks, and swollen lips all from his lovemaking and possession. He wanted to make this good for Ella. She pushed her lower body upward, touching his dick and sliding it into her wet entrance. She gasped and he stared as her pupils dilated so much the blue almost dissolved. He nudged his sex, teasing her, and used his knees to push her legs wider as he tried in vain to take it slow the first time, but lost control as she grabbed his bottom and pushed upward. Sensing her desire, he let go and thrust all the way inside. There was a moment of resistance, a whimper from Ella, but he lost any patience or restraint and bucked, pushing through her tightness until her hot insides clamped around him.

Ella cried out and he covered her mouth with his own, demanding ownership. As her body adjusted to his size, she discovered and matched his frenzied rhythm, clawing his back with her nails. He slowed his movements and withdrew slightly before he plundered deep back inside, savoring the delicious feeling of her. Ella's body undulated beneath his and he rocked back and forth inside her until she screamed. He saw stars and he kissed her breasts roughly, nipping the tips and sucking them.

"Marcus."

Ripples of her orgasm echoed through him and he grunted with satisfaction, kissing her breast and sucking her nipple as he thrust his sex deep inside her as far as he could. Her muscles tightened around him and sent him off into his own ecstasy. He collapsed onto her moist, hot body. *Mine.* Their bodies joined and fused with moisture. He lay spent and exhausted for a while, unable or willing to move, but fearing he was crushing her, he lifted his body off a drowsy Ella. Kissing her neck and shoulder, he moved her on her side and pulled her against his body and tucked her into his chest. He draped his arm possessively over her abdomen and smoothed her satiny skin with his fingers. His breathing slowed as his hand trailed over her breast; the need to join with her again rose.

Ella lay on her side, her breathing low and slow. A contented sigh escaped her lips.

Discovering she was a virgin was a shock; he had not expected that. It should have made him stop immediately, but he couldn't. Would she hate him? Had he hurt her? She had whimpered for a fleeting moment but after that, her moans and screams were not due to pain. He kissed her cheek and a smile stretched across her face. It thrilled him more than he was willing to admit; she was his and would always be his— wasn't that what she said? A fierce need to possess her again swamped him. He had no right to such thoughts after he had told her he was not capable of being that man, but it seemed his heart and body were not willing to listen to his mind. Was he simply fooling himself? His hand stroked the sensitive and already damp area between her thighs and she whimpered. This was bad and yet, how could it be when it felt so absolutely right?

"Marcus, don't stop. You've started an itch and I feel the same need you do. I need you, again." She sighed, turning, and climbed on top of him to watch him through glazed eyes. Her hand skimmed the fine, dark hair on his abdomen and down toward his solid and very erect sex.

"Ella, we need a condom…"

She lifted her hand so that her fingers covered his mouth to stop him from speaking.

"Sh, we don't need to. I get an injection for birth control, so the risks of getting pregnant are slim to none and a child has never been on my to-do list." She moved her hand down and massaged his manhood. He groaned and dug his head back into the pillow as he let the pleasure consume him. Ella positioned herself just above his hard sex and plunged down, gasping at the friction and tightness that invaded her.

She moaned and rocked back and forth, sitting astride him and clenching her tight insides.

But within seconds, he grabbed her wrists to stop her and rolled her over, keeping their bodies fused until he sat astride her, in control. Marcus liked her taking the first move, but if she carried on, he wouldn't last long and he wanted to make this time last longer for both of them. He kissed away the frown on her lips.

"It would've been over in seconds, baby, the way you were behaving."

She continued to frown and he lay over her, whispering in her ear, "You didn't do anything bad—quite the opposite." Ella squeezed her internal muscles and he kissed her lovely neck, sucking on the soft skin until it left a purplish mark that he licked with his tongue. Marcus raised his head, dug his hands on the mattress and thrust deep inside Ella, who grabbed his hips and pushed her body up to meet his forceful pushes. Lightness invaded him, like he'd never experienced ever; he laughed at their lovemaking because for the first time in his life, he felt whole. Gazing down at Ella, who smiled in a sleepy way, his rising orgasm rocketed and coiled around him, lifting him far away. Feeling the waves of her orgasm consume her, he stared deep into her eyes. Bliss, absolute bliss—and then he exploded, hurtling him into space.

A little while later, still joined, he reached for the only bedding he could find—a thin cotton sheet—and covered them. She snuggled against him; her arm stretched across his chest and his arm held her tight to his side. This wasn't him. He wasn't into cuddling and holding after sex. After sex, he made it clear he liked his space and usually asked the women to leave—only a few pretended to be annoyed; most merely complied—but his arm tightened possessively around Ella.

The afternoon slid into evening, and they continued taking it in turns to please and explore each other's body so that Ella knew every part of Marcus's body—all the scars and bullet wounds that had been patched up over the years, his tattoos, of which he had three. They laughed and talked whilst sipping on Champagne and dining on chocolate covered strawberries before falling asleep. As her eyes opened some time later, a fresh yearning for him started again. Would it ever stop?

As she reached her hand over where his body should be, Ella realized she was alone. Her body jerked and then fell back against the soft mattress. She smiled, remembering all the lovemaking they had shared. Her body trembled and ached in places she never imagined would get sore, but it was a delightful feeling. Her stomach fluttered as her fingers once again probed her delicate velvet folds, already moist with desire, and she closed her eyes. Yesterday, she could not think of anything except her need for Marcus; today, that sensation was easier to bear and her mind floated to the reason she was in Wales at all. She had to go to Tregowen House and see whether anyone there still knew something of the old ways. It was a long shot but at the same time, her instincts were calling her there.

A sudden dip in the mattress announced that Marcus was back. Ella opened her eyes, feasting on Marcus, who prowled over her and stared at her, fresh from the shower with his dark hair glistening blue-black from the water and totally naked. He covered his hand over hers and plunged deep inside her hot, moist core in a rhythmic routine she found hypnotic. But he stopped too soon and removed his hand, trailing it up toward her belly. He shook his head; beads of water fell between the soft peaks of her breasts and he lowered his head to lick the water. He left a blazing trail of heat as he continued his way down to her belly button, which he tongued. He pulled her hips up to meet his, pressing his arousal at her wet entrance and plunging inside.

"I know you must be sore, Ella, but watching you please yourself is too much to ignore. And God help me, but I have a craving only you can satisfy. See what a monster you have created." With that, he thrust deeper into her depths; she lifted her bottom off the bed to meet his thrust and moaned as her orgasm reached its crescendo and took her over the edge. As the waves of her orgasm pulsed around him, he slowed his rhythm, loving the tightness and heat of Ella around him. He was amazed how well they fit together and how quickly she had learned what pleased her, and how to return the pleasure and then some. Never in his life had he ever been with such a generous woman. A passion rose inside himself and he thrust again and again.

"Deeper, deeper," she pleaded and he did as instructed until they climaxed together and he collapsed in a heap on top of her. It would never be enough.

CHAPTER TWELVE

Marcus raised his head an inch off the pillow, opened his weary eyes and rubbed his face with both hands. He raised his arms high above his head, stretching like the cat that ate the canary. He cricked his neck from side to side and moved his legs. He was in excellent shape, having been in the SEALs, but having been in bed for nearly twenty-four hours, cramps plagued him. Their lovemaking had not been interrupted by anything; hell, they hadn't even stopped to eat anything beyond the strawberries. When was the last time that he had utterly forgotten about his problems? The answer was simple. Never!

He chuckled like a naughty schoolboy, a well satisfied one, and he was certain that Ella must be suffering after their incessant lovemaking. He shifted onto his side and rested his head on his bent arm as he drew lazy circles around her pink areola, and she sighed in her sleep. Marcus had told her it was just sex, and she had agreed, but as he dipped his head to kiss and suckle her nipple, soaking in her musky scent, his dick jerked to life with a fury and he knew that he was lost. She belonged to him and he was never going to be able to let her go. Never. It was eleven thirty in the morning, and they should be heading out. Staying in the hotel for the past almost twenty-four hours was a huge indulgence but it had been necessary. Ella should now be sated and feeling better and stronger; at least, she would after he claimed her once more and then a hot bath was in order.

Ella woke with Marcus's hand stroking a rising flame between her thighs and she responded by bucking her clit closer to his hand and moaning for release. Every muscle in her legs and her core throbbed and ached, but the need for him to fill her outweighed the pain and within seconds, his cock impaled her.

"God, Ella, I'm sorry, but I just can't stop myself." He thrust in and slowly receded out, driving Ella to distraction as she dug her nails into his bare back and rode the same wave of delight that he was on. She wanted him filling her and driving her crazy with an intoxicating pleasure. Moments later, after they rode the crest of ecstasy together, she fell back into the mattress, and Marcus collapsed next to her body for a second before he rolled to one side. He leaned over and kissed her belly.

"I'm so sorry, Ella. Stay there, while I run a bath for you. I'll be just a minute."

The pain burned and she ached everywhere, but she couldn't be happier. She had never felt this complete before in all her lives. Any minute, she expected to wake up from this wonderful and erotic dream. Instead, a naked Marcus reappeared and lifted her into his arms as if she weighed nothing and carried her into the steaming bathroom, where he had filled the tub with hot water. The smell of roses permeated the air. Sighing contently, she let him slowly lower her into the water and she leaned back against the coolness of the tub. He lathered a cloth with soap and rubbed it all over her body. Her eyes closed, she let him tend to her, unable to argue or resist.

"That's it, baby, relax and just feel the sensations. I promise I won't touch you until you're no longer sore." He kissed her lips and lathered the soap over her breasts and arms. Ella let the hot water soothe her aching muscles and the stinging from their lovemaking. Clenching her legs together, she wandered over the past several hours and smiled. As the water lapped against her silky skin and she sank into a dreamy abyss, a memory rose, vivid and sharp.

It was the night of the full moon and for weeks, an unsettled sensation of not being quite right was getting stronger inside Lady Elizabeth Dempsey. Memories of other people and lives plagued her dreams, which sent her screaming at shadows. Her husband, Sir Charles Dempsey, was concerned but she was not sure whether it was because he thought her simply mad. Barnaby Jones, a stableman, had only the other day caught her as she fell and after noticing her strange mark on her wrist, insisted she need to meet with him in the darkest part of the woods that stretched out beyond the well-tended gardens and extensive grounds, just where the forest began, and he would explain why her dreams were filled of a witch hanging.

Fear consumed her but her need for answers overrode that. She stole out into the chill of the night, seeking him out, wrapped in a plain long gown without her corset, simply donning her chemise under her dress along with her woven stockings and shoes. Heaven help her if she be found. Indeed, her personal maid had undressed her, ready for bed, and she couldn't explain nor ask for help. Anyway, it made breathing easier and she could run if need be. Her long black velvet cape shrouded her.

She raced through the grounds, in her front lacing half-boots, which were made of a tough cotton material, trudging through the squelchy mud and grass until the dark woods rose to greet her. The pale moon looked enormous as it gazed upon her and her blood stirred at its nearness. The bushes rustled and the trees swayed; a night owl cooed and out of the black night appeared Barnaby, his face grave and his dark eyes intense. There was a wildness about him and more so than ever tonight as he stood dressed in his black leather breeches, tall black boots, and smoldering black shirt open to reveal a thatch of dark, sooty hair.

He wore his hair longer than other men of the time and he secured it back by a leather band, the length longer than his shoulders, and stubble shadowed his jawline. Yet, fear was not what entered her mind when she stared at him. Her heart sped at an alarming rate that made her breathless. Her husband, Sir Charles, was older than her by at least four and twenty. He was a serious and quiet man who promised to look after her and not cause her any harm. Their marriage was an arrangement behind closed doors and although Elizabeth was not unhappy because there were far worse fates, it was a marriage on paper alone.

There was no love, no passion or desire. They had been married for over two months and he did not seek to enter her chamber and was frequently engaged elsewhere. She suspected that her husband was secretly meeting with another woman, his lover. Rumors were rife through the house that he visited a certain lady friend and Elizabeth was lonely. If she were caught alone with such a man as Barnaby, it would cause a scandal, but when he caught her the other day, the way his strong arms held her close against his chest and feeling his strength beat against her breasts, she wasn't sure she could stay away.

He was mesmerizing and addictive. Standing here now, she couldn't even meet his gaze but she had to discover the cause of her nightmares for her own sanity. However, as she sucked in a breath at the sight of him, the effect his presence stirred within her. She was not certain he even liked her, as his eyes grew darker, glaring at her. His mouth held tightly closed as he stared down at her; his eyebrows dipped sharply. He looked as if she was merely an annoyance, an irritation and yet he had summoned her here.

"Milady, you're late," he said sharply, eyeing the fields behind her.

"Sir, I came as soon as I could but I needed my maid to believe I was sleeping. I fear she watches me under orders of my husband." She fiddled with her hands. Was this just a waste of time? Her boots, despite the fact they were made for outdoors, were wet and her feet soaking.

"Well, we best make haste. It's close to the witching hour and there are too many risks as there is."

Elizabeth stood her ground as he made to enter the still and shadow-filled forest; her heart beat wildly against her chest. What if he meant to kill her or ravage her and leave her for dead? An uncertain doubt rose as to the reason she was truly here with him. What could he possibly know or want with her?

Barnaby stepped one foot into the dense woodland, twigs snapping and bushes rustling, but he hadn't taken two steps before he realized he was alone. Swiftly turning around, he gazed at the delicate and pale face that captivated him from a distance. Lady Elizabeth Dempsey stood, shaking with the coolness of the night or a fear that she was in danger, and yet her face shone bright, her sapphire eyes twinkled and her head tilted up. Unconsciously, his heart squeezed and the need to protect her stirred deep within, just as it had the day she had fainted before him.

That day he discovered she was from the clan of Ariana, the moon goddess. For centuries, his people, Romany travelers, had helped throughout old Europe people just like Lady Elizabeth and hid them from those who would do them harm, taking them in when no one else would and over time learned about their magic and kept the secret, working with the moon goddess herself. They traveled all over the world, forming networks and creating an alliance; in return, their children were blessed with knowledge of the future and money. His people were camped out in their many caravans far in the woods and had been drawn to this location six months ago and given a job helping on the land. Now, as he faced Lady Elizabeth, he knew why and yet he wished he could turn around and walk away.

Her natural beauty stole his breath and captured his heart. Her kindness and innocence was a well-known fact throughout the household, and gossip about her virginity and loveless marriage grew daily amid fears that the lord and master of Tregowen House, Sir Charles Dempsey, for all his seemingly quiet and harmless manner, was plotting her demise. He raised his head to stare at the stars and clenched his fists. Why did men of such power crush the innocent? With her dowry secured, another lady was rumored to be his next wife. The gossip below in the kitchen and stables was endless. Yet, Lady Elizabeth would never accept him and she was way out of his reach but he wished to help. Barnaby scowled upon seeing Lady Elizabeth's mark. Any hesitation over intervening evaporated and an overwhelming desire to carry her away from her devious husband and their loveless sham of a marriage grew daily. All he needed was to convince her. He stretched his hand out flat before her and motioned for her to join him.

"Lady Elizabeth, you can trust that I mean you no harm, but you must come with me now. There are many creatures of the night of which you are unaware of and *discovering something as rare and precious as you would be far too tempting for them to resist."*

A gasp escaped her mouth and she flicked her pink tongue outwards, sweeping it across her full lips. Desire flooded his loins, rendering his cock rigid and making his breeches uncomfortably tight, and he groaned. The tips of her fingers touched his hand; a bolt of fire surged straight into his heart and jerked him forward.

"Where are we headed?" Her softly spoken words brought him back to the present and a vision of another time and place disappeared. If he could carry her away right now, he would, but she needed to learn about who she was and what she was capable of, and that would take time. She needed to meet with her clan and Ariana. He nodded toward the mysterious woods.

"A place not far from here where your kind gathers, but we must be quick."

Elizabeth shivered but stepped toward him.

"Ella, Ella—you have to get out of the water. It's stone cold." A rough hand shook her shoulder, and she shivered. Darting forward, the cold water sluiced down over her pert breasts. She gasped as if she had woken from a deep slumber. Her previous lives often revisited her in dreams but never where she felt a connection with another person. In this memory, she knew exactly what Barnaby was thinking, and the resemblance to someone now was striking. Shocked she couldn't speak and blinked as the realization sunk in.

"Ella, are you all right? You look like you've seen a ghost." Marcus's face loomed in close toward hers as he crouched next to the tub and brushed her wet hair away from her face.

She stared at him with her mouth wide open. Okay, his hair was shorter, clothes different but it was him. He was Barnaby, which was impossible because he wasn't a soul-shifter. Was he?

"Come on, you must get out. You are freezing." Marcus held up a warm fluffy towel in front of the bath and she stood up, letting the water fall down over her body as he wrapped it firmly around her. Ella tucked the towel between her breasts and opened her mouth to speak as she lifted her leg to navigate her way out of the wrought-iron clawed tub. She followed back into the bedroom. How could Marcus have existed then and now if he was not a soul-shifter? And surely she would know her own kind because they had a certain distinct scent—with him, there was nothing. Was that because he was her mate? Did he know he was a soul-shifter? Until recently, he was completely opposed to the idea that his mother was gifted with foresight. Added to the fact that he also had dreams of her indicated that he probably had inherited his mother's gift, but could he also be from her clan? She wanted to say something but without sounding weirder than normal and after everything they had shared, would this be too much for Marcus to hear? Barnaby did not resemble Marcus identically but as she remembered his eyes and the way their hands had touched, something reached inside her soul and told her they were one and the same.

If Barnaby was Marcus, then how many times had their lives been intertwined or overlapped, only for fate to intervene and send them in different directions until now?

"Ella, you need to get a move on. We have a rental car being delivered soon. Tregowen House has a Halloween event going on today, so there will be lots of people, which will be good as two more won't stand out too much." He watched her as she rubbed the fluffy towel along her wet skin.

As their gazes locked with each other, she realized the inner struggle he was fighting because his face was rigid with control. She might desire him incessantly, but it seemed he, too, felt that burning need. The power she held over him filled her with such elation and confidence that she let the towel drop to the ground so his gaze could feast upon her.

There was a groan and within seconds, he gathered her into his arms and impaled her up against the bedroom wall. Her skin was still moist from the recent bath but tingles exploded throughout her belly as he kissed her pert and ready nipples. A cry escaped and she realized the noise came from her own mouth as Marcus sucked and pulled at her breast. His rough, early-morning stubble grazed against her skin but she moved her body against him, needing his lips to carry on creating the ecstasy that was building. She raked her hands through his hair to pull him closer, but he pushed against her. His hoarse voice echoed in her ear. "Lift your legs up and wrap them around me. I'll hold you." Marcus placed his hands along her hips and lifted her as she complied with his request. The hard arousal of his cock was evident in his jeans as he pushed against her throbbing clit and she moaned, needing him as much as he needed her.

She grabbed hold of his leather buckle and undid the belt, pushing his trousers down to the ground. Underneath, Marcus was naked and his eager and ready erection sprung upward, ready to sink inside Ella's warmth. He paused from kissing her neck and lay delicate kisses along her collarbone as his sex nudged against her silky entrance.

"I cannot help it any longer—forgive me." He pushed his way into her wet entrance, and she let her head fall back against the wall; her fingers dug into his shoulders as he pumped and pumped inside her.

She lifted her hips to match his rhythm and skin smacked against skin. Marcus claimed her mouth, possessing every inch with his tongue to mark her as his. Ella was certain she even heard him mutter the word *mine* as he pushed in as far as he could. Wave upon wave of ecstatic sensation built and then erupted inside her, and finally she screamed his name in release before she rested her head on his shoulder.

Feeling her muscles clamp so tightly around him as she came and hearing her call out his name sent him over the edge into his own euphoric release, and he spilled his hot seed inside her before he leaned his arm against the wall for support. Marcus was still partly dressed with his shirt on—minus a few buttons—but he didn't care. He gave Ella a gentle kiss just below her earlobe and eased her to the ground, feeling her silky skin with his hands as she slid down his body. God, she was beautiful and he just couldn't get enough. After telling her in the bath that he would leave her alone, he had succumbed as soon as he saw her stark naked, standing brazen like the goddess Aphrodite. This needed to stop; he couldn't think straight around her and that would put them both in danger. He needed things to get back to the way they were when he felt in control and in charge, not like some lovesick teenager who was beholden to his dick.

Sighing, he let go of her and moved back, not looking her directly in the face. "Ella, go and get dressed. I need to have a quick shower and then we're leaving." Marcus walked straight into the bathroom and slammed the door behind him.

There was no doubt in Ella's mind that something just changed and the temperature turned arctic. He was in a mood but why?

CHAPTER THIRTEEN

Ella squirmed in the leather seat of the sleek silver Range Rover Sport HSE TDV6 that Marcus rented for the trip out to Tregowen House. There was no need for any words or directions as the state-of-the-art SUV already had the route plotted on the GPS, and so there was an awkward silence. Marcus had barely spoken to her after the shower and Ella did not want to speak now because she knew that something was about to erupt between them that would spoil the blissful contentment that she had experienced over the past twenty-four hours. So, rather than confront him over his blatant indifference and mood, she thought about Tregowen House, the mansion built in the seventeenth century, a place of grandeur and manicured gardens and even a maze that she once was lost in. It had once been home.

Back when she lived there, it was 1816 and she had married a titled man, Sir Charles Dempsey, in a simple ceremony. She was Lady Elizabeth Dempsey, eighteen years old and an orphan until her marriage. Sir Charles was a friend of her father's and she had been betrothed to him for several years. Her mother died in childbirth and her father died fighting the war in America. Life on the Welsh country estate was quiet but good and she was safe, until the truth emerged about her alliance with the clan of Ariana and her fondness for Barnaby.

The marriage, from beginning to end, was an elaborate hoax that left orphaned heiress Elizabeth Dempsey a prisoner at the mercy of the Elusti. A complex operation was in play from the beginning to get rid of her quietly; Sir Charles had contacted the Elusti, a mercenary group that for centuries traveled through Europe under the proviso that they were working for the church. They were hell-bent on righting the error of human weakness and evil ways and used the "Bloody Code" as a way to bring criminals to justice if they refused enlightenment. They doled out severe punishment in secret and underground dwellings, where spectators could gather and watch as the victim was tortured. The reluctant converts who refused to admit guilt achieved eternal justice by death. Sir Charles Dempsey conspired with a bunch of local scoundrels to abduct her and Barnaby, only for them to be discovered and confirming that they were lovers. He had conducted this elaborate plot to rid himself of her and thus allowing him to be free to marry his real love, a lady of little wealth, and keep all the inheritance. Elizabeth would be left with men who were merciless and bloodthirsty.

A startled cry escaped her lips as she remembered the thrashing of the cat-o'-nine-tails and the unbearable burning pain as it sliced through her skin on her back and feet. The torture went on and soon the pain-filled days ended in a blur. She longed for death. Ella suffered repeated duckings in the filthy river while tied and bound to a chair. She was submerged into freezing water until she almost drowned. The final degradation came as she lay stretched upon a large wooden table as she faced a variety of men who demanded her confession and the whereabouts of her people. Various pointed tools and instruments were plunged into her battered and weakened naked body until finally her soul departed, finally succumbing to the torture and multiple doses of a tincture made of a highly potent laudanum mixed with red wine. A delirious Elizabeth Dempsey slipped away.

Tears fell unchecked down her cheeks as she bit her lip and twisted away to stare out at the passing cars and buildings. After being drugged at bedtime by her maid, she was carried to a place of ill-repute and dumped in the local inn; she awoke to find herself in bed with a naked and equally drunk or drugged Barnaby, whose real name she learned later was Raven. They were carted off by a jeering band of men and women, who pulled them out onto the dirty street and threw rotten vegetables and all manner of waste at them, neither able to defend themselves or correct the errors. They were found guilty and carted away. He was bound and gagged but as he made an attempt for freedom, he was kicked in the back and downed in seconds with a heavy blow to the head. They never had a chance.

No, returning to this grand house was not out of choice, for the memories of the time she'd spent there were bittersweet. This place haunted her and the possibilities of what could have been lingered unspoken. Now she sat next to Marcus. A sense of déjà vu swept through her. Would history and fate combine to destroy her for good this time? Under Barnaby's careful tutelage, Elizabeth had discovered the reason for her dreams of death and the images of the women from the past. He had given her a special gift, one still in her possession: the bracelet, an ancient relic, that held a secret opening for messages for when they would meet. She touched her right wrist and stared over at Marcus, frowning. Under a sky full of glittering stars, and surrounded by a circle of ancient stones, she was introduced to her people, the soul-shifters, and to Ariana the Moon Goddess.

Marcus pulled off the highway and signs for the National Trust Manor were clearly posted. A shiver of fear trembled down Ella's spine as she stared at the sky, blanketed a deep gray and black and threatening a downpour any minute. Marcus sat with his shoulders stiff; not a word had been spoken since they left Cardiff. Swiping away her tears and sniffing had caused a slight twitch of his cheek muscle as she glared at the side of his profile; he flicked a glance but quickly faced the road again.

"Stop looking at me with those eyes, Ella."

Sucking on her lower lip, Ella forgot her past and the suffering as her body rose, once more wanting to be touched. A need so strong rose inside her already aching limbs that she had to bite back the desire to cry out his name. Surely, after the last twenty-four hours of lovemaking, she should have had her fill of him and the desperate thirst for him should have subsided? Why was her body such a traitor? And for Marcus, of all people, when even after she had explained he was her mate, he explained it was only sex to him? Was it simply sex? True, they had not known each other long but if she was correct in believing that Marcus was Barnaby/Raven, they had known each other before, and the chemistry they shared was there, only this time she could not deny it or hide from it. Her body craved him like oxygen and without it, she would not be able to exist.

Each nerve ending jumped to life. Sparks of desire rippled through her veins and surged around her body as flames leapt and raced down her arms toward her chest and exploded in her core. She could not believe how close she was to climaxing just at the thought of his touch alone. She clamped her thighs together just as Marcus turned his head to study her and creases lined his forehead in deep rivers.

"Are you all right?" He maneuvered the Range Rover effortlessly around the roundabout. Driving on the left side of the road didn't faze him at all—he was an experienced driver—but the traffic was horrendous and impatient people beeped their horns and irritated him. He swiped his hand through his hair and turned off to the left, driving down a wide and mainly tree-lined road. The roads here were less busy and quieter. A sign directed him to take another left, which he did, and the fast cars and irate drivers seemed a million miles away as he drove down a long, smooth driveway and parked in the gravel area designated for cars. Open, flat, green pastures stretched before him and to the right were row upon row of neat one-story red brick buildings and a small courtyard with black iron gates, which led into the main estate and large mansion house beyond.

Turning to face Ella, he saw her quickly wipe away tears; he reached for her but she shook her head. He didn't want to get into an argument with her but could sense one brewing inside her and he couldn't blame her. He'd been cool and distant and it didn't sit well on him but he didn't know what to say or do. For the life of him, he was swimming in uncharted waters.

"I'm sorry, I cannot seem to help it. I thought that after we...after we had sex, that I would be fixed, but I'm not. I'm a mess. The *need,* if anything, is worse."

Marcus blinked and swallowed. His heart pounded in his chest: she wasn't mad at him—she was still aroused and wanting him. His breathing sped up as he glanced around to search the vicinity and then watched her as she squeezed her knees together. A need he couldn't explain to himself drove him onward.

"It's all right. You don't need to be fixed—this is part of who you are. You're beautiful, Ella. I've never witnessed anyone as beautiful as you." As he spoke, he moved his hand over to her silky knee, moving the short skirt up as his fingers smoothed across her silky skin and moved closer to her heat. Ella stared at him, unblinking, and pushed her back into the seat and moved her body closer to his hand, his touch. It was erotic and she was totally hypnotized by him. No one else existed. He inserted one finger inside her hot, wet core; she let out a long breath and pressed her hand at the glass passenger window, bucking as he added another digit to fill her. She closed her eyes and sucked on her lower lip as if trying to hold back but he felt the waves of her passion wash against his fingers. He stroked her sensitive spot in tender circles over and over until she groaned loudly, pushed her head back and turned away from him.

"Ella."

Hearing her name, she turned to face him; he kissed her moist lips and possessed her mouth. He would be happy to watch Ella consumed with passion all day long. It didn't matter to him that his arousal went unattended. No, he was more than pleased to help relieve Ella in whatever way she needed.

Breaking away from him, she breathed. "Marcus, I want to please you." Her hand moved to stroke the front of his faded jeans and he glared at her.

"You do more than you realize." He kissed her waiting lips and removed the keys from the ignition before he got out of the car.

Ella didn't want to move and chuckled as she stared at the steamy windows. She adjusted her panties and couldn't believe how totally brazen she had been, letting Marcus give her an orgasm in the parking lot of all places. Brushing her hair away from her flushed cheeks, she pushed the car door open and stood on the gravel. Despite being October 31st, a warm breeze greeted her as the leaves swept around the ground and rustled at her feet. The sun peeked from the thick clouds and promised to linger for a while as she smiled. Marcus walked around the edge of the sleek Range Rover and picked up her hand in his.

"Well, we're here, milady."

His voice caught her by surprise and sent her back in time to when the house was very different than today. There was no parking lot, simply endless stretches of green land with trees, hedges, and the long dirt driveway that went on for miles, ending up at the palatial three-story red brick mansion that was set in over ninety acres of parkland and beautiful tended and manicured gardens with stone statues and mazes dotted around the impressive grounds. The influential family had owned the house for several generations and the entire building had been reconstructed and changed from the dull gray stone that was easily available when the house was first constructed to the more refined and hard to purchase stately red brick. At the time, the family prosperity affected the lives of the surrounding population in many ways. Yes, Sir Charles Dempsey was a lucky man who inherited the wealth of his family and wielded great power.

Hearing Marcus's voice, she released his hand, unable to concentrate and unsure whether to divulge what she believed to be true as they walked toward what now resembled several workshops and gift stores selling tea-towels with the grand house emblazoned on the front. When they stopped by the wide and open door, she listened as a weaver demonstrated how to work the loom and in the far corner, a potter threw wet clay on the spinning wheel. A small crowd of people gathered in both corners of the room, listening, and kids watched eagerly. Marcus disappeared for a moment, only to reappear behind her, whispering over her shoulder.

"I bought us two tickets to explore the house and grounds. Come on—unless you want to paint some pottery?"

Ella glanced at him briefly, smiling, and nodded. They moved away from the warmth of the white-washed studio and walked over the stone pathway, headed toward the black tall gates that opened into Tregowen House. Heaving a deep breath, she marched forward. She didn't truly have a plan. It was here in Wales that she learned that she wasn't entirely human, that she was gifted with magic and that she had lived other lives. She had stood next to a group of men, women, and children: some aware of their history and confident of their magic—others, like her, haunted and terrified. All that vanished the minute that Ariana, the most beautiful woman she had ever laid eyes on, walked among them and told her story. The moon that night was larger than she had ever witnessed and it glowed yellow.

"I don't really wish to enter the house but if you wish to, we can. This isn't a walk in the park for me, Marcus. I know you find it impossible to accept that I have lived before, but this was once my home. It's where I discovered I wasn't entirely human, that my soul had been reborn several times and each time I died, it was at the hands of the men in my life."

The wide gray stone path was deserted and Marcus strode off ahead with his hand clasped behind his back. Ella glanced at the beautiful mansion to her distant right and knew that the long glass windows that overlooked the pretty gardens and lawns let in an incredible amount of sunshine when the sun was out. Her gaze lifted toward the farthest corner, where her rooms as mistress of the house had once been. Tall ceilings, long windows, a small four-poster wooden bed and a writing table overlooked the lawns. Her room was sizable, with a large marble fireplace and chairs on either side but not warm or cozy. The two long, wide windows each had window seats and many hours she had spent sitting there, when the weather was inclement, dreaming of a different life.

She swallowed down the thick lump stuck in her throat as a gush of wind lifted her hair and blew it around her face; the gates banged against the brick pillar. As she walked down the flat cement pathway with the green grass laid out like an emerald ocean as far as the eyes could see, the beauty and tranquility of the place washed over her. She knew the gardens and the stables were straight ahead and to the left. A small enclosed garden architecturally designed with colored stones and a mosaic design of roses and mixed plants awaited them before the cobbled courtyard that bordered the stables, which used to be full of horses, including her beloved Arabian Spirit. She shuddered, remembering how her husband Charles increased his tactics to bring about her downfall by shooting her beautiful stallion. The horse, along with Barnaby, were innocent victims caught in the cross fire of her life. The sound of a pistol firing had Ella screaming and clasping her hand over her mouth.

Marcus charged over and wrapped his arm around her waist, embracing her in his strength as she forced back the tears and allowed his presence to comfort her.

"What's wrong?"

Ella stood halfway down the path, studying the lawns and thick outcrop of trees that bordered the land and led the way to the forest with the ancient stones, if they were still there. She stared back at the brick wall that hid the formal gardens and the gate that led to the courtyard and stables, unable to move.

"I-I think I have to leave. It's too much. There are too many ghosts here. I can't breathe."

Ella shook, stuttering the words, but stopped speaking. At that moment, a small group of loud visitors strolled past. The children were all dressed in Halloween costumes. A little girl swirled around in a ballerina outfit and Ella watched, fixed on her pretty pink tutu and wild blonde curls. A bright yellow and black bumblebee costume worn by a younger girl buzzed past and the melancholy drifted away as Marcus squeezed her hand and pulled her down the path toward the house. Facing the ghosts was something she knew she had to do at some point.

"We all have ghosts but I'm here, and I'm not leaving."

Ella held his hand and stared up at his soulful eyes, unsure whether he meant he wasn't leaving now or ever. She sighed, knowing it was wrong to want any more than they had, as it always ended in disaster. She knew deep down she had to face whatever was calling her and she needed answers. A sign stuck in the ground advertising the marvelous talents of the fortune-teller Meg Cauldwell quickened her pace; she practically dragged Marcus to the gates that led into the mansion. Maybe this mystic would be the answer.

"What's the hurry now, Ella? What's going on inside your head? Tell me—I'm not a mind reader."

More people passed, with children dressed as witches and ghouls and carrying plastic bags decorated for Halloween, to gather the candy that was being dished out inside the house, if you dare enter. The sign had also said that the Tregowen House was haunted and decorated to the hilt for the Halloween festival that was well underway. There were pumpkins to carve, games to be played, a competition to judge the best costume, music, food and a haunted maze to walk through for those brave enough later on in the evening.

"That woman, that fortune-teller Meg—she may be able to help us. The old Romanian gypsies—they looked after my kind; they helped us when no one else would. I told you about Barnaby. Well, his people traveled across Europe, helping people like me and in return, they were gifted by the goddess with foresight."

Marcus hesitated as people pushed roughly past them through the gates. It was still early afternoon but the sun that had greeted them earlier was now absent and a chill from the brisk wind ruffled his hair. "I thought you didn't want to go inside?"

Ella stepped closer to Marcus, blocking out the wind and smiling at the strangers who wandered past.

"Do you know what déjà vu is?" She twisted his shirt in her hands and stared up at him, holding her breath.

"Of course. It's a sensation of having done something before, a weird feeling inside that this isn't new."

Ella blinked and continued to gaze at him. "Correct. Have you ever felt that?"

Marcus shook his head.

"Are you sure?" She shivered.

"Ella, I'm not good at playing games. Are we going inside or not? Because standing here isn't getting us anywhere."

He was such a narrow-minded man, unwilling or unable to explore the possibilities. If Marcus was Barnaby, she couldn't understand why he was so hell-bent on ignoring issues. Or was he so shut off to anything that his ghosts never emerged? She huffed and walked ahead; the wind pushed against her back and she tightened her jacket around her chest, blocking out the wind and wishing she had a scarf.

Marcus strode up the stone steps next to her in silence, his hands shoved deep in his pockets. The wide oak door was open, inviting visitors to enter. The heat of the house billowed out as the glow of orange and gold from a million candles and fairy lights greeted them. A wave of walking back in time swamped her and instead of the sea of children and guests, she saw a busy hallway with servants in their black and white uniforms, scurrying around and ferrying large silver platters of food into the large dining room, the clink of glasses and laughing, dancing in the air along with the smell of lamb and rosemary. The hallway was elaborately decorated in its rich ruby wallpaper and tall ceilings that held intricate wooden moldings. Dark wood paneling covered the lower half of the walls and at strategic places, terrifying wooden carvings of gruesome animals gave a wild feel to the room.

"Ella, are you all right? You look very pale." Marcus had hold of her elbow and it was enough to pull her back to the present.

The smell of burning wood and incense wafted around her, along with the scent of cinnamon. Gaudy bright Halloween lights and decorations hung around the magnificent wooden fireplace and people dressed as ghostly servants in torn shirts and pants walking like zombies wandered around, offering cookies and glasses of apple cider. A large cackling witch moved and screeched as she flew across the ceiling on her broom, making Ella squeal. A monstrous bucking corpse sat up in a coffin and winked at her. Ella laughed as she moved around the crowded room, losing sight of Marcus as she was jostled among the throes of people. Haunting music played in the background and the doors squeaked. Howls of ungodly beasts groaned loudly around her and the room became a swirl of bright flashes and whispers she couldn't focus on any longer.

Ella pushed through the milling people and stumbled into the grand gilt room, which glowed from all the gold painted on the walls like a treasure chest. A magnificent gilt and almost baroque-like fireplace heralded center stage, and rich and beautifully intricate paintings were tucked away on each wall and ceiling. The details and delicate brushstrokes and vivid colors were amazing and stunning. This was the room where Sir Charles held his fancy and private parties from which she was always excluded, but she could admire the splendor of the room even if now it was not entirely as she remembered. As she gazed around the lavish paintings, a flash of dark hair leapt out at her and she thought it was Marcus, but the scratchy voice that accompanied the mop of hair belonged to an older woman. One who wore her witch's costume snugly, revealing two bulging bosoms that practically spilled over her corseted bodice. Bright red lips smiled at her and her long nails pointed at her and beckoned her forward.

She stepped closer, glancing at the table in front of the colorful witch, whose other hand rested on top of a milky-white crystal ball. The witch stroked her hand over the ball in a smoothing motion and Ella lifted her gaze to stare at the woman. Breathing in all the senses around her, there was nothing: the scent was normal. The woman was human and absolutely no use. Her dark wig slipped to reveal a patch of bleached hair underneath. A roar of disappointment clawed at her belly.

"Come on, a tenner and I'll read your fortune. I'll tell you if you're going to meet Mr. Right or Mr. Wrong or if you're going to travel the world. Come on, a tenner, and I reveal all your secrets."

Ella's blood boiled. A fury jettisoned from inside that had her reaching forward toward the woman to shake her. Realizing what she was doing, she sharply dragged her hands down. This woman knew nothing of the future; she was merely an actress, a con artist trying to earn a living. Some unsuspecting and yet willing victim placed a ten pound note in the witch's hand and she swiveled away, beckoning for the customer to enter her covered lair. Behind her was a small enclosed tent and she quickly strode inside as the customer followed on her heels. Ella let out a deep breath and turned away. Well, that was it. What on earth did she do now?

The room swirled around and the heat licked at her feet. She couldn't swallow and her skin felt on fire. She had never been burned in any of her previous lives but she had felt the heat of the poker branded on her shoulder. Wincing, she tore through the crowds, needing fresh air, and pushed past men and women, not stopping as people toppled and twisted away or grunted as she nearly knocked them over. Voices called out to her but she ignored them as she raced and ran away to safety. She didn't stop in the hallway but charged upstairs past the gruesome body in the coffin and hurtled down the carpeted hallway, past all the portraits of the people of importance who had once owned or lived at Tregowen House.

She knew where she was going and took a sharp left, fleeing down the end of the corridor and opening the door that led to her private quarters. Once inside, she slammed the heavy oak paneled door behind her and shut out the rest of the world. She breathed in the past and let their voices echo around her, and she stepped away. The room had been painted a different color, and the bed wasn't hers; neither was the furniture. There was nothing of hers inside the room: it was simply a shell, a place she had once slept in for a while. There were no feelings of love here, only heartbreak and loss. The wide wooden floorboards creaked as she stepped over them to the farthest long window that overlooked the front red brick walled gardens. She studied the long stretch of immaculate lawns directly in front before she gazed at the dark woods where she had met Barnaby that fateful night. The day was turning into early evening and it was already dark. The not quite full moon hung, suspended by an invisible thread with the mottled gray patches like ghostly eyes watching her and waiting.

A hand rested on her shoulder, and she swiveled around, ready to thump or throttle whoever was there. With her right hand tightly coiled into a fist and raised above her jaw, she posed, waiting to hit out, but Marcus faced her and grabbed her hand with his.

"Ella, stop. I know being here is difficult for you but when you run off like that, you draw attention—namely security—after you. This is a National Trust house—you cannot just run around like you own the place." His dark gaze stared at her and she laughed, unable to hold it all inside.

"I did once!"

He sighed and swept her into his arms, clinging onto her tightly; she blinked away the memories of this room—the hurt, the pain—and snuggled into his warmth, resting against his hard chest as she sniffled. Removing his hand from her waist, he grabbed her hand and walked with her to stand next to the window and stared outside. Ella lifted her hand and pointed to the far right.

"Over there are the stables, and that's where Sir Charles shot my horse Arabian Spirit dead. He said the animal was wild and uncontrollable, but that wasn't the case. I adored her. He liked to be in control, and it was one of the ways he tried to break me. Another was locking me in my room for days with no food. The servants were ordered not to speak to me. They were told I was mad and that being locked away was for my safety. Of course, it wasn't like that in the beginning. For the first two months, I was treated with mild curiosity. I came from England. I was an orphan, but I had an inheritance, which was quickly put to use by my husband, who seemed to plot my demise after the second month and after the discovery of my growing friendship with Barnaby."

"Were you and Barnaby lovers?"

Ella gasped and massaged her neck as she stared at him and then back into the darkness. "I wish we had been. God, I wished it were so but no. For all that Barnaby was, he wouldn't take another man's wife, even if he wished to. He was a Romanian gypsy and I've yet to meet a more loyal or honorable man."

"Did you love him?"

Ella pivoted around. There was no point to this conversation; it was in the past. Even if Barnaby was Marcus, he didn't have a clue and the man was dead because of her.

"It doesn't matter, Marcus. We didn't get the time to explore our feelings for each other. Sir Charles put his plan into action and our fate was sealed. After we were both captured, I watched him die before my very eyes, trying to save me. Down there is where I discovered who I was and it's where I met Ariana." She pointed out into the midnight blue sky and in the distance, a tiny flame of yellow light glowed.

"Oh, my God, there's a light out there, Marcus. That's right where the ancient stones are. We have to go there."

Marcus peered in the direction of her finger. A glimmer of a light waved in the utter darkness, as if beckoning for them.

CHAPTER FOURTEEN

Trudging out into the misty and now freezing eerie night was not uppermost in Marcus's mind but he'd come this far and he wasn't about to let Ella wander out alone. Watching the perimeter and dark corners, it was impossible to know whether anyone was out here lurking or lying in wait, which he didn't like at all. He had pointed out several times that the light had since disappeared but it signaled that someone had been here. He'd grown angry when she refused to listen to his protest to return in daylight; she'd stomped off in a huff and declared that he was scared of the dark. That made him laugh out loud and earned a scowl from Ella. She didn't know his history and he had no desire to share it with her, but he had completed an extensive number of tours, executing them in the dead of night. The big difference from then to now was when he was in the game, he was totally prepared and geared for that mission. He knew the conditions—hell, he'd earned the badge of experience dealing with the terrain of Afghanistan, fighting in the war zone—but here, with her at his side, the danger was insurmountable and the risks too great. He swore as he followed the stubborn woman.

Marcus didn't have a face for this enemy but as he marched into the darkness, his back tensed as his ghosts sat on his shoulders, watching. He didn't know what the Elusti might use or what their ultimate goal was. He didn't know their weapons or what to expect while lying in wait. He was going in blind and he cursed at their exposed position. Ignoring everything else, knowing he had to deal with the situation, he followed behind her sure footsteps like a lamb to the slaughter; he watched all around, listening for any sign of company, and then he would toss her over his shoulder and hightail it out of there. He wasn't good when it came to sensing a woman's emotions but Ella was different. She didn't moan or complain; she held back her tears as she retold the story of her life as lady of the manor. She had suffered in each life. She had never found peace. He ground his teeth as he fought the growing rage and need to kill this man, Sir Charles. What kind of man would shoot an animal as a display of power or abuse a woman the way he had Ella so cruelly? As for this man Barnaby, why didn't he simply take Ella when he had the chance? He didn't seem much of a man either, especially if he knew the rumors and suspected what Sir Charles was up to.

God, this tiny woman who, in the freezing fog, was searching for answers, unwilling to give up, had suffered incredible torture over the years and yet she endured. She wasn't a basket case. She was a living, breathing woman of incredible strength and resilience, if only she would slow down and be reasonable.

"Ella, are you trying to lose me? It's as dark as Guinness out here, which makes me feel the need for a stiff drink after this little adventure. But seriously, Ella—stop." He grabbed her arm and swiveled her around. The moon glowed behind her, illuminating her pale blonde hair and heart-shaped face. Her pink lips were plump and her blue eyes sparkled. Her stubborn face told him she was intent on her mission but another face stared back at him.

A picture clear and sharp.

A delicate, untainted face with her hair coiffed and pinned back into a waterfall of rich auburn curls. She wore a gown of lavender silk; diamonds glittered at her neck and he stared at her breathlessly through the long window that looked into the dining room at the grand house he worked at. She was a rare beauty, young, and smiling. Lady Elizabeth had arrived not two days ago, all excited and eyes wide at her new home, but as he stared at her much older and very stern-looking husband, this was not a match made of love. Was she here because of his money? A stirring inside his breeches told him it was no business of his.

It was none of his affair except she stirred his heart and watching her as she was swept around the grand room as the violins played, he found himself entranced by her.

Marcus coughed loudly and searched the trees around him before he pinned his gaze on Ella. That scene he pictured—he'd never seen it before and yet it was like a sharp memory. He couldn't speak as the night surrounded him and he stood in the mushy earth. The damp smell of the forest filled his nostrils. He was caught. Dreams as a child had captivated him, dreams he outgrew as a man but now he faced a woman who had appeared to him in them. With his hands on his hips, it was like atoms colliding and spinning around him or he was on a fast merry-go-round, swirling him around. He wanted to get off because the dizziness wouldn't let him focus and think straight. He needed to process and understand what he was seeing.

Marcus opened his mouth to speak but the words wouldn't form. He battled inside his mind with everything that he had learned from Ella over the past couple of days and the words that his mother Josephine had spoken about, so matter-of-fact.

Your father was a soul-shifter. Ella's your mate. I didn't think you would live to discover your fate.

Damn it, he had never fainted in his life but an overwhelming sense of spinning out of control shifted his balance.

"Marcus, what's wrong?" Ella stood so close to him he could smell her sweet jasmine and a hint of orange. The scent drew him close and the need to touch her rose. He stared at her as if for the first time, gazing into the depths of her vivid blue eyes that seemed to say *whatever it is, tell me; I can take it!*

"I *know* you…I've met you before." He forced the words out but as they left his mouth, the air was sucked out from his lungs as the realization of what that meant sank in. He dropped to his knees on the ground.

Ella quickly crouched down next to him, kneeling on the ground, her hands on his shoulders. "Oh, God, Marcus, you're scaring me. Of course you know me. What the hell is wrong with you—are you ill?"

Finally, he sat back on his haunches, letting out his breath and he rubbed his shaky hands down his jeans.

The night he died was bitterly cold, just like this one, and the moon stared down upon him as a witness. His back jerked violently as his arms were wrenched from their sockets. A hulk of a man dressed in a brown leather tunic and wearing a black face mask continued to wield the long whip, lashing it across his back and slicing the skin open raw. Blood dripped in tiny rivulets down his back. Waves of pain assaulted his brain but he absorbed the sensation. He had learned over time how to let his soul wander above, not feeling the bite and sting of the sharp leather. But he twisted as two men dragged forward a woman whose beautiful gown was torn to shreds and her bodice ripped open, revealing her naked and heaving breasts. Her hair was disheveled and hung in matted curls. Her gaze heavy and dazed. A guttural roar tore from his throat and he pulled on the ropes that bound him to the wooden posts. To torture him, he accepted—but her? He would kill them all. The dirty scoundrels dragged Lady Elizabeth to stand next to him and pushed her onto the ground on her hands and knees. Then they untied his bound wrists and shoved him toward her.

His legs gave way and he fell in a heap next to her. He moved his arm to lift her face from staring at the ground to look at him. His body dragged over the damp earth, his chest bare and he was covered in dirt, blood, and sweat, but he didn't care and it didn't stop him from tasting her just once. He pressed his lips to hers softly. Whatever their plan was, he knew they weren't leaving here. He grabbed her around her shoulders and held her tight against his chest.

"Know I will find you. This isn't over. I will search for you always and they will suffer."

The look of wonder on her face as she stared at him as if he was mad gave him a spurt of energy; he released her. He jumped up and twisted around but a single shot fired from a pistol. He stared, stunned, gazing quickly back at her frantic and hopeless stare. He opened his mouth as blood dripped down the front of his chest and poured down his skin like a gushing well. A scream sounded behind him. All he could see was the beautiful and perfect face of Lady Elizabeth as his heart stopped beating and his life ended.

Marcus inhaled a deep lungful of air and his head snapped sharply up. He had lived before and died. The night sky above him was clear and a million bright lights twinkled, saying hello. Marcus jumped up and shook off the grass and dried leaves stuck to the wet patches on his knees. As the missing pieces to his past were placed, he knew with certain knowledge what lay beyond the trees but he needed confirmation that he wasn't simply going insane. Grabbing Ella's hand, he raised her off the ground. She stumbled to follow him, but he marched them straight ahead through the tall evergreen and oak trees.

"Where are you going? How do you…Marcus, speak to me!"

At the concern and the confusion in her voice, he turned abruptly around and raised his hand to stroke her cheek; his thumb rubbed on the high cheekbone and he drank in her perfection. He pressed his forehead onto hers and kissed her parted lips tenderly before he wrapped his arms securely around her waist and joined their bodies in a tight union. The kiss he gave Ella was slow and soft. He didn't demand; he took his time, savoring the feel of her soft lips as he stroked and kissed her. Tasting the sweet and tartness of her mouth that was her alone.

When she softened against him, he broke the kiss and moved his head back a fraction to stare into her huge eyes that waited for his explanation as his heart beat like a war cry. He couldn't bring forth words. He slackened his embrace and tugged her through the croft of trees as the moon shone down on them both. There, before them, as they pushed back the overgrown bushes, Marcus fixed his gaze on the misshapen and some snapped in half pale gray monolithic stones, of which there was nine. One lay completely on the ground like a felled tree.

"I remember bringing you here and meeting the moon goddess with her flowing flaxen hair and milky complexion as she talked to us all and told us of what was to come and who we were. I remember thinking I should leave, that I had only meant to bring you to her, not stay, but as I rose to leave, her hand stilled my movement and she spoke directly to me without the need for words. From that moment on, everything changed and yet like the sands of time, everything she said came true and there was nothing I could do to stop it."

Marcus reached for both her hands and pulled her as he walked backward, leading them into the center of the stones.

"I'm a soul-shifter, too, and that night, as Ariana spoke to me, I longed to tell you of my love for you but I wasn't sure you felt the same. Times have changed but there's a lot that hasn't. I still don't know the face of our enemy and yet he is out there." He wrapped his arms around her, feeling for the first time in his life this was absolutely right and that no matter what happened, he would do everything in his power to keep Ella safe and with him. He kissed the top of her head.

"Ariana isn't going to appear. I remember her telling me that was the last time she would make such a journey, that we were on our own and that by telling us what we needed to know that was all she was able to do or she would be cast out of the heavens by the angry gods. We need to leave it isn't safe here. You're exhausted and so am I."

As they moved away from the stones, the bushes rustled, twigs snapped and several hefty men dressed entirely in black stood with guns aimed at them. Marcus quickly pushed Ella behind him but the numbers weren't in his favor at all. The row of mercenary-looking soldiers parted as a man of medium height with dirty blond hair, narrow gray eyes hidden behind square spectacles, and a pointed nose strode forward. Ella gasped behind him and she pushed into his shoulder, trying to charge forward, but Marcus grabbed her arms and held her next to him as she twisted and kicked out at his legs.

Damn it, she hurt. She was a real vixen when she was fired up but charging after the guy was only going to end with her getting hurt. The professor had no qualms when it came to hitting a woman; he'd already seen him in action and damn it, he needed to think before they made a move but time was slipping away.

"You bastard, you're alive. I should've known you were behind this."

She struggled against his hold. Marcus stayed silent and analyzed the scene. He gripped her firmly, not wanting her to break free as he glared at the men and their rifles and mass of weapons strapped around their waists. He'd brought a small army along and all he had was a gun and his knife. Nice move. Had they been under surveillance the entire time? How did they know she was here?

"Nice to see you again, Ella, you're positively glowing my dear. All this fresh air must agree with you." The professor stepped closer, not too close but enough that Marcus could stare into the man's cold, steely eyes that glimmered with a peculiar excitement as he stared at Ella. He clasped his hands to form a steeple and rested his middle finger on his chin as he pondered for a moment.

"I'm sure you're both wondering why and what is going to happen next." The professor tilted his head up at the moon and smiled. His lips widened into a wide, long grin bracketed by deep lines that made his mouth stand out as his jaw narrowed to almost a point. He was pure evil.

Marcus remained calm. He knew to stay alive, he needed to be alert, cold, and as equally deadly as his opponent. He turned his emotions off and again weighed the odds of getting out of here alive because he needed to stay alive and he needed Ella to stay alive.

"We hoped you'd lead us to the goddess herself but as that hasn't happened, we need you for something else. And with the full moon coming in forty-eight hours, we needed to rein you in, dear. I have something that is going to make you feel wonderful."

Marcus tightened his fist; whatever happened from here on in, the professor was his. He would kill him without a moment of regret once this was over. He didn't know what their intentions were but it was obviously to do with the cycle of the moon and that meant Ella's sexual state. He gritted his teeth, not giving anything away, which would only make it worse, and Ella stiffened beside him; he knew she was thinking the same thing. She didn't respond and neither did he. The professor nodded and two of the soldiers strode toward him, heading for Ella. He couldn't stop Ella from being taken this time but he could escape and be ready for next time because there would be a next time if he could break free. The soldier nearest to him, with his military buzz cut and face streaked in green and black grease paint, didn't make eye contact with Marcus, which was a big mistake because he was ready as his hand touched Ella. Marcus lifted his knife from the belt and grabbed the man around the neck, throttling and pinning him back against his chest.

Ella screamed but the man holding her dragged her away.

"We're leaving. Deal with him."

As the soldier tried to drag Ella away, she stomped on his foot and lashed out with her leg.

The professor slapped his hand across her cheek; she went flying. The soldier roughly launched after her and hauled her away through the trees as the professor followed, not looking back at him. Four mercenaries faced him, equal in size and stature, ready to kill him. Holding the man up against him to cover his chest, he squeezed his throat, and his team watched. Marcus coldly sliced the man's throat open and blood gushed out. Stealing the gun from the man's side holster, he fired off rounds in quick succession, peppering the air with bullets and scattering the soldiers into the bushes. Without hesitation, Marcus shoved the dead man away from him and disappeared into the forest.

CHAPTER FIFTEEN

Marcus charged through the densely knitted forest and twisted branches that slashed across his cheeks and ducked behind a thick oak tree. With his fingers, he swiped the damp earth and smeared his face with moist brown soil. His heart was tapping along but he breathed very slowly through his nostrils. His gaze was alert and watchful in the dark as he ran over the scene of events that had unfolded moments before. Ella would believe he had abandoned her, which he had, but it had been necessary to regain control. The professor was alive and more than just friends with the Elusti; he imagined he was quite high up in the ranking system as he was here in charge of this little get-together but not for much longer. Once he dispatched the others, he would be right on their tail. He needed to be quick and deadly. A movement behind him and a sudden change in the wind had him leaping at the dark shadow to his left. The solid silhouette shoved him hard in the belly and gripped his arm.

"Boss, it's me."

"Jake, what the hell are you doing here?"

Jake eased his grip on Marcus and shoved him away. "Saving your sorry ass." Gunfire sounded in the distance and Marcus stared at Jake. "You didn't think I would come alone, did you?"

Marcus hissed and strode off through the bushes and undergrowth until he was back by the stone circle. Two men lay inert and sprawled on the ground, including the one Marcus had killed from earlier, which meant there were the two others out there either in hiding or had fled. A skyscraper of a man stood next to the dead bodies, as black as the night sky and as broad as any oak tree. His nut brown eyes connected with Marcus. He nodded and gave him a wide grin as he secured his rifle over his shoulder. Shadow and Bear were a pair; they were his sniper team back in SEAL Team 5 based back on the West Coast but he didn't have a clue why they were here.

"Good to see you, boss. Sorry we didn't get to the meet-and-greet earlier."

Marcus wiped his forehead and stared at the two heavyweights Bear and Shadow, dressed in full combat gear and boots, covered with face paint as if this were a routine mission. *What the hell.*

"What the fuck are you up to? How the hell?" He didn't move and the men eased back and shifted their glances toward Jake. Marcus turned his angry stare on Jake.

"You have exactly two minutes."

Marcus could feel the blood pump inside his veins and he was ready to spew like a volcano. They once were his team and they never made a move without him.

"Marcus, you knew that I'd left the SEALs, just like you. After Dallas died, it wasn't the same. You were injured and hell, it wasn't the same. Anyhow, Captain Steel was leaving and setting up a worldwide private security team. He's collected quite a few impressive clients who wanted to hire him immediately. The work is the same: covert, don't know if we'll get back alive—that kind of stuff—but the pay is way much better. Look, shit, I should have said something back in New York but, man, you caught me on the hop. You were running blind from the FBI. I was scared shitless you were going to get yourself killed, man. Your head wasn't screwed on. Hell, you've never given a skirt the chance to pull one over on you, ever. And she pulled a doozy on you!" Jake chuckled but Marcus remained unmoved.

"I knew she was up to something. I had it under control."

"It didn't look like it, all trussed up in handcuffs. Anyway, when I knew you were going to keep chasing the skirt and you asked for help to get airborne, Steel came to mind. The jet you flew in is his and he—"

Marcus flipped his hand up and clenched his mouth; he'd heard enough. "I know we were flying on Steel's plane. What I didn't know was that he has his own army and that I'm your *mission*. Again, what the fuck is going on, Jake? My patience evaporated thirty minutes ago. Ella, the woman you keep referring to as the skirt, is not just some woman. Do I make myself clear?"

The two men eyeballed each other.

"Seriously, you think we don't know that, boss?"

This, coming from Shadow, who stood to his side and who was as silent as his name, was like a blast of cold water over Marcus. He paused and took a breath as he rubbed his forehead. He was bringing his emotions into play here, something he never did. That wasn't good on any mission and this was his hardest. Staring down at Jake, not giving an inch, now wasn't the time to appear weak or nervous, especially around his team. He shoved his emotions into check.

"Steel is investigating Aidan O'Connor, the professor. He's known to mix in some very bad and influential circles that deal with arms trafficking worldwide. They also deal with drugs, sex trafficking, you name it. When I mentioned what was going on with you back in New York, Steel jumped on it and this became a mission. Ella Masters, the Witch, became our mission."

Marcus didn't blink an eye. Months ago, Ben Steel—a man whose life had been the military and he had enough medals to prove it, his former and very well-respected captain—had contacted him out of the blue to offer him a job. At the time, he wasn't in the right frame of mind to talk to anyone who reminded him of the past but now, as he stood in the chilling temperatures and stared at his former teammates and knowing Ella was a prisoner at the mercy of this psychotic group the Elusti, he couldn't be happier. It evened the odds somewhat and he could take a breath. This would be his hardest mission yet but he could complete it and bring her home safely. He strode over to Jake, who backed away, but he grabbed him by the scruff of his thick black sweater and slapped him roughly on the back.

"Ella never had the upper hand, man, never. I knew her game from the beginning because I'm exactly the same as her. She was trying to survive any way she could. Failure is not an option on this mission, understand? Now, where's Payday?" If Jake and the sniper team were here, he knew that Steel would have recruited other members. Maybe it wouldn't be so bad being part of this band of fierce warriors again.

"How did you...he's our surveillance. He bugged the transportation and he's keeping eyes on the ground. He's already on the road with Preacher Boy. We're here to bring you in for a full debriefing. Steel's waiting at the operations center."

Marcus breathed a sigh of relief. Operation center. That meant it wasn't some scrambled, put-together mission but a bona fide, well-organized tactical team in place. With Steel at the helm with an unlimited financial back pocket—well, if the rumors were true and certainly your average Joe didn't have his own jet!—maybe it was time to talk about this job he'd been banging on about to his deaf ears until now. Marcus stared at Jake's steel-gray eyes and nodded.

"We'll get your lady back, boss. Don't you worry," Bear chipped in as they trudged their way back through the moist earth.

Shadow spoke into his mouthpiece and swatted away a fly. "I'm counting on it."

****

"Just let me get this straight, Steel. You've been watching me since New York, since I touched base with Gateway?" Marcus stood almost nose to nose with his former captain Ben Steel, who, at six two, was the same height as him. They had been arguing for hours. The sun had come up and daylight streamed in through the windows that fronted onto Cardiff Bay. Copious mugs of coffee had been drained, which hadn't helped his urgent need to move, to find Ella, but Steel wouldn't let him go until the air was totally cleared between them and ensured that they were on the same page, whatever the hell that meant. He did have a sneaking suspicion he was being drawn into something he had little choice in, which only got his back up even more.

He studied his former boss who, although he carried a little more weight around the middle, was a formidable man. He knew he trained every day. Most of the team did because they believed warriors were made through training hard to increase their strength and speed. Their motto, *The only easy day was yesterday,* was ingrained on his brain. He also knew that Steel wouldn't give up until he got what he wanted.

Ben Steel wore his hair closely shaved at the bottom with a longer length on top of thick silver hair that he parted neatly to the side. Thick swatches of stray strands flopped over his lined forehead. His wide eyebrows, also silver, arched and his neatly trimmed horseshoe mustache twitched as his hazel eyes narrowed. He scratched his mustache and sighed.

They stood alone in an old deserted brick warehouse somewhere down on the waterfront in Cardiff. The water taxis honked their horns as they passed by and tiny sailboats fluttered on the horizon of the deep blue waters that he could see through the broken windowpane. Seagulls squawked and Marcus wondered not for the first time how Ella was and he shook his head.

"Drayton, if you must know, you've never been off my radar. I've been biding my time and waiting, but I knew at some point you would make the right decision and join us. You know me—you know my loyalty is to my country and to my men. Hiding mistakes and covering up bullshit for evil because they have bigger purses or are influential politicians—it's never been what I'm about. You knew I would never simply retire. I've been dreaming of creating this elite group for years. The timing is right. I need men like you. A natural leader willing to do anything to get the job done and the men respect you. Hell, I respect you and what's more, I trust you when you're thinking straight and your head is in the game. I pay well but loyalty isn't bought. I'm creating an elite team of specialists who will be committed to the mission first. As usual, anything we do is covert and undercover but we're still the good guys. We fight for justice and to help those who cannot help themselves. Each mission is agreed by the team and I want you as my second-in-command. I want you to help with recruitment and to have a say in accepting or rejecting the assignments. I have two teams in the making but it's early days. Some of the men you know. Others you don't. Most are ex-SEALs but I'm not restricting recruitment to just military backgrounds. I need men and women with certain credentials and abilities. Experts who are driven and are the best in their field: scientists, doctors, psychologists, linguistics as well as soldiers. Like I said, I'm creating a very specialized team that will work worldwide. Are you in?"

Marcus was excited by Steel's vision and enthusiastic recruitment bullshit but his mind was focused on Ella. He walked over to a wall that held a multitude of photographs stuck up on the massive whiteboard that housed the main players in the Witch mission. Ella's picture was at the center, her eyes pleading and tugging at his heart. He rubbed both his hands over his face. Staring at his platinum Rolex watch, it was eleven hours since he'd last seen her and the thoughts of what that madman was doing to her was driving him mad.

"We know exactly where she is and we'll free her but I need Aidan O'Connor. He's not the main player of this group we know to be called the Elusti but he is one of the Masters. We need him as leverage to discover who the ultimate leader is and gather the intel about this group's network. Once we have Ella Masters secured, you do realize she will never be safe? She will be a target forever. If you care at all for this woman, and I think you do, you must let her go, for both your sakes."

Marcus swiveled around and banged his fist on the tall black filing cabinet. "Fuck you." Who the hell did he think he was to dictate to him about his personal life? Even if he took the job, his personal life was his business. But as he flicked his gaze back at the photograph of Ella's pale and perfect face, he knew that wasn't true. As a SEAL, the job always came first. It played a big part in the reason he never settled down: a) he didn't believe he would be any good at it and b) he was the job. Leaving a wife and some kid behind didn't sit well in his gut and most guys who had taken that plunge in his line of work ended up divorced fuckers anyway. It didn't matter whether they were soul mates or not; if he took this job, he would be married to it.

"I'm not trying to mess with your head but you know the rules. You know the life and the risks we take. When we get Ella back, the only chance for her to live a normal life is to start over, with a new identity, and I can provide all that as well as security that will watch over her twenty-four seven...*if* you agree to work for me."

Steel's words made him laugh. Ella never had a normal life and she never would. Steel didn't know who the hell he was dealing with. Or, for that matter, who he truly was and what that meant for him and Ella. He still felt torn in opposing directions and he wasn't sure he would ever resolve that conflict. It was as if he stood on the precipice of the Grand Canyon. Did he take the offer and get Ella to safety or run after her on his own? It seemed both sides had been following him and he'd been totally unaware; his skills as a SEAL were already compromised because of Ella. His personal mission before he met Ella was to seek the Elusti out and eradicate them from the face of the planet. With Steel, he could do that, set himself up financially for a change, and ensure that Ella was safe, even if she wasn't with him. Could he do that? After all he said to her, could he truly walk away? Money wasn't the only issue. He needed a job, and he was certain; he no longer had one. Staring around the empty but technology-filled warehouse with long, dust-filled glass windows that housed table after table with electronic devices, screens, and state-of-the-art computers, he was amazed at the speed and efficiency of Steel's group and how quickly they had set up base camp.

"What about the FBI? They're not going to like the fact that I absconded with one of their most wanted and left the country. They will have me arrested—won't that be a bit messy for you?"

Ben Steel picked up a beige folder from the collapsible table next to him, walked the few steps it took and shoved it in Marcus's chest. "Like I said, Drayton, you've been on my radar since you left the SEALs. I've been charting your progress, and just because I'm not working for the government anymore doesn't mean I don't have contacts there. As far as the FBI is concerned, you're working with me as a favor, which is another reason why when this is all cleared up that you need to give the lady up! She's hot, she messes with your focus, and to be fucking honest, you're not at your best when she's around. You make mistakes and I cannot afford any. I want this task force to be legitimate as far as possible and I don't want to piss off the government agencies if I can help it. They were ready to haul your ass to jail for treason until I told them that you were working for me. Your boss Philip Jackson is gone. He just up and disappeared. They're too busy trying to figure out, what, if any, information he took because his sudden departure was mysterious to say the least. Luckily for you, I was able to give them something. I'm trying to save your ass, but you don't make it easy. I'd rather try to work with them and not break too many rules. You know that word teamwork? The code you used to live by? Now, make yourself worthy of the dog tags you wear around your mangy neck and make her proud."

Marcus opened the folder that Steel had given him. All his personal details—height, weight, eye color, parents' particulars, his father's death, his school, education, his juvenile record—hell, everything was in this file. Ex-girlfriends, every mission he'd served on, the number of kills and the list of medals and achievements. Finally, there were two pictures of Ella: one as she was when he first met her, barely recognizable with long, nondescript hair and brown eyes behind timid glasses and a picture from days ago at the airport with her wavy blonde hair and vivid blue eyes. He swallowed and abruptly closed the file.

"I choose my own men. I get to choose who watches over Ella, and she doesn't get to hear about this conversation we're having right now. Another thing: there are a few things about Ella and me that you should know."

Steel leaned back against the table, crossed his arms and pinched his nose with his left hand.

"Does what you need to tell me affect your decision?" Steel didn't look at Marcus; he just stared at the ground.

"No, but—"

"Drayton, it will have to keep. The tactical team is ready to move and if you want to save your lady, you need to leave now."

CHAPTER SIXTEEN

Since Ella had been dragged through the woods on Saturday evening, she had been hit repeatedly across the face by the man who held her as she struggled and when she kicked out at the muscled thug and landed her foot directly in his torso, a swift stabbing pain sliced through her neck and brought her to the ground. Hours later, she woke up, her eyelids heavy and her gaze woozy as she lay on her side coiled in the fetal position; wet drool ran down her cheek. When she lifted her head, her cheeks throbbed from the bruising and her mouth was bone dry. A nasty bitter taste lingered, making her long for a drink, and her head thumped in pain, along with an incredible wave of déjà vu. Looking around the tiny cell, there wasn't much to see. The walls were chalk-white and covered in graffiti with slogans like Go Fuck Yourself and a variety of names with dates surrounded in a heart shape.

A small window no bigger than ten-by-ten inches let a fraction of sunlight in but she wouldn't be able to reach it and wouldn't be able to fit through it even if she could somehow smash the pane of the glass. The smell of urine was overpowering and her skin itched, making her want to scratch all over. A tickle on her shoulder made her jump; a huge brown cockroach wriggled into view. She screamed and brushed the bug off her but the sudden change in momentum caused bile to rise up in her throat, which she pushed back down. At that moment, her jailor and the man who didn't hold back when it came to hitting a woman opened the wooden door wide, letting brisk but clean air enter. He blocked her exit.

"Don't even think about giving me any trouble. The master said I can do anything I like to get you to do as you're told, bitch. Do you hear me?" His large grubby hand rubbed his crotch.

Ella stared up at the greasy slime ball. His face was round and dirty stubble covered his chin and cheeks. His weasel brown eyes pinned her to the spot. She didn't want to be cornered in a room with this bulldog of a man; she'd been tortured in her previous lives but she'd never been raped and the thought of this man touching her was enough to make her want to die right now. A heaving sensation wouldn't settle and, unable to gain control, her stomach reached up and she vomited on the ground.

"You dirty bitch." The man's hand walloped right across Ella's head and she crashed to the ground. She didn't lose consciousness quite then as she heard a ringing noise in her ear and Aidan's sharp shrill voice yelling at the man. A sting in her arm made her jerk forward before she blacked out again.

Ella gasped and jerked her head as freezing water shocked her face and ran down her exposed and mostly naked body. Her gauzy top and jeans were missing; all she wore was her skimpy bra and barely there thong. Two large and silent men in camouflage pants and dark tops held her upright as her legs buckled and someone hosed her down in the tiled shower cubicle. She blinked as water rained down her cheeks, drenching her, and her body was numb with the cold but an explosive fury was gathering up a storm.

"Get her out of there and get her dry." Aidan's voice boomed from the back as he hovered behind the man who hosed her down. The man who had hit her was absent. Her head lolled as the two men lifted and carried her out of the shower.

"Ella, put this on before one of the men loses control. God knows I have to keep my men happy but it won't help my plans any. So cover that delectable body of yours before it's ravaged."

He flung a thick white gown at the guard and when she stood on her own bare feet with her head low, the men on either side of her released her and handed her the clothing. She sunk her arms inside the material, letting the thickness of the plush cotton warm her. Ella thought briefly about kicking out at both but didn't want to end up injected with any more drugs. God only knew what they were giving her, but as she was losing consciousness, the burning sting in her arm was the last thing she remembered. Standing here, despite her terrifying circumstances, an unbearable and incontrollable heat gathered in her core, almost overwhelming. She tightened the gown with the white soft belt. She refused to look at any of the men but pinned her gaze on Aidan, who lowered his head down and pointed his sharp chin at the ground as his eyes met hers.

"How are you feeling, dear Ella?"

A nervous sensation raced through her. He smiled, as if he knew something that she didn't, and it made her more on edge than ever, but she tried to remain calm, not wanting to show any fear. She spat in his face.

He bounced back and raised his hand way up in the air, ready to strike her, but he stopped. Instead, he looked over his shoulder at one of the guards. "Bring her into the examination room. I don't think she's had enough. She needs a bigger dose, and then we can begin the first test, Ella, which may be your last if you don't cooperate."

Once again, the two goons who said nothing but simply nodded to Aidan, gripped an arm each and dragged her down the corridor, taking a left and after several feet, dragged her toward a door. She pressed her feet on the linoleum floor, but they pulled her and eventually hoisted her off the ground to carry her inside a huge laboratory slash medical examiner's room with virgin white walls and gleaming shiny steel cabinets and steel tables. Cupboards hung on the wall, along with shelving with every manner of surgical supplies and dressings. There was a long steel shelf with a range of different size jars and glass containers that held eyeballs, a heart, a liver, and other parts of the body pickled in a clear liquid solution. The aroma in the room was strong and suffocating. The room was modern and antiseptic-looking but memories of the dungeon where she was splayed open and exposed for everyone to gawp at as she was tortured gripped her throat.

They were going to keep hurting her. Ella shook her arms, trying to break the hold the guards had over her, but their grip was unyielding, and they led her farther into the room and dumped her in the gray metal chair positioned in the middle of the room. With her head tilted up slightly, she breathed in through her nostrils, trying to steady her frantic heart, and stared at Aidan, now dressed in a white coat and wearing rubber gloves, with a long needle in his hand. His hair stuck out at odd angles, as if he'd been pulling at the roots, and his eyes stared wide behind his glasses.

"I know you want answers, Ella, but the only answer I can give you is that the pay a professor gets sucks. This little sideline is not only far more satisfying, but it pays extremely well. I am a scientist, but after a few issues with my trials in which everyone overreacted, I lost my license and was discredited, forcing me to reconstruct my whole persona. Thanks to a very eager but very stupid history professor who ended up as a corpse, I found my new identity. You see, I have a gift for memorizing everything. Becoming the professor was easy but this is me, here in the laboratory, experimenting, and you're my latest guinea pig, Ella."

Ella sat there, legs inches apart, and watched as the professor waved the syringe with yellow liquid back and forth like a flag. Her heart pounded and she wet her lips. Just as she was about to pounce for Aidan, a shot fired directly at her from the left. The bully of a man who had hit her for the third time stood there with a black eye, wielding a gun, and he fired. *Pop, pop, pop.*

In a split second as Ella charged at the professor, the bullet penetrated her and she staggered before she dropped to the ground. Blood pooled out around her belly. She expected pandemonium but the professor very calmly knelt over her, injected the fluid into her neck, and whispered, "It's up to you now, Ella. Show us your gift—show us, or you will die."

Ella's body jerked and twitched. She was cold; the belt around her waist unraveled to expose her creamy skin now soaked with oozing blood. Yet, hovering in the background, a fever was brewing, a rising sensation of needing something. She licked her lips and stared up at Aidan. How could she be feeling desire when she was dying? She pressed her hands on her belly, pushing hard, and screamed out at the agony.

Spasms of pain ricocheted throughout her body. She was going to die if she didn't fix the gunshot wound. As her hands splayed across her body, Aidan pushed her over so she lay on her back and gazed up at the ceiling as her eyes rolled back.

"I want to *see* your magic, Ella."

For a moment, Ella drifted away to another plane as memories of her previous lives clashed and the voices called out to her: *Come on.* Her finger touched the small hole in her belly, rubbing around the site in a circle as she squeezed her stomach muscles and grunted. She visualized the bullet, which hadn't exited through her back but sat between her stomach and spleen. Bleeding internally, it wouldn't be long before she became unconscious and died. This would be it. She and Marcus weren't mated. She wasn't immortal. If she couldn't withdraw the bullet, heal the ruptured organs, and stop the bleeding, she would die. In every life, Ella was alone and it would always be that way.

No one was going to save her except herself, and she wasn't going to die today. Calling out to the forces of nature, she collected the energy of the air around her; she called to Ariana to help her, and on the spirits of her dead ancestors to give her the power to heal her injured body. Her heart pumped faster and faster, sending urgent blood to where it was needed to repair the damage, and her body shook violently.

The professor stood and shouted but she couldn't make out the words. Gunfire sounded but she focused on her heart pumping blood and the need for the bullet to be removed to stop the bleeding. She screamed and rolled onto her side, grabbing her belly, and bucked as shooting pain exploded inside. A stampeding of several heavy boots charged across the room but as she blinked, all she could see was a beautiful angel, all golden and white with arms outstretched.

"I'm ready."

"You must fight, Ella."

****

Flashes of the past twenty-four hours replayed inside Ella's head. She knew she was alive because she could hear soft whispers around her but she was almost too scared to open her eyes. Lifting her eyelids open gently, she lay still, afraid and too weak to move. The images in her head made her breathing speed up and a cold sweat rippled across her shoulders. She tried to be brave but pain was pain and she was too weak to numb it. A stray tear fell down her cheek. She moved her head to the side, straining to see clearly and attempting to understand where she was.

Marcus sat in a chair near the bed, with his hands on his knees, and stared at her with his black coffee-colored eyes narrowed as she met his gaze. Dark stubble spread over his chin and strands of his ebony hair flopped over his forehead in disarray. He was dressed in worn jeans and a thick brown turtleneck sweater. Casual, but he looked good enough to eat to her. She smiled; she didn't want to but she couldn't help it as his dark eyes probed her face. Her heart soared to life and did a crazy dance. He was here. He had saved her. It didn't matter that he hadn't actually been the one to stop the gun from firing; he hadn't stopped her from being hit but he was here now. She blinked just in case he wasn't real but when his warm, strong hand touched hers gently, she gasped and the jolt of heat pulsed through her body, shocking her awake. A tingling from her belly spread out and she gripped his hand, unwilling to break the contact. Her mouth was dry and her throat ached but another ache ignited like a fever; she couldn't help but squeeze his hand tightly. Marcus inched closer and leaned over the bed; the smell of his aftershave filled her.

"You need to get me out of here now because I need something the nurse cannot give me and I need it stat."

Marcus's eyes darkened and instead of moving away, he closed the gap and kissed her lips with the softest of kisses.

"Aren't you in pain?"

"Yes, the kind only you can relieve." She stared at him with her bright blue eyes.

"Your wish is my command but we need to have a serious talk later. I'll go and sign the discharge papers while you get changed. I brought some clean clothes, which are in the locker. Can you do that or do you need me to help you?"

Ella stared up at Marcus, who hadn't smiled since she'd woken up, and knowing that they needed to have a talk was confirmation that something bad was about to happen. But he was here with her now and that was good enough for the moment. She would deal with the loss later but it was there in his sad eyes: he was leaving her. Hiding her devastation and sudden emptiness, she carried on as normal.

"If you help me get dressed, we won't be leaving here for a while and this bed isn't big enough."

No smile; he simply nodded curtly and disappeared out of the room. Ella hopped out of bed, wincing, but rubbed her belly to ease the pain. She ripped off the pale blue hospital gown and stared down at where she had been shot. There was no evidence of the gaping bloody hole at all. She threw the gown on the bed. She was naked and hoped when he said clothes, he had included underwear. In the bedside locker was a plastic bag with a red and black checked shirt, blue denim jeans, and a set of red silky underwear. She stared at them. Marcus knew her size and the thin satin wisps of material increased the rising desire that had been there from the moment her eyes rested on his. She didn't want to talk about what had happened; she didn't want to talk about the future; she didn't want to talk—full stop. She just wanted to feel him against her, inside her. Dressing quickly, she buttoned her jeans as Marcus walked back in the room; he stopped as his eyes roamed over her entire body. Her hair was a mass of unruly waves that rested at the top of her breasts.

Two seconds later, he wrapped his arms around her so tight she couldn't breathe and he stroked his hand down her hair before he tipped her chin up to meet his lips.

"Are you wearing the underwear I brought?" His voice was low and hoarse.

Ella nodded, unable to speak.

Releasing his hold, he moved her forward, his hand on her waist as he pushed the door open and a nurse stood there with some papers.

"Like I said to your husband, we're happy to discharge you but you need to be looked after for the next twenty-four hours just to be on the safe side. Here's a list of signs and symptoms to watch out for. If you're worried at all, just call the number on the bottom of the page and come straight back in. You had a lot of blood for a nosebleed. Do you get them often?"

The small dark-haired nurse looked seriously at Ella, dismissing Marcus, and for a moment, she wasn't sure of the story that had been told but she smiled and nodded.

"Since I was a little girl. Even the smell of the blood is enough to make me keel over." She held Marcus's hand tighter.

"I'm sorry. I just have one more question before you go. Do you feel safe at home?"

Ella was so taken back by the question she didn't answer immediately and stared up at Marcus, who remained stiff and expressionless at her side. During the shooting, Ella had been fixated on the abdominal wound but she now remembered the several direct hits she'd received to the face and as she smiled, felt her cheeks throb. Realizing that the bruising must still be evident, it was enough to make the nurse concerned as to whether her *husband* was abusing her.

"Yes, I am safe at home." Unconsciously, she palmed her cheek. "Do I look a mess?"

The nurse looked at her but Marcus answered. "You never look a mess, Ella, and the bruising will fade. But we need to be more careful from now on. Come on, so I can take you home."

The nurse shifted a sideways glance at Marcus, who was at least a foot taller than her. "Make sure that you do." The petite nurse didn't smile at him at all and for once Ella observed a female who wasn't completely bowled over by his swoon-worthy looks. She handed Ella a card, which she looked at and pocketed. She stared up at Marcus and they walked out of the room. Walking down the corridor and outside into the cold, early hours of Sunday morning, she shivered. The sirens of passing ambulances drowned out any conversation but Ella continued to shiver.

"You're freezing. Take my coat—I didn't think." He removed his leather jacket and placed it around Ella's small shoulders, pulling it tight across the front. He tugged on her hand and led her to the Range Rover. He settled Ella inside before he moved to his side. Ella sat in the leather seat, waiting…knowing he was going to leave her. Already, a sense of loss invaded her the more time they were together. She placed her seat belt over her and placed her hands under her bottom, in case she couldn't help but reach out to touch him. Staring ahead and resting back into the seat, she let him drive her away from the early-morning traffic and flashing lights.

"Ella, are you asleep?"

She must have closed her eyes without even realizing it and warmer now from the heater and the jacket that surrounded her, she opened her eyes. They were in the parking lot of the hotel. Marcus had turned to face her and had his hand on her cheek, smoothing the skin in unsettling sweeping circles.

"Ella, I need to tell you something."

She took a deep breath; she knew what was coming and was prepared for it. He had said all along that he would walk away, that all they had was sex. She hadn't wanted to believe it but here it was. A coiling, fluttering need gripped her and she placed her hand on his, moving it to her breast, and she applied pressure.

"I know what you're going to say, Marcus, but I need you one more time and then you can walk away. That's what you want, isn't it?"

She stared as the muscle twitched in his jaw. Ella squeezed his hand, which squeezed her breast, and she moaned. At this moment, she didn't care about tomorrow: there was only now. Hours ago, she thought she would never take another breath but here she was, still alive in this cursed life. He may not love her the way she loved him. Ella sucked in the air; she stumbled as her heart missed beats and tried to catch up. She loved him—why did that surprise her? Never before had she given herself so willingly to any man knowing so little was given in return and here she was, exposed and needing his touch, his kiss. She swallowed and gazed at him as she moved his hand down over her belly to the juncture between her legs. She pressed his fingers down into her heat as she arched back, savoring the feel of friction and what it did to her.

"Please."

CHAPTER SEVENTEEN

Ella lay on the soft but firm mattress of the king-sized bed and allowed her fingertips to smooth their way along her silky skin and wind their way down to her most intimate of places as she remembered vividly all the pleasure she had experienced with Marcus before he had left her. They had barely made it back to the room after her declaration in the parking lot and then as soon as they entered the elevator, Ella unbuttoned her shirt and moved her hips from side to side in the journey up to the eighth floor in the elevator. Marcus had pinned her against the steel wall and unbuttoned her jeans so he could place his hand down into her panties. Feeling the wetness between her legs, he groaned and inserted first one finger and then another as Ella kissed his neck. As the heat in the elevator soared, Ella coiled her leg around his hip, locking them together.

When the elevator shuddered to a halt, Marcus whisked her out and as soon as they entered their hotel room, both stripped off their clothes, dropping them on the ground. Ella backed away, headed for the bedroom and shimmying out of her jeans, only leaving her scanty underwear on. She didn't make it to the bed before he grabbed her around her waist and lifted her up against his naked body and she squealed. Automatically, she wrapped her legs around his waist, fusing their bodies. His hard erection nudged against her moist core and she stared at him, unwilling to breathe or say anything, just needing him to be inside, filling her. He pushed his erection slowly while he kissed her neck and panted against her skin, making her shiver and want him more.

"I thought you were dead. I saw all that blood and I thought you were fucking dead."

His voice was savage and filled with a barely controlled anger. He eased the hold he had around her waist, letting her legs slide down against him. They leaned against each other for precious moments, warm bodies connected, but the mood shifted from dizzying, uncontrollable desire as he leaned his forehead against hers to something deeper. Ella stood on tiptoes and kissed his mouth with soft little nips, smoothing her body against his as if smearing her scent all over him to reassure him.

"I'm not dead, Marcus. I'm very much alive and in need of something only you can give me. Please."

Ella kissed him on his chin, his neck, and then she crouched lower to kiss him over his taut and firm chest, over his toned abdomen. She licked his belly button and she smoothed her hands down over his hot flesh, stroking his groin and hips until she touched his very alert and throbbing cock. He wove his hands into her hair and pulled her head back slightly so they gazed at each other. She looked up at him as he held her away from his manhood, stilling her.

"I want to please you, Marcus, like you pleased me," she said quietly. Her small hand grabbed hold of his sex and she stroked the length back and forth, adding some pressure at the base.

"Ella, you always please me."

"Just one last time. I don't want anything more." She didn't believe her own words and didn't stop to wonder whether he did. A shudder raced through Marcus and he eased his hold on her hair. She continued her teasing massage of his sex from the base to the tip. Within seconds, any reservation that Marcus may have had disappeared and he gathered her up in his arms and carried her to the bed. For the rest of the day, he made tender love to her, taking his time and wringing out every orgasm until she was exhausted and completely sated. The way they made love this time was completely different than before. Marcus didn't simply ravage; he took his time, touching and tasting every part of her body. The sun filtered into the room through the sheers, but they wrapped their bodies around each other sleeping the afternoon away.

When they awoke, it was night and the giant full moon shimmered through the windows. A yearning grew and their last union was the most wild and frantic coupling. Ella lay on her back as Marcus drove his shaft into the deepest part of her as if it would never be enough. He clutched her and bucked, yelling out, and kissed her neck. Ella bucked as her orgasm spread and the waves carried her away. A deep, sharp sting—a bite at her neck—had her pushing at his chest and wriggling but a deep growl and a strong weight pushing her down deeper and deeper made her resist as the world shifted on its axis. *Mine.* She heard the words like a command.

Say it, Ella. I want to hear you say you're mine. Mine.

She wasn't sure whether it was a dream or whether Marcus was talking to her inside her head, but after giving him everything, saying this little word seemed like nothing.

I am yours.

As if the word unlocked the door, Marcus slumped against her body and they lay entwined, not moving for a while but wrapped in each other's arms. Ripples of euphoria rocked her body back and forth in a drugged stupor. Fireworks exploded in the pit of her belly and fiery tingles screamed in her veins as her body undulated and trembled. The sense of being united and feeling of total completeness was overwhelming. The pain in her neck disappeared and she floated like a butterfly on the breeze, feeling the warmth of the sun on her skin. She clenched her nails into the mattress; something magical had taken place as her body continued to pulse. She fell into a deep slumber.

Hours later, a sense of loss and coldness surrounded her and she jerked awake, stretching her hands out to the side where Marcus had been, only to find the spot empty and the sheets cold. The door to the bathroom swung open and a shaft of light fanned into the room. Ella fell back against the pillow.

"Ella, I need to talk to you." Marcus stood, already shaved and dressed in his jeans and dark sweater. His hands raked through his wet locks despite the early hours on the clock. He spoke with a distance that was impossible after all they had shared but it was there on the edge of his tongue. Ella gathered the single cotton sheet and covered her body, shielding herself against his stare and wanting to hide away from this moment of heartbreak. She sat forward and wrapped her arms around her knees, bracing herself. She was ready.

"I have a new job, working for Orion Corporation. My old Captain has set up a private company. It's a good job. I get to handpick my assignments and my team but I have to leave now, today, and that means leaving you. Steel promised me that you will be taken into protective custody. There's a man waiting outside the door, ready to take you until the Elusti is blown apart. I've made sure that provisions will be made for you so that you can live comfortably with a new identity. He will brief you with all the details later when he takes you in. You will be *safe* and it will be my on-going mission to hunt them down."

He stopped and scanned around the room as he chewed on his lower lip. She'd never seen him do that before and almost felt sorry for him as he looked so awkward. She didn't know how to respond, or what he had expected her to say. The loss she'd felt earlier was replaced by a void and empty feeling but she couldn't say anything. She simply nodded. There was nothing to say. He hadn't made any declarations, or real promises; he'd only ever been honest that it was only sex, even when confronted with the knowledge that they were soul mates. He'd never truly believed any of it, and although she knew irrevocably that things had changed for her, there was nothing to suggest it was the same for Marcus. He was walking away, even after discovering they were the same, and knowing their shared past. There was nothing left to be said.

Her fragile heart ached and throbbed but she wouldn't cry or make a scene. No, she would let him go. Ella straightened her shoulders and flicked her messy hair away and bravely swallowed as he grabbed his leather bag off the ground and picked up his keys from the bedside table. He moved to step closer but she bent her head.

"Thanks for everything, Marcus. I do wish you all the best, but don't worry about me. I'm a survivor and I've always taken care of myself." She ripped the sheet from the bed and wrapped it around her like a shroud. She jumped off the bed and headed toward the shower. *Don't look back—just let him go!*

"Just go in to the debriefing, Ella, and let them handle everything."

She didn't move to look back but gritted her teeth at his words. "Sure, whatever you say, Armani." Pushing the door open, she escaped into the still steamy shower and closed the door behind her. She rested against it until she heard the door click closed in the other room. Turning the shower on to full force, she stepped into the pouring heat and let the water pummel her skin. With her head in the cascading water, she let her tears fall. After the shower, she returned to bed, reminiscing over the past with Marcus. Her fingertips quickly traced over the sensitive places he had recently been.

As Ella applied a generous smear of red lipstick to her pouty lips, she stood back and admired her handiwork. She fussed with her newly styled, bouncy blonde tresses and pulled the front of her Victoria Secrets red satin corset with matching diamanté studded thong. By the time she finished, Marcus would get this piece of gossip in triplicate and it was going to be so satisfying. If his final parting words had been slightly more caring or showed a modicum of true feeling, she may have found another way to gain her freedom but no, she decided he deserved everything he got. She knew it would eat him up as much as it would hurt her to even touch another man.

But there was no way she was going to be tucked away safely, like some ancient relic, watched over by Marcus's friends. It would be unbearable; the distance alone from him might drive her insane but to have constant reminders flitting in and out of her life was worse. At least, if what she had been led to believe about being parted from your mate was true, but not having experienced it before, she wasn't entirely sure the rumors were true. She was fine. She wasn't a blithering mess. She could do this. There was a loud *tap, tap, tap* on the door that divided her bedroom from the main suite. It was her escort. "Miss. We need to leave. Mr. Drayton said to make sure we left at eight thirty sharp."

The male voice on the other side of the door sounded young and she didn't recognize it at all, which melted away any last-minute nerves as she went into her role of seducing siren. She settled herself comfortably on the large bed and dimmed the light switch, praying that she could pull this off. "You'll need to come in, unfortunately. It's a bit embarrassing but I need your help."

She wriggled on the bed, attempting to stay calm as her heart fluttered. She stretched her left arm above her head as if it was attached to the handcuff she had looped around it. Of course, it you were up close and personal, you would realize it wasn't actually locked. The broad white door swung open and there, dressed in a dark suit and white shirt and holding a gun, was a shorter version of Marcus. Or was she seeing double? She shook her head to clear her vision. He was much shorter but broad with shoulder-length dark hair—lighter than Marcus's color—and his eyes the color of whiskey. But his face was baby soft, as if he wasn't old enough for facial hair. He was young, maybe in his late twenties, and his eyes widened to the size of soup bowls when they finally rested on a squirming, semi-naked Ella on the mattress. His mouth practically dropped to the ground as he soaked up every inch of her body. She pouted.

"That son of a bitch left me handcuffed. You'll need to get over here and unlock me if you want me to move. The key is on the side table, just out of my reach. Look there." Ella was positioned smack in the center of the bed so no matter which end he tackled her from, he would have to actually get up on to the bed to help release her. He stared and closed his mouth shut, frozen for a moment as his brain ticked over. Without saying a word, he put the gun down on the table and stared at the small key, swallowing. After taking one step toward her, he stopped.

"Mr. Drayton never mentioned handcuffs." His thin eyebrows lifted as he looked again at the scene in front of him, staring openly at her curves. She twisted her long, slim body, baring her mostly naked ass, and bounced up and down on the bed.

"Well, I guess he forgot but either way, he likes to be in control and there's no way I can be out of here by eight thirty if you don't free me and stop gawping." Her angry voice rose and that shifted him into gear as he grabbed the key, knelt on the bed and stretched his hand to cover hers. He stared at her face and her lips as she flicked her tongue over her ruby gloss-streaked mouth and that was his undoing. She kicked him right in the groin, leaving him in agony and dazed. It was easy to slam him down on the bed, forcibly switching her wrist for his and snapping the cuff to the bedpost. Stunned, he lay there groaning and then as awareness dawned, he yelled angrily. She blew him a kiss as she grabbed her discarded clothes from the chair and closed the door behind her.

"Never trust the enemy."

CHAPTER EIGHTEEN

The waves crashed violently on the shore below in rocky Skrinkle Haven with its impressive sandstone cliffs and slim headland that split the beaches in two, as if man-made. She wrapped the gray infinity scarf another loop around her neck to stop the blustery wind from the coastal breeze. The turbulent aqua-marine waters stretched endlessly and seagulls screeched in the air above her. Ella added some final delicate brushstrokes to the canvas before she settled the small paintbrush back onto the easel and admired her work. Without turning around, she shifted her stance and dug her hand inside her pocket.

For a moment, the wind stilled and a movement behind her alerted her to the fact she wasn't alone any longer. Living in the small village of Manorbier in Wales, it hadn't taken very long for the locals to get to know her and the story she had created of a single artist painting the Pembrokeshire Coast at different spots and times of the year. She had rented a small self-sufficient cottage in the tiny village on a month-by-month basis; it was better that way, giving her the freedom to leave with little notice. One month had passed by quickly enough with no news or unexpected visitors and Ella was surviving in her lonely, isolated existence. The sudden scent of a human presence had her spinning around; her left hand rose to shoulder height, curled into a fist, and her right hand clenched tight, ready to fight off a would-be attacker. A tall, statuesque man about the same height as Marcus stood there but there the similarities ended. Why she compared every man she met now to Marcus, she had no idea but she did. Intelligent hazel eyes stared at her and a thick, neatly trimmed mustache twitched as the man gave a tentative smile. He wore dark-gray cargo pants and a thick navy sweater with a short black leather jacket on top and heavy brown boots.

"I'm Ben Steel. The postman said I would most likely find you on this rather isolated path, Miss Jessica Smith. Look, to cut a very long story short, I know you're Ella Masters, *the*

Witch. I know that because Drayton works for me and told me where you would be. Did you really think he would simply let you escape? To cut to the chase, Miss Masters, we've allowed you some space and privacy but it's time to come in."

Ben sucked in the fresh, salty air and looked around, narrowing his gaze back toward Ella. "It's undeniably beautiful here and you're a gifted painter, but aren't you the least bit bored?"

The way he spoke and learning that he was Marcus's friend and boss did two things: it made her cheeks flush crimson at the thought he must know all her story, including the very last chapter at the hotel, and that Marcus had known where she was and her new name the entire time. How was that possible?

"I'm not sure what Marcus told you about my company Orion but it's an elite and private task force that I have set up purely to hunt down those who need to be captured and dealt with. I have only just begun setting up the ground crew but I want a global team committed to defeating the enemy, whoever they might be, and ready to move at any time and to any location. I know you have an extraordinary set of skills and I believe you would be an asset to my team. I'm offering you a job, Miss Masters, and with that comes a hefty sign-on bonus, added to the fact that you instantly get enrolled into the family. We protect our own. No disrespect, Ella—may I call you Ella?—but you cannot hope to fight everyone off on your own out here. Or do you plan to keep moving every couple of weeks?"

His voice was rich and sincere. She hadn't quite worked out what her game plan was going to be long-term; all she knew for sure was that she couldn't count on staying anywhere for any length of time and eventually she would run out of money. Staring at her golden bracelet, she moved it around her wrist and stared out at the sea.

"I can help you get the Elusti, Ella. Isn't that what you want?"

Ella breathed in the air and let the energy of the wind clear her head as her hair, which had stopped growing since

she had arrived, blew back and forth. Living secluded,
pretending to be someone she wasn't, left her few options. It
meant a lifetime of being on the run, hiding and always living
in fear. If Ben Steel was true to his word, she would not only
have money to live on but important work that would bring the
Elusti down. She may not have the means to tackle them alone
but as a team and over time, that was a possibility. There were
still many unanswered questions about other people like her.
The way the Elusti was set up, with Aidan at the helm as some
sort of mad scientist—shivers raced down her spine at the
memories, which made her believe there was much more
going on. He was playing games and conducting experiments.
Her hand rubbed her neck; he had injected her several times
with an unknown substance and she didn't know what the
effects of it was but she feared she wasn't the first or last to be
tested on. She hadn't even told Marcus. Working for Steel
would give her a sense of purpose and it would give her some
answers.

"Are you all right?"

Ella blinked and crossed her arms over her chest. She
lifted her gaze and stared at Ben Steel. The size and power that
emanated from him alone should intimidate her but she was
way beyond that. If he wanted her, there was good reason;
either way, maybe it was better to be on the inside watching
rather than being hunted for a change.

"What's the sign-on bonus?"

The Silver Fox, her new nickname for her boss,
smirked as he felt inside his jacket, removed a checkbook and
pen, and promptly filled out a check.

Ella's heart churned. Was she really going to do this?
She had never worked as part of a team; she only ever worked
alone. She pulled on her lower lips as another thought entered
her brain.

He extended his hand and passed her over the slim
piece of paper.

"What about Drayton? Does he know about this?" She
waved the check in the breeze before she even glanced at it.

When she did, boy oh boy, the staggering number of zeroes made it impossible for her to stop smiling.

"If you agree, you will leave in the next twenty-four hours. I will give you instructions as to where you need to go. Your contact with be Jake Meadows. I think you know him as the Gateway? He'll bring you in. And no, Drayton doesn't know yet but he will. I do not foresee any issues, but I need to know right now if that will be a problem for you because if it is, the deal is off the table. I do not need romantic liaisons between team members, do you understand, Masters? It makes everything complicated and I don't like it when it gets complicated."

He was straight to the point, and she liked that about him. If he had any clue about their sexual relationship, he didn't bat an eyelid. Perhaps he was another man who believed that sex was simply sex. Anyway, it brought her right back to the problem she faced: namely, Marcus. What if she couldn't handle being around him? What if he was with another woman? How would she feel? Could they keep things simple and work together? Her head spun with all her worries.

"You need to complete a series of training. I know you're fit and strong. I've heard the story of the young recruit at the hotel, but you had the element of surprise in that situation. I need you to be war-worthy, ready for anything, and that takes training. Lots of training. You may wish you had never started by the time I've finished with you but you will become a member of an elite squad that will not only be men but women as well. Any good with languages? I hear you have some medical training."

The world spun precariously. *Lots of training.* The only training she had really undertaken had been self-defense with Aidan. She was strong but war strong? Maybe this wasn't for her. As if he knew she was torn, he spoke.

"Meet with the team, Ella. Whatever you decide at the end of the training, that check is for keeps. If you decide to bail, you keep it, but you will have to go into a legitimate witness protection program and I cannot guarantee where that will be. You have to understand you're known to several worldwide security agencies and one or another of them will pick you up, or worse, the Elusti will hunt you down. I don't know everything about your past but one way or another, it will catch up with you. You either choose to work for me or for some unknown. This will never end, you know that."

He was giving her a choice but not much of one. The spinning sensation settled. Ella made her choice and she would deal with the repercussions, come what may. After pocketing the check in her back pocket, she lifted her hand and gave him a firm shake.

****

Making the decision to accept Ben Steel's very generous offer was, in hindsight, made very glibly. Facing not only Marcus but all his men filled her with a sickening dread but she had absolutely no idea as to how she would even survive the training. She swallowed down all her thoughts and fears, telling herself that whatever she faced, this was professional, this was business, this wasn't going to be personal and she wasn't going to be one of those women who cried in front of men. No, she didn't want to be seen as the weaker sex; she wanted to be treated by them as an equal and she would focus on doing her best to prove that to them. Ella wanted to show them that as a woman, she was as capable as they were. Steel had said the six-week training would be based upon and be very similar to the Basic Underwater Demolition/SEAL training, which was much longer at six months but they simply didn't have the time. It would be grueling and intense. The training would be comprised of men and women and a strict regimen would be enforced at all times. If she passed the physical fitness, she would then proceed to incorporate other aspects like weapons, linguistics, and intelligence.

Steel had left her as soon as they shook hands, saying that she would hear from him very soon. No sooner had she folded her easel and gathered her paints into her arms than another human scent wafted around her, and a familiar man walked into view. Wow that was quick! Jake Meadows strode over. She stood, unmoving, as he helped to pick up the drying canvas off the ground, studied it intently and then gazed at the view before he swung back to look at her.

"You have a very good eye, Ella. It's quite breathtaking. You certainly are a woman with many talents."

There may have been a little edge to his voice but the fact that he didn't simply launch into anything that involved Marcus was slightly comforting. He was trying to find neutral territory. Deciding to keep Marcus out of the conversation was probably better for both of them.

"I didn't expect you so soon. I'm not even packed."

Jake nodded and removed the easel from her hand. "Come on. I've been here watching you for weeks, Ella. You didn't even notice me. You don't have much to pack, that I know because I've been in your house. I could go on about security or the lack of it, but it's a moot point. We're leaving. And let's just clear the air before we head off. Like I said before, Drayton is family. I would do anything for him. He's one of the good guys. We were in the SEALs together and if you pass this training, you'll be part of that family and I will be there for you. We all back each other up. We work as a team. Of course, I'm not sure you'll even pass the training because the way I look at it, working as a team will push you to the ultimate limit—you don't trust anyone, which may have worked for you before, but it sure as hell won't now."

Ella listened to his speech and marched up to his side, pulling the easel out from his hands. She was ready to take him down. Her anger skyrocketed when she realized he'd been inside her makeshift home and looked through her belongings.

"I don't need you to carry my stuff. How dare you follow me and invade my privacy, you jerk."

"Honey, you don't get to have privacy when you've been on *America's Most Wanted*. Drayton tagged you the first chance he got and switched the bug on after that sexy romp with my pal Stevens, who will never live that shit down. Gotta say, you have spunk, Ella Masters, but I wouldn't like to be you when Drayton catches up with you and he will. Like I said, you need to be able to work as a team and even if you don't need me to help you carry your blasted easel, it will make you move faster, hence we will make it back to the cottage quicker. Why do you insist on struggling?"

Ella was focused on the words that involved Marcus tagging her. How the hell had he managed that? She scratched her head. And using what as a bugging device? The only thing in her possession that she wore all the time was her amulet. She removed the bracelet. Jake stopped and watched her.

"Shit."

She ignored him but held the intricate bracelet between her hands. She studied it carefully. The top looked untouched as the stones twinkled and shone, all except one that looked duller than the others. She pressed it and it moved, dislodging itself from its position. She held up the tiny glass bead and scratched the surface to reveal a tracking device, which she threw to the ground and smashed with the heel of her boot before replacing the bracelet on her wrist.

"Thanks, teammate. I'm learning things already. I won't be caught out again, believe you me, and if you think I'm not a team player, well, maybe you're right. I don't trust people. I have good reason not to. Give me a reason to change, but until then, all I can promise is that I will do my best to help my team survive because I'm a survivor and I will do whatever it takes."

Jake stared at her, unblinking and cursing under his breath. "I can deal with that. Are you going to tell Drayton?"

She left the coastal path behind her and in an odd way was eager and excited about her next step, although a reunion with Marcus might cause some problems she'd rather not think about at the moment. Sighing, she glanced over at Jake, who was taller than her and walked at her side.

"What's to tell? I have one request before we leave."

Jake caught up to her, removed the canvas from under her arm and grabbed the easel.

"What request?"

"We need to go to church first."

Jake's eyebrows arched at her reply but without saying a word, he nodded. An hour later, they stood in the small church of St. Agnes in the tiny village of Twi. The brisk wind of the coast was absent and stillness lingered in the empty and silent graveyard. Many deserted headstones lay eroded through time and the elements of nature. The ancient yew trees shaded and protected the abandoned resting places of dozens of men, women, and children; some names were clearly visible, others broken and the words once lovingly carved washed away by time. Ella knew immediately where the final resting place for Gwendolyn Smythe lay. After her death, her remaining family, who had never believed she was a witch, petitioned for her to be laid to rest in the grounds on the local parish church but the vicar refused, saying it would be unholy.

Years later, when the witch trials were denounced as nothing more than an excuse to murder innocents, the descendants petitioned again and removed the remains to inside the grounds of the church in the far corner in the shade by the biggest and oldest yew tree. Ella planned to use some of the money from Steel to replace the headstone with a large granite one that would stand for the rest of time. There were no other gravestones out there of her other lives, at least none she had discovered.

Gwendolyn called to her, and she felt the pull from the middle of her stomach, leading her to the corner. This was not her first or second visit to the cemetery and each time, Gwendolyn spoke and comforted her. Approaching the steel-gray mottled and eroded headstone always brought her to her knees, and she dropped into the wet earth. Jake stood directly behind her, leaned over and touched her shoulder. He crouched low.

"Are you all right? Whose grave is this?"

She didn't answer but dipped her head low and smoothed her hand over the curved top of the headstone. There were no chiseled flowers or ivy adorning the front, no symbols to honor her love of healing or belief in God. The stone lay bare except for her name and a date that screamed of murder and misjudgment. This was where her first life ended at the hand of people who were swept up by the hysteria and gossip that branded her an evil witch capable of murder and bewitching others. Tears fell. They always did as the noose tightened around her neck and she watched the screaming crowd of delighted onlookers, not one of them stopping to save her. The tears splashed on her cheeks, and she let them.

Let it go. The past is the past. Live on for us all, Ella. We live on in you.

"I will."

This was the last time she would visit, or maybe she would come once more when the new headstone was in place. She touched the top of the stone and made a sign of the cross over her chest before she stood.

"Why are we here?"

"I'm just saying good-bye."

She walked away and allowed herself to glance over her shoulder once, knowing that Gwendolyn would be standing under the yew to watch her depart. She waved, and the ghost waved back before it vanished.

CHAPTER NINETEEN

Ella lay on the small cot with the thinnest mattress she had ever slept on in her plum camisole and black cargo pants, waiting for the sun to rise. For weeks now, her routine was emblazoned on her brain: sleep for a few hours but be ready as often her trainer would wake the dorm up with early-morning drills and if you weren't ready in two minutes, there were severe penalties, like missing food or having to clean the men's restrooms, and even though the food tasted like cardboard, it lined her stomach. Steel hadn't mentioned the sleeping arrangements or the fact that the food at the secret camp somewhere in deepest Maine was disgusting.

Since being escorted by Jake the *Big Mouth*—as she renamed him back in the States—she had been holed up in the middle of a dense forest of evergreen trees surrounded by a wide crystal lake with barely any decent facilities for weeks in freezing temperatures in December. Christmas had come and gone by in a blur. Everything she ate had the same bitter taste and made her stomach queasy but she pushed on. Her muscles in the beginning rebelled, stinging and aching with pain, but after a while, the endurance paid off and she was able to power through even as others collapsed. In fact, by week two, if the training commander Hawk said they needed to do fifty pushups, she pushed herself to do fifty-five. Her adrenaline for pushing herself to the maximum to achieve her goal fed her as nothing else was. Ella was never a big girl, not even in the breast department but since she'd been training and taking into account the mornings in which she emptied her stomach completely, she'd lost several pounds but her arm muscles were more defined and toned. She figured the vomiting was due to the lousy diet. She was getting good at sneaking the protein bars from the makeshift kitchen; they were the only snacks she could eat that stayed down, that and her incredible thirst for milk. She drank it by the gallon.

The shrill noise of the whistle had her leaping up out of bed and she quickly dashed out of the long, narrow dorm room that held ten other women. She was one of the smallest but not the youngest; there was a girl who was just twenty-one and had a talent for moving objects by thought alone. It had taken Ella twenty-four hours to realize the recruits that Steel was bringing together were not your average private soldiers and some weren't even human. The smell was an eclectic mix of races and supernatural forces; it was odd that no one addressed or talked about that fact. Instead, everyone focused on getting stronger and reaching the end of the training, apart from those who quit.

Since joining the room, she had formed a bond with the young slim girl with long auburn hair always tied back in a ponytail. She was in the bunk next to her. The girl had the most striking emerald eyes and although her features were delicate, she was a strong opponent in combat. Because of the similar heights, Ella had been placed opposite her and at first the temptation to go easy on the young girl was overpowering. But as she let her take the upper hand in some vital moves, she realized the girl wasn't giving an inch. Her name was Isabella, Bella for short, and she couldn't help feeling a sense of connection when she was around. She hoped later at dinner time that she would get the chance to talk to her privately, if their training finished at a civilized time—which was unlikely. Most evenings, by the time training finished and everyone sat for dinner, exhaustion kicked in. Most left the table and by the time they reached the dorm, undressed, and showered, they were asleep inside of minutes.

Today, after their twenty-mile hike carrying a load on their back that weighed around fifty pounds, they were told there would be a swimming exercise in the lake. For Ella, the hike wasn't an issue; she was happy with that and knew she wouldn't have a problem but the swimming brought her out in a cold sweat. Memories of the past and the drowning on the ducking stool, the burn of her lungs and gasping for air as all hers was squeezed out almost made her throw up again as she took the stairs two at a time to stand in the front row and faced Hawk, who blew the whistle again. She quickly glanced around and every one of the recruits was present.

A collective sighed buzzed around her. She smiled and nodded at Bella.

"Well, ladies, you're into week four. Only two more to go, which means you're more than halfway. As a celebration, we've turned this exercise into a competition. We're putting you into pairs and you will work together to find your specific color flag at a set location, retrieve it and return to base camp. The first pair to collect the flag will be rewarded by being excused from the swimming exercise for this afternoon."

His words were like music to her ears and she chewed on her lip, determined that she and whoever she was partnered with would win, even if she had to bring the heavens down to get them to the destination. She jumped up and down on her feet, gearing herself up for the long trek and stretched her muscles as the trainer called out the names of the teams. Hearing Bella's name, she instantly froze, waiting to hear her name next but Adelle was called. *Damn.* Ella's name was next and she was partnered with the tall and well-endowed Kelly. She smiled at the woman, who was about the same age as her but she didn't reciprocate. This was going to be interesting.

As the group divided into the five teams, they were each handed a backpack with their load, which also contained water. They were given a map and a compass. Each map showed the team where their flag was located, so all they had to do was navigate their way to the *x* that marked the spot on their map. The hike was a round trip of over thirty miles, longer than Ella had imagined but the sun was just rising and the forecast for the day was a frigid thirty-five, which, for December was about average but at least there wasn't snow.

"You any good with maps?" Kelly still didn't smile, rather frowned and pouted, but as Ella tentatively smiled at her, she decided any ill-at-ease sensations she was catching best be buried because to win this, they needed to work together.

"Yes, this is a breeze. Come on."

Ella heaved her backpack over her shoulders, slipped her arms through and pushed the backpack up until she felt the weight rest between her shoulder blades and settle into place.

She swallowed a generous mouthful of cold water and glanced over at Kelly, who was tying her laces on her boots. Taking this chance, she walked over to Bella to wish her luck just as they were leaving and as she turned, Kelly was directly behind her.

"Ready?"

She nodded and they left in the opposite direction. The five teams all split up, walking toward their goal and each headed away at a steady pace; to start off running would simply burst their energy—slow and steady won the race. They needed to finish. The talk was kept to a minimum as they set off walking through the shady forest, the sounds of wildlife a muted hum and buzz. Branches snapped and the occasional woodpecker knocked on the tree. Ella was glad she had slipped on her thermal shirt and had added a lightweight jacket for layers. If they made steady progress and didn't encounter any unusual terrain or company, they would be fine. About an hour in, Kelly stopped and stretched, bending and stretching her shoulders; Ella did the same, as well as knocking back some refreshing water.

"So who recruited you? The fuck-me Drayton or take-no-prisoners Steel?"

Ella's head instantly picked up at the mention of Drayton from the woman's lips and her stomach twisted in knots.

"Rumor has it that Drayton sleeps with the women he recruits as part of the test. Personally, I don't think that's the case, just those who can match his stamina. He's a bit of a bad boy, if you know what I mean."

Ella stared over at the woman and gave her a vacant smile. She wasn't going to let what Drayton did bother her. She ground her teeth and strode ahead not answering. The sun shone through the shaded trees and a wave of nausea swept over her that threatened to have her barfing again. This was ridiculous. The sound of water up ahead had Ella moving toward it without explaining why and seconds later, she dipped her head into the clear and freezing stream to soak up the energy, refreshing and charging her. She flicked her head back and the water cascaded all over her jacket but she bounced up.

"We need to move faster, this way so that we're heading north. Come on, or we won't stand a chance of winning."

Kelly grabbed up her backpack, swung it back over her shoulders and again they took off, climbing up the incline, and headed farther into the forest. Her legs ached and they were almost at the site where their camp should be but a yelling stopped Ella in her tracks. She twisted her head to her side as if trying to detect which direction the voice came from. As she listened, the sound grew louder and she instinctively knew that it was Bella calling for help. As she moved toward the yelling, Kelly shouted at her.

"You're heading the wrong way!"

"Bella's in trouble—I can hear her calling. I'm going to help."

Kelly charged over and grabbed her arm, yanking her back to head in the other direction. "I cannot hear anything. Are you crazy?"

Ella pulled her arm away and stared at her. Her head shook. "I know she's in trouble. I cannot just leave her."

"This is about winning and being the best." Kelly shrugged and gazed in the opposite direction. It was obvious the woman didn't want to help anyone except herself.

"Go if you must. It's not far, about another mile if you keep heading straight, but I'm going to help Bella. It's not just about winning; it's about teamwork and I'm not leaving her behind."

Kelly glared at her and then stared over in the direction of the persistent yelling and back at where they needed to walk to in order to find their flag. She let go of Ella's arm and trudged off.

"Suit yourself. It's probably a trick and you're falling for it, but I'm going to complete my mission with or without you."

Ella watched as Kelly plodded up the hill and disappeared from view. She hesitated for a second. What if she was right and it was a hoax? She'd just let her partner wander off, knowing she didn't have any skills for reading the map. It was a short distance to their flag and if she had listened to her, Kelly would find the flag and make it. Spinning around, she moved through the thick bushes and scratchy weeds as fast as she could.

"Bella, I'm coming! Can you hear me?"

There was no response, so she kept yelling out loud and ducked as she avoided the low branches and pushed the trees and bushes out of her way. The woodland was more dense here and darker. A trickle of sweat dripped between her shoulder blades and she wiped her forehead with the back of her hand. She was warm in all these layers. She had been walking for around ten minutes and was about to walk back in the direction she came, fearing she had been fooled, when she heard a low whimper.

"Bella?"

Again there was silence and then a strangulated yell. "Ella, over here! Ella."

Without waiting another second, Ella lifted her legs and pushed the ferns out of her way. Her boots squelched in the soft and damp earth as she raced forward. The ground sloped away steeply and Ella almost fell with the weight of her backpack as she bent her body but she pushed her back up and slowed her descent. The forest floor was carpeted with autumn leaves in red, orange, brown, and yellow but they hid the uneven ground. As Ella reached the bottom of the slope, she tripped over branches and stared as a few feet in front was a sheer drop that she would have plummeted over had she not tripped. She tiptoed toward the edge and there, about four feet down on the muddy bank below, was Bella, lying in a twisted and unnatural position.

"I'm coming down. Don't move." Ella removed her backpack and dumped it on the ground. As she searched through the contents, she realized that she didn't have any medical supplies. They should have been given at the very least a basic medical first-aid kit but there was nothing. Lighter now that the backpack was removed, she crouched low and held her arms out to the sides to steady her descent as she made her way down the steep grassy and slippery bank. Reaching the ground, she quickly moved over to assess Bella's situation and the woman gave her a tentative smile.

"Thank you. I thought I could manage when I sent Adelle off to get help but the pain is really bad."

Ella removed her jacket and covered Bella with it. Her pale face and shivering body told Ella that shock, possibly from the injury and blood loss, was setting in. Bella didn't attempt to sit up, which was good, and Ella placed her hand on her throat to take her pulse. She studied Bella and her left leg, which lay at an odd angle. It was more than likely broken. What was worse was the fact that she had her hand over the top of her thigh where blood seeped out. Ella crouched down by her side and knelt, dipping her head down low to Bella.

"Bella, I'm going to have to stop the bleeding, okay? It's going to hurt but if we don't stop it now—"

"I will die…"

"We're not going to let that happen."

She couldn't see the extent of the damage unless she ripped her pants but was reluctant to move Bella's hand in case it started to bleed fresh blood again. She didn't have a belt but Bella did.

"My leg was hurting the most but now not so much. I'm just so cold and tired."

Ella quickly unbuckled Bella's leather belt and pulled it out from around her waist and slipped it under her left thigh, high above where Bella's hand was.

"Bella, this is going to hurt like hell but it will help you, I promise. When I tighten the belt, move your hand. One, two…" She pulled with all her strength and Bella screamed out loud, lifting her body off the ground and trying to move away from Ella. The forest echoed with the scream but Ella pressed Bella down, keeping her still against the ground until she slumped to the side, unconscious. Ella felt her carotid pulse, which was strong but fast, faster than it should be but hopefully now that the bleeding was stopped, it should slow down. With Bella unconscious, Ella used her small knife to rip the pants to examine the leg more closely. As the material separated, she was able to see part of the femur bone sticking out; blood trickled but did not gush.

Ella scanned the vicinity. Bella was asleep, so she placed her sweaty palms on either side of the protruding bone. The skin was clammy and where her hand touched the skin, heat radiated outward. She closed her eyes and the wind around her increased as she pushed her energy into the wound, realigning the bone until it was in the correct position, and the cells were working to heal the fracture. She had never before attempted to heal another person because she risked exposure. But at this point, she feared Bella would bleed out and she couldn't be sure how long it would take for anyone to reach them. This way, when Bella woke, she would be able to stand and beside some residual stiffness or soreness, she would be able to walk, giving them a chance. She glanced at her watch; it was one o'clock and she was certain by now Kelly had reached her destination and would be heading back. Would she tell them what had happened? They had no way of contacting headquarters or Hawk and again she wondered how that was possible. Surely there should have been some means of alerting the trainers if they were in trouble. She pondered this as her eyelids fluttered heavily and unable to stay awake, she slumped up against Bella and fell asleep.

The hoot of an owl woke Ella, who bolted up and in doing so, Bella stirred and shook her head, sitting forward with ease.

"Ella, where did you come from?"

Before Ella could say anything, Bella touched her hip and leg and stared at her torn pants and bloodied leg. She gazed deeply at Ella and attempted to stand; Ella jumped up to help her. Bella stood, stroking her side and staring at the blood, dirt, and large black bruises on her thigh. She winced as her hand smoothed over her thigh and then she snapped her head around to glare at Ella.

"Y-You fixed me. How?"

As her voice rose with anger and fear, the wind around them increased and the trees shook violently. The leaves rained down on them. Ella stared at Bella, her heart pounding inside her ribs. She wasn't a soul-shifter or a vampire but she had a strong suspicion she was a caster, a witch. She'd never met a real witch before but standing in front of Bella, whose emerald eyes glowed and her hair, dislodged from the ponytail, flapped behind her, she brimmed with a potent energy.

"Bella, your leg was broken. You were bleeding out and barely conscious. I did what I had to do to save you. It's my gift but not one I use lightly. It's my secret, but you have a secret, too, don't you?"

They were inches apart. Bella licked her lips as she raised her hands straight up into the air and snowflakes fell covering the surrounding area creating a beautiful winter wonderland all around them. Ice droplets hung from the trees and sparkled liked diamonds. Ella shivered and smiled at the scene, but twisted her wrist to glance at the time on her new multi-purpose watch, which not only told the time but was a compass. It was now half past two. If they worked together, they might still have a chance, even if it would be cheating. Who would know?

"That's amazing but I'm thinking we need to find your flag and get back to base camp. Can you use your skills to get us there?"

Bella ran her hand over her trousers and the fabric repaired itself. "I didn't want to use magic. I was scared of what the others would think but you're like me. Come on, I know where we have to go."

Ella returned up the incline and collected her backpack. Fifteen minutes later, they were back on the trail. After pocketing their red flag, the return journey was uneventful and hours later, they marched back to base camp, feet weary and backs aching but a friendship formed. Ella wanted to collapse and vomit—she wasn't sure which was going to come first. The last mile was a killer and every part of her body throbbed. Walking into the quiet camp, the first person they saw was Hawk, who shouted and screeched out commands to the other recruits who stood around. Ella stared at the scene as the other women raced over. Her body shook but nothing prepared her for the magnificent sight next to Hawk. As he bellowed, Drayton's hand stretched out to hold the man's arm, silencing him. Hooded moody eyes zoned in on her, his mouth held in a tight line, and dark shadows filled the hollows under his socket. A mean, almost unrecognizable Marcus stood dressed in black combat gear with his hand still resting on the man's and his other trembling slightly.

"Where's your partner, Masters? What the devil are you doing with Fields? We had a report that you needed to be extracted, that you were injured? A full medical team is out there right now looking for you."

Hawk's words registered in Ella's brain but the world was foggy and his voice distant and far away. She shifted her glance back toward Marcus, unsure whether he was real or simply a hallucination she had conjured up due to the fact that she hadn't been eating properly. The energy that kept her going all day was depleting fast. Standing still, her legs trembled and she knew she needed to get her backpack off, but she couldn't move. All the action going on around her was a blurry whirl of white and black shapes. The shadow that was Marcus charged toward her but too late as her body gave up the battle and dropped to the ground.

CHAPTER TWENTY

Ella reluctantly shifted her position in the bed, which was far more comfortable than the one at base camp, and she longed to stay snuggled and in her cozy state. As soon as she had woken up, she realized she was no longer in the forest in Maine but in a private hospital. The smell of disinfectant made her gag, and a constant beeping noise to her right told her that her heart was still beating. She was also attached to an intravenous infusion that delivered fluids, and she tried to swallow but her mouth and tongue were dry. Forcing herself into a sitting position, she poured some ice water from the jug into the small tumbler just as a nurse in a maroon top and pants walked in.

"You can leave soon. Your vitals are all stable. We're just waiting for the results of one further test, but Dr. Smith said he's happy and the gentleman who escorted you in, Mr. Drayton, left your clothes and said he will be back very soon. He told me you needed to wait until his return, but as he's not your next of kin, I'm not obligated to keep you. I thought you should know. I don't like pushy men, and he's definitely that."

Ella smiled at the nurse and nodded. She swallowed the refreshing liquid and savored it. As soon as the nurse mentioned Marcus, the world halted. He wasn't a dream. He was back and sniffing around. A panic rose sharply and a need to run had her jumping out of bed. She was free to leave, and that was what she was going to do. She tore out the plastic needle and pressed on her skin to stem the bleeding as she eyed the room. Next, she removed the hospital gown and tore off the stickers attached to her chest. She spied her clothes and changed into her muddy black pants and top. She didn't care any longer how she looked. Her face stared back at her in the bathroom mirror. For weeks, she had stopped applying any makeup, and her skin looked clean and fresh, if a little pale. Her blue eyes stared back at her, clear and alert. She couldn't face him. Quickly, she splashed her cheeks with cold water and brushed her teeth. A knock on the door made her turn around. It was another nurse, who entered and passed her a slip of paper.

"This is a prescription for your prenatal vitamins. You can get them at your local pharmacy. We didn't have the details on file, but Dr. Smith says you will need them. He has also booked an ultrasound scan for four weeks' time, back here. Congratulations. He says you're about eight weeks pregnant and everything looks fine."

The ground underneath Ella shook, and she grabbed onto the cabinet to steady herself. She snatched the prescription from the nurse's hand and forced a smile. She stared down at the prescription. Realizing that the last shot of Depo was months ago. With everything that had been going on it had completely escaped her, which wasn't like her at all. She pressed her forehead, momentarily stunned and unsure. A baby. She shook her head.

The baby was Drayton's but this didn't change anything between them. They didn't have a relationship, there was no *us* and this wasn't the time to play happy families. She didn't even know what that meant. She had never wanted to be a mother and especially not now. Her life was a complete mess. A strangled sob caught in her throat, and she pressed her hand against her chest. A need to move even faster now reared its head. Lifting her head, she stared at the prescription. What if the injection Aidan had repeatedly given her affected the baby? Maybe, he had given her something that night when they had fought, and it wasn't a baby at all but something else?

Ella couldn't think rationally. Since she'd landed back in the States and agreed to work for Steel, everything had changed. She only held one passport; her other identities were all removed and the money that she had stashed away was dwindling fast. If she used Steel's money, she would be followed; she would be found. As she charged out of the hospital door, all she could think of was running as far away as possible but in her confused state, she blindly stumbled, not looking where she was headed until two strong arms grabbed hers and held her prisoner. The familiar scent wrapped around her and she couldn't move or raise her head to look at him.

"Ella, where are you running to this time? The time for running is over, sweetheart."

Click. His sweet endearment was her undoing and she tugged forcefully to make a break away from him, only to feel her left arm wrenched awkwardly. A cold metal bracelet rubbed against her wrist. Snapping her gaze to his, she couldn't believe it. He was doing it all over again. Open mouthed, she watched Marcus snap the remaining cuff onto his wrist; he pulled her along passing patients and staff, who stared at them as they exited the hospital. A black truck pulled up to the curb. Jake nodded as Marcus hoisted a struggling Ella into the back seat.

"You two sure have a thing for handcuffs."

Ella refused to say a word and stared out the window. Her stomach churned while she bit the tip of her finger. He couldn't possibly know about the baby yet—hell, she had only just this minute found out. But he was the father; maybe she should say something. She swiveled her head around to gaze at him but Kelly's face zoomed into view in her mind and her words about his sexual prowess. She didn't owe him anything. He'd left her.

"Don't you have anything to say, Ella? It's not like you to be so quiet."

Avoiding his eyes and his inquisitive stare was uppermost in her mind because when she allowed him to drink her in, there would be no stopping the need to be closer and she feared she would tell him everything. It simply wasn't fair and he knew it.

"I know Steel offered you a job, but he had no right in hell to do so and even if you had completed the training— which is now over—you wouldn't be joining Orion. Do you hear me? The money he gave you is yours to keep but you're going into protective custody instantly. It's all been arranged and you don't get a say in this, Ella. This is my decision."

A growl deep in her belly exploded. Hearing him dictate again how things would be uncorked the fizzing bottle of anger. Placing her left hand on the metal handcuff, the metal softened and she snapped it in half, shoving Drayton away from her, still refusing to meet his gaze. She shouted at Jake and instantly the car jerked and started weaving all over the road, sending them back and forth.

"Stop it, Ella! Stop it now!"

The truck came to a shuddering stop in busy traffic as horns blared around them. She pulled the door handle and jumped out, running as fast as she could and dodging the oncoming trucks and cars. Ella didn't care about the danger of the fast-moving traffic; she needed the distance from him. Pushing her leg muscles to work harder, she acknowledged she was a survivor; it's what she did. She would manage on her own again.

More horns blared, but she sprinted as fast as she could, certain Marcus would not give up the chase and would be in pursuit. She ran down the narrow and pedestrian-filled street, but she didn't know what town she was in. There were no familiar landmarks. She kept running until a squeal of brakes announced that her luck was about to run out. Glancing back, she saw Marcus and Jake in the big black truck. As she slipped down the side alley, she noticed as she sprinted there was no exit and at the end was a six-foot-high chain fence. She was cornered but kept running, even as the roar of tires over the gravel and smell of burnt rubber reached her nostrils. She didn't dare look behind. Her hands grabbed onto the chain link fence and she pushed her body up, clambering over but hands grabbed her around the waist to pull her down. Letting go, she grunted at her capture again. Standing apart, they faced each other but did not touch. Refusing to meet his gaze, she looked to her side.

"Ella Masters, you're the most stubborn, exasperating woman I've ever met! Will you just dial down your I-can-survive mode for one second? I said no more running, Ella—that is nonnegotiable. What's got into you?"

His hands rested on either side of her hips and the world suspended as a need to touch him and have him hold her flooded her. What was she doing? If she was pregnant, she needed help. The Elusti were still out there. She didn't know what had happened to Aidan; she hoped he was dead, but instinctively knew he wasn't. On the run, pregnant, would make everything harder.

"I'm not going into protective custody, Drayton. I'm not going to be shoved away somewhere on a desert island—I will go insane. I am joining Orion. For the first time in my life, I have a sense of purpose, a direction, and you are not taking that away from me. No one is. Do you hear me? What gives you the right to tell me what I can and cannot do, anyway? It was just sex, remember, and you soon replaced me anyway, so what's the big deal if we work together? If you can't handle the heat, get the hell out. We're not married— you're not my boss. I'm an adult, capable of making my own decisions."

Marcus pushed his shoulders back to his full height and his dark eyes narrowed as he closed the gap between them. She stepped backward until she reached the chain fence and it rattled. He grabbed her hands and lifted them high above her head. Ella knew what was coming and she tried to resist as best she could, moving her head to the side and refusing to look him in the eyes. He pressed his firm body against hers and kissed her neck. A gathering need exploded in her belly as he continued to kiss and lick; a blissful sensation overtook her anger. He parted her legs with his knee and rubbed her core; automatically, she moaned in response. He released her hands, which fell around his neck and pulled him to her as she melted into him.

"This gives me the right, Ella. You're mine. You gave yourself to me and I'm claiming you. Do you hear me? I want you right where I can see you all the time. No more running, Ella. Say you'll marry me and the rest we'll figure out together."

The air stayed in her lungs and a weight pressed on her chest. He was asking her to marry him but he hadn't even said he loved her. This was crazy. She shook her head but he pulled out a huge square cut solitaire diamond on a thin platinum band. She was speechless. If she had ever taken any time looking at rings, this is the one she would have chosen. It was perfect. She stood back and blinked away tears with her hands crossed over her chest as her heart beat wildly.

"When I said you were going into protective custody, Ella, I meant me. I will protect you from harm always."

Ella looked from the ring to Marcus, who stared at her, waiting.

"I can't, Marcus. This isn't right. You don't love me. It was just sex, remember?"

He grabbed her left hand and pulled her into his arms. "It was never just sex, Ella. Seeing you shot—it almost killed me. I thought you were dead and I had lost you. I had my reasons for leaving you afterward but never again. When I heard about your sexy romp—damn it, Ella, I nearly killed the guy who spoke of the beautiful angel in a satin red corset and thong. Were you trying to kill me? Seeing you carry your load, dressed like a soldier in training, blew my mind into outer space. Maybe I can concede in certain areas. I'm willing to try, but only if you agree to be mine in name as well as in every other way, Ella. I'm dead inside without you and when I said I have a right because you're mine, I forgot to add that I'm yours in return. Without you, I am nothing." The ring hovered over the tip of her third finger on her left hand.

Tears formed in her eyes but she couldn't let them fall. Everything was so uncertain and Kelly—she had hinted that she had slept with Marcus. Would he do that? She studied his features and sighed.

"What's it to be, Ella?" He wrapped his arm around her waist, drawing her closer.

She could feel his heat. With him, they would be a team; she wouldn't be alone.

He ducked his head close to her ear. "I love you, Ella, and I know you love me, so say yes."

He kissed her lips and she floated, surrounded by his strength and love. He said the words she longed to hear and suddenly she had no option but to tell him.

"I'm pregnant, Marcus."

As he had watched Ella trudge those last steps into camp, carrying her heavy backpack and walking next to Bella—who he later learned she had helped as well as retrieving the flag—filled him with a fierce pride for the woman he loved. Yes, he realized not long after he had let her go it was a huge mistake but he didn't have a choice. When the story circulated about her escapades with the young agent, he'd seen red and almost squeezed the life out of the new recruit, who talked about *his angel.* Yes, he had learned that letting her go wasn't going to work for him at all. Even when she wasn't around, she replaced his ghosts, night after night, until he didn't sleep at all. Despite Jake watching her at her cottage on the Welsh coast, it didn't ease his worry over her.

He requested overseas duty to recruit members for Steel's team but memories of their time together invaded his thoughts constantly. Even when women, beautiful women, threw themselves at him and offered him sex freely, he couldn't follow through. He knew it might ease his need but if he came close to another woman, Ella's face would surface. He was ruined. She had ruined him for all time and all other women. She was it for him, which had led to his earlier declaration of love. He knew it was mutual but instead of her saying yes, she had told him she was pregnant! Her face as she revealed her news was crestfallen and along with the admission was a quick but determined declaration that she wouldn't be for long as she pushed away from him and headed toward the truck.

Dumbstruck, he stood there, unsure of his next move. His forehead creased with deep lines of fear for her and their unborn child; he knew she was holding back on something vital. Knowing she was carrying his child held any words he wanted to say inside because he quite honestly didn't know what to say. It was like the final piece in the puzzle that had been jumbled dreams until this moment. Now, he couldn't ignore the facts. They were the same and they belonged together. A buoyant feeling made his chest puff out with pride and a desire to cart her over his shoulder and handcuff her to him until she was his bride filled him but her eyes weren't their usual sparkle. She was terrified and he didn't understand why.

He blew out a deep breath. He had to handle this situation carefully. As he marched back to the truck, he commanded himself to stay calm. Although he'd never imagined Ella as the maternal type, recalling the vision of her with a child and the love that was overwhelming, he knew in his heart she would be. He knew she loved him but there was still something she was keeping secret. She didn't trust him enough to share whatever her fears were and that made him crazy. Once he sat in the back of the truck with Ella, the atmosphere was colder than the Antarctic.

"No handcuffs? We're making progress." Jake's humor did nothing to ease the tension and they both harrumphed.

"Where to, boss?"

Marcus was so deep in thought he didn't realize the truck hadn't moved. As he thought about Jake's question, he glanced over at a pale and distant Ella. He grabbed her hand and stroked her palm. The only way to get her to answer his questions was his touch.

"Back to see Dr. Smith."

Ella yanked her hand but he tightened his grip and stroked her wrist gently. She could fight him all she liked but he knew she would cave before too long. She wasn't going to shut him out anymore.

"You can fight me all you like, but know this, I'm not going anywhere. I'm yours. I'm here to stay and any fight that comes to your door is mine too. Let me in, Ella. Let me help. Tell me what is going on in that beautifully stubborn brain of yours because despite my many talents, reading your thoughts isn't one of them. I'm not sure if you were running from me at the hospital but now I'm worried you were running from the news you could only have just learned. Either way, Ella, I want you checked over because, honey, you're not yourself."

The truck roared to life and pulled away; the wheels tore up the uneven and gravel filled road.

"You know I can hear everything you're saying up here, right?"

"You keep that big mouth of yours shut, Jake Meadows."

Hearing the words roll off Ella's lips made Marcus smile. She would always say what was on her mind and he liked that about her. Jake liked that about her, too; he'd told him she was a keeper. He was worried she had trust issues but hell, didn't they all. Maybe letting her join the team wouldn't be such a bad thing but with her being pregnant, there was only so much stress his heart could take.

"If joining Orion means so much, we can talk about it, but you need to tell me what's going on, Ella. If what we have is going to work, you need to let me in and let me help you."

The truck bounced away and soon left the congested streets, headed back toward the private medical clinic that Steel had set up. Marcus kept hold of Ella's hand as her body trembled and he shifted closer, knowing she couldn't resist the pull between them when he started to arouse her. He didn't care that Jake was in front; he wanted answers and he wasn't going to let her keep any secrets between them any longer. Looking out the window, she refused to answer him or look his way, which called for drastic measures. He pressed his hand over her right breast and squeezed the nub between his fingers. He watched as she remained stoic but bit her lip. Turning so his back faced Jake to shield her as much as possible, he unbuttoned her cargo pants and dragged them down to her hips. There was a gasp and a wriggle as she glared at him but he could see the rise and fall of her chest as her heart raced with excitement and arousal. There was no stopping his assault and he pushed his hand down into her warm and wet core as she bucked back against the leather seat and he circled her hot and wet entrance in a hypnotic motion. A low moan escaped between her mouth and he covered her lips to swallow it, invading her there and continuing the slow torture below. Removing his mouth from hers, he whispered, "Tell me, Ella, and I'll give you what you want. Tell me."

Her body rose to his touch, eager for more. She melted next to him, unraveling with need. Still, he toyed, stroking and circling her sex. Ella placed her hand on his and gazed into his eyes as tears dropped onto her flushed cheeks and he stilled, unable to move. He'd never seen her cry openly before. He pushed his fingers in, wanting to take away her pain. As the waves of her orgasm washed over him, she softened against him; her head rested against his shoulder and she gazed up with her luminous eyes.

"Aidan drugged me, several times. I don't know what the drug was or what it's meant to do but I'm pregnant. I'm not meant to be pregnant, Drayton—do you understand? "

He watched her wide eyes as what she told him sunk in. A violence burst inside that made him want to commit murder. Her soothing hand as it stroked his cheek dampened his anger and instead, he wanted to hold this woman beside him forever. He wrapped his arm around her small shoulders and turned back, bringing her across his lap and kissing her lips, softly nudging them. He hadn't told her yet that Aidan was a free man but he wouldn't be for long. And when he caught up with him, he would be dead once and for all—after he revealed what he had done to Ella. Maybe the pregnancy was a coincidence but he didn't like it one bit. He kissed the top of her head.

"Marry me, Ella."

EPILOGUE

Ella admired her trim figure in the long mirror, twisting and turning to gauge whether there was any evidence of the fact she was now twelve weeks pregnant, but staring at the fitted lace bodice with its sweetheart neckline and dainty capped straps, her flat stomach hid her secret. The morning sickness had subsided leaving her feeling well and strong. After explaining to Marcus her concerns regarding the baby, some of her fears receded. He was a powerhouse, a force to be reckoned with when it came to getting what he wanted and he didn't play fair. She brushed her hands down over the long flowing dress that spread out from her hips and rested on the ground. The cream sheer skirt was hand stitched with delicate embroidery and tiny Swarovski crystals that sparkled, and the material underneath was the softest cream satin.

She'd never worn anything so beautiful in her life. Her blonde hair was blow-dried and sleeked into an up-do, held together with an antique diamond and pearl studded clasp. Marcus had presented her with beautiful pear-shaped diamond earrings, but she would have been equally satisfied to say the I Do's in Vegas in jeans and a T-shirt. The pomp and ceremony held little meaning for her; she was just happy they were together at last, even if there was still so much of their past that had been left unspoken about.

There was a knock at the door and in walked Josephine, Marcus's mother, who, the minute she saw Ella, covered her mouth with both of her hands as tears bubbled in her eyes.

"Oh, my dear, you make the perfect bride. You're beautiful."

Ella spread her hands over her flat abdomen. "Hardly perfect, Josephine." Tears welled up in her eyes as she thought about the tiny life that innocently lay curled inside her belly. The life that four weeks ago she had threatened to end amid fears as to what Aidan had done, but Marcus, in his usual way, had convinced her after plying her with copious amounts of

sex that she needed to wait and undergo more tests. Maybe she
was more petrified of becoming a mother, something she had
never truly considered. She wondered whether she would be
any good at the nurturing and loving, as well as the fact that
there may also be something wrong with the child she carried.

Josephine, as usual, looked regal and elegant in her
champagne-colored gown with her hair pinned back into a
fashionable chignon. She walked to stand in front of Ella and
gripped her shoulders as she looked up at her.

"Your child will be perfect, ma chérie, because he was
created out of the love you have for my son and as such, you
will love him or her unconditionally. And of course, I will be
here to help for as long as I can."

Ella couldn't stop the tears that trickled out at
Josephine's words and she quickly swiped them away. She
moved into the older woman's embrace hugging her tightly. In
a short time, she had grown to love Josephine as if her own
mother. Another knock sounded on the door and a rather
abrupt and gruff voice addressed them.

"It's time, ladies."

The door swung open. Ben Steel, in his dark black suit
with white shirt and long black tie with a pale pink rose
attached to his jacket, walked in. With both her parents long
gone, Steel had offered to escort the bride down the aisle,
although a heated argument had taken place when their
impromptu nuptials had caused a major row and threats of
walking out of Orion were launched. Steel eventually backed
down and considered the altered arrangements he now faced
with a reluctant acceptance. Marcus had relented and agreed
that Ella could join Orion but only to work on certain
missions, under strict guidelines and not in the field while she
was pregnant, a fact they both agreed to keep hidden from
Steel. After the baby was born, the rules about her working
would be discussed again. Ben Steel straightened his tie and
bent his arm.

"You look absolutely stunning, Ella. Drayton's a lucky
man. I hope he knows just how lucky because if he doesn't,

I'll be waiting in the wings." His mustache twitched and Ella laughed at his gruff declaration.

"You leave those two alone, Benjamin Steel. My son knows he's met his match in Ella Masters and there will be no other." She walked out the door and Ella picked up her small bouquet of blush pink and strawberry pink roses before she looped her arm with Steel's. As they walked out of the cottage perched on the East Coast, the sky above was a Tiffany Blue, with not a cloud on the horizon to blot out the winter sun. It was late January, and the light snow showers last night added to the romance, but were melting fast. The long garden had been given a complete overhaul and one which she wasn't privy to until now. The stunning vision before her brought another bout of tears, which she wiped away.

White and silver lanterns hung from the multitude of branches and bushes. To her left, a long wooden table was set with an antique lace runner, ready for the twenty guests and glass jars lined down the center their flames flickering. On a small side table covered in white table linens stood a three tired wedding cake and on top instead of the traditional bride, and groom was a set of slate gray handcuffs. Ella smiled. More roses in shades of pink were positioned in tall glass vases down the aisle to her right where two neat rows of side chairs covered in white cotton with bows at the back were positioned. Dividing the chairs was a long white pathway where she would walk to greet her groom. At the end was a carefully constructed arched canopy made from thin branches and twisted with strings of pearls and white flowers. The sweet scent was overpowering. The roar of the ocean in the background made her want to race forward. There was no fear, no wanting to back out, no wanting to run away. Marcus stood there with his solid broad shoulders set back, and his hands clasped together in front of his black fitted suit. He was the most handsome devil she had ever met with his dark hair disheveled and his obsidian eyes gazing directly at her. He gave her the strength to take the steps she needed; he looked at her, as though she was the only woman on the planet, and she couldn't breathe. He smiled at her and her heart beat faster.

Ella passed several people she didn't know and smiled at Bella and several other women she had worked alongside while training. She noted that Kelly was absent, which she was glad about, even though Marcus assured her nothing had passed between them. A dislike for the woman lingered but nothing was going to spoil her day. She smiled at the handsome and strong men on the other side, all of whom were military and part of Orion. She nodded and knew that in time their names and faces would become like family. She stared at Jake, who stood next to Marcus, and he nodded at her. Lastly, she rested her eyes on the man who had captured the last Welsh witch, heart and soul.

Marcus bent forward and kissed her lips in greeting as the small crowd clapped and roared. The priest started the ceremony, and Ella said good-bye mentally to each of her ghosts, laying them all to rest. They reminded her of all the past hurts and ill-fated love affairs but this time was different: this time, her husband loved her and wouldn't let her down. They both exchanged their vows and placed simple platinum wedding bands on the other's hand, joining them. They were now man and wife. An explosion of confetti and rose petals rained down on them, and Marcus wrapped his arms tightly around his wife's waist. He drew her up against him, kissing her and stealing her breath away as whistles and more cheers sounded around them. After only a moment, he released her and held her hands out between them, bending close.

"I love you, Mrs. Drayton. I told you a long time ago, I would find you, and now I have. I'm never letting you go. There are parts of me; you don't know, parts, you may not wish to know, but I want to share everything with you, the good and the bad. In return, I want to know all of you, and together we'll face each ghost and say good-bye to the past. I will never let anyone hurt you ever again. I will protect you *forever*."

Ella's heart beat wildly and she opened her mouth to reciprocate his words of love, but his speech played around in her mind as tears bubbled in her eyes. The last few weeks and days had passed in a flurry of activity, and all the while, she was focused on her training, surviving a life without Drayton, and convincing herself that the baby was healthy. She hadn't processed what had taken place between her and Drayton on the last night they had spent together before he'd walked away from her until now. She'd tried to erase the exotic and wondrous memory from her brain, but it burst to vivid life in her mind. As she tenderly touched her belly, carrying his child, standing here as his wife and staring at a future together, she realized their powers would magnify and grow. The night Ella believed she conceived, Marcus had bitten into her neck, which completed the ancient mating ritual which bonded them together and rendered them immortal. Did Drayton realize what he had done? Stepping on tiptoes, she kissed him and smoothed his cheek with her thumb.

"I love you too. Forever is a long time, Drayton, but I'm willing to give it a go."

THE END

AUTHOR's BIOGRAPHY

J.M. Davies is the author of Capturing the Last Welsh Witch which is her debut adult paranormal romance. She has also written a young adult romantic fantasy trilogy called Children of Annwn under the name of Jennifer Owen Davies.

In general, she loves creating character driven stories that touch your heart and take you away to a magical world that leaves you craving more. When she isn't writing, she loves to read and her tastes include Nora Roberts, Catherine Cookson, Jane Austen, Jodi Picoult, Deborah Harkness, Cassandra Clare, Suzanne Collins, P.D. James, Patricia Cornwell, Pittacus Lore, Diane Gabaldon and many more.

In her spare time, she enjoys managing a local writers group and maintains an Alzheimer's support group on Facebook, a cause close to her heart. She also loves discovering old treasures at yard sales and revamping them, watching Grey's Anatomy, Madam Secretary, and Vampire Diaries, walking on the beach, cooking, and when there's time the gym.

Jennifer has been married for twenty years, and is mother to four boys. Jennifer and her husband are originally from

Cardiff in Wales, but they now live on the East Coast of America in North Andover with her family and two cats. Jennifer fell in love with New England, and among the pages of the books are references to both local beauty spots and historic sites from the area and from back in the UK that have captured her imagination. She loves to hear from readers and here's some links to stay in touch.

FB Author page https://www.facebook.com/pages/Jennifer-Davies/1421409368089313

Web-site   http://www.jenniferowendavies.com/

Email   Jendaviesuk@gmail.com

.

CPSIA information can be obtained at www.ICGtesting.com
Printed in the USA
LVOW11s0210080316

478108LV00001B/113/P